W9-ACU-498

CHASING DOWN A DREAM

Center Point
Large Print

Also by Beverly Jenkins and available from
Center Point Large Print:

Destiny's Surrender
Heart of Gold
Destiny's Embrace
Destiny's Captive
For Your Love
Stepping to a New Day
Forbidden
Breathless

**This Large Print Book carries the
Seal of Approval of N.A.V.H.**

CHASING DOWN A DREAM

BEVERLY JENKINS

JAMES RIVER VALLEY
LIBRARY SYSTEM
105 3RD ST SE
JAMESTOWN ND 58401

CENTER POINT LARGE PRINT
THORNDIKE, MAINE

This Center Point Large Print edition
is published in the year 2017 by arrangement with
William Morrow, an imprint of
HarperCollins Publishers.

Copyright © 2017 by Beverly Jenkins.

All rights reserved.

The text of this Large Print edition is unabridged.
In other aspects, this book may vary
from the original edition.
Printed in the United States of America
on permanent paper.
Set in 16-point Times New Roman type.

ISBN: 978-1-68324-482-0

Library of Congress Cataloging-in-Publication Data

Names: Jenkins, Beverly, 1951– author.
Title: Chasing down a dream : a blessings novel / Beverly Jenkins.
Description: Center Point Large Print edition. | Thorndike, Maine :
    Center Point Large Print, 2017.
Identifiers: LCCN 2017024400 | ISBN 9781683244820
    (hardcover : alk. paper)
Subjects: LCSH: African Americans—Fiction. | Large type books. |
Domestic fiction.
Classification: LCC PS3560.E4795 C47 2017 | DDC 813/.54—dc23
LC record available at https://lccn.loc.gov/2017024400

To the dreamers

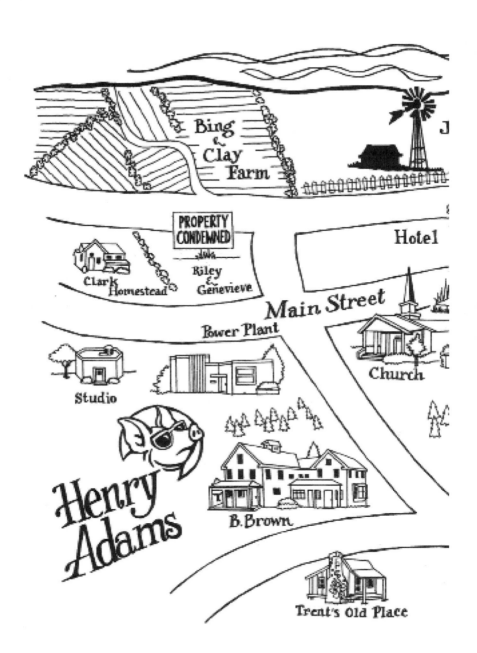

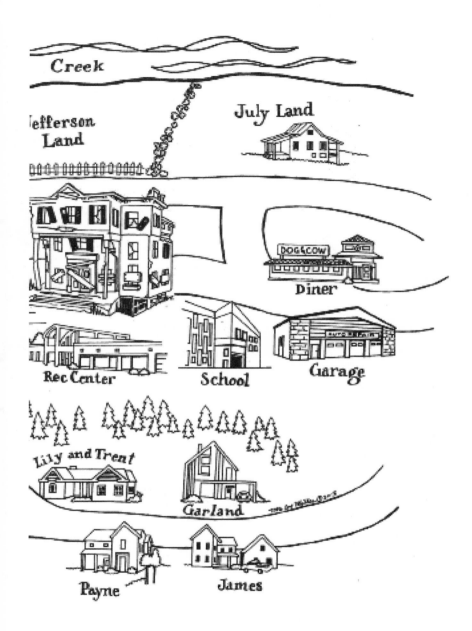

PROLOGUE

Ten-year-old Lucas Herman, riding in the backseat of the SUV with his eight-year-old sister, Jasmine, saw her jump with fright in response to the booming claps of thunder outside. She didn't like storms, never had. But he was the oldest, way too big to be afraid of the violent weather, or at least that's what he told himself. Hoping his fears couldn't be heard in his voice, he asked the driver, their uncle Jake, "Should we stop?" Rain was coming down in sheets and the SUV's wipers were swinging back and forth like crazy.

"Where?" his uncle called back, attention glued to the road. "We're out here in the middle of nowhere."

And they were. Kansas, if Lucas remembered correctly. They'd passed a small town a short while ago. At that time, the sky had been bluer than any he'd ever seen back home in Dayton. A few minutes later it went dark as night. Then came the wind followed by pouring rain, crackling lightning and ominous growling thunder. He didn't know how his uncle could see to drive, but the big black SUV crept on through the deluge. Uncle Jake Gleason wasn't really a relative. He was their dad's fraternity brother. Two years ago, their parents, Daphne and Elliot, died in a car accident. When no family members stepped up to take in Lucas and Jasmine, they became wards of the state of Ohio and placed in separate foster homes. Jake had been trying to adopt them ever since. A few days ago, he finally gained approval and was now driving them across the country to Sacramento, California, where he lived with his wife, Leslie. Lucas didn't know what the future held but being reunited with Jaz was the most important thing. Little sisters could be a pain in the butt but he loved her and had missed her just as much as he did his parents.

Another boom of thunder filled the car and Jasmine jumped again and put her hands over her ears. Lucas reached out and took her hand. "It's okay, Jaz. Don't be scared. It's just a storm."

But it seemed to be more than that. The thunder and flashing lightning were increasing in frequency.

Uncle Jake shouted over the din, "We have to stop. I can't see anymore!"

Lucas peered out into the rain and shouted, "There's a house!" It was set back from the road. The flashes of lightning made it pop in and out of view like something from a scary movie but he didn't care. Apparently, Uncle Jake didn't, either. He drove up to the house and stopped. There were no lights on inside.

"You two stay here. I'll see if anyone's home."

Before getting out, he turned to them and said in a serious voice, "If anything happens lock the doors and stay in the car. I'm leaving you my phone. Okay?"

Lucas took the phone and tried not to acknowledge the icy sense of foreboding he suddenly felt. He wanted to tell him not to go, but rather than act like a baby, he stayed silent.

"Take care of your sister. I'll be right back."

The door opened. Rain and wind screamed in. Uncle Jake bolted out, slamming the door behind him. Lucas saw him climb the stairs before the rain hid him from view. He and Jasmine waited tensely.

"I hope somebody's home," Jasmine said.

"Me, too." He prayed Uncle Jake returned quickly and wished he could see him but the storm continued to rage. The wind was now so strong the car was rocking. He heard what sounded like a train, and time seemed to slow as the SUV began tumbling end over end. Windows shattered. Jaz screamed. A terrified Lucas undid his seat belt and threw his body over hers to protect her from the stinging debris and rain now swirling inside the car. Something struck him in the head and everything went black.

CHAPTER
1

She was making her way through the thick tropical vegetation of a rain forest. She had no idea why she was there or where she was going but there was a yellow brick road beneath the boots on her feet, so she followed it. This wasn't Oz, though; there was no Tin Man, Lion, or Scarecrow. No Dorothy or Toto, either. Just humidity, the yellow brick road, and towering fern-like foliage that dwarfed her six-foot frame. Suddenly the vegetation vanished and she stood on a coppery-reddish plain that reminded her of the flat openness of desert. Off in the distance a gray mountain range loomed against a cloudy sky. The harsh cry of a bird drew her eyes up to a majestic black-and-white harpy eagle flying above. Its huge wingspan and distinctive crested head made it instantly recognizable. It screamed again, circled her a few times, and flew off toward the mountains. Raptors were the spirit animals of her Black Seminole clan, so, taking the harpy's presence as a sign, she followed.

The eagle returned every few minutes, circled above before flying off again as if urging her forward. When she finally reached the rocky base of the mountain, she glanced up. The summit was shrouded in clouds but the urge to climb was strong, so after searching, she found a narrow path and began the ascent. The eagle sounded once again and flew directly at her. It now wore the face of a dark-skinned woman. That startled her so badly, she woke up.

Tamar came out of the dream sitting up in bed. The harpy's harsh caw seemed to call to her across the distance. The lighted dial of the clock on her nightstand showed it to be 5:00 a.m. The details of the dream lingered. She'd never been a vivid dreamer. In fact, she rarely remembered them at all, but this one was memorable if only for the scenario. What had the rain forest represented and what would she have discovered at the mountain's peak? The woman's face on the eagle had been as dark as her own. And that made her wonder if it was somehow tied to her ancestor, the First Tamar, who'd died in the 1880s. Per legend she walked in the dreams of July family members, a legend proven true a few years ago, when she showed in the form of a hawk to Tamar's adopted great-grandson Amari.

Tamar drew her hands down her face. It hadn't been a nightmare but it had left her shaken.

She slowly swung her legs over the side of the bed and sat there for a moment to let the aches and grumbles of her ninety-plus-year-old bones have their say before she could move. *Age ain't nothing but a number,* she scoffed. In truth, though, she was thankful for the discomfort because it meant the Spirit had blessed her with another day to keep an eye on the goings-on in the town of her birth. Henry Adams, Kansas, was founded in the late 1870s by freed slaves. The Julys took up residence in the 1880s. Back then, her Black Seminole ancestors had been famous all over the west for their train-robbing outlaw ways, until Hanging Judge Isaac Parker threw his gavel at them and turned the family into law-abiding citizens. In the years since, Henry Adams had its ups and downs, but by the beginning of the twenty-first century it hovered near death's door. No tax base, no young people, no jobs. Salvation arrived in the form of outsider Bernadine Brown, who purchased the town lock, stock, and barrel on eBay. Thanks to Bernadine's vast wealth and business acumen, the town where Tamar reigned as matriarch now boasted brand-new buildings, new residents, and a state-of-the-art infrastructure that made it the envy of every small city around.

Tamar finally stood and slipped on her robe and

her slippers. Crossing the quiet room to the open screened window, she looked out over the plains surrounding her home and the small creek that ran behind it. Elements of the dream returned but she set them aside. The area had had a series of violent storms yesterday and she wouldn't be surprised to learn a few tornadoes had touched down. Kansas summers often brought terrible weather and she hoped no one had been hurt. All was well now, though. The sun was rising red against the pink-and-gray sky of dawn, and the air was cooler, free of the humid mugginess so prevalent over the past week. The town's new swimming pool would be opening later that day and she was looking forward to the celebration. There was no telling what else might happen before sunset, because something was always going on in Henry Adams. With that in mind, she left the bedroom to start her day and hoped the dream would let her be.

Rochelle "Rocky" Dancer was a co-owner of Dog and Cow, Henry Adams's only diner. At 6:00 a.m., she entered the kitchen by the back door to the sounds of pots and pans being slammed around by her young head chef, Matt "Sizzle" Burke. She didn't know what had him so upset, but she stood and watched as he smacked a skillet down on the flat top then stormed to the big standing fridge, withdrew a carton of eggs from inside, and slammed the door as if it were the object of his rage. Before he could damage her kitchen or himself, she cleared her throat.

He turned to the sound but the anger on his face remained. "Hey, Rock."

She placed her purse on the steel prep table. "Morning, Siz. What's up?"

"My boyfriend and I are fighting. Again."

"Boyfriend?"

"Yes, boyfriend. His name's Stephen and he's a controlling jerk."

Rocky was still stuck on the boyfriend part. "How come I didn't know you were gay?"

He stopped cracking eggs. "That a problem?"

"Of course not. I just never knew, that's all."

"Guess it never came up."

"Guess not. So, do you want to talk about it?"

He blew out an impatient-sounding breath. "I've known I was gay since middle school. My family knows."

"No, Siz. Not about that. Why are you and Stephen fighting?"

"Oh." He smiled ruefully. "I got an offer to work for one of the best chefs in the country at his restaurant in Miami. Steph says I'll be abandoning him if I say yes."

"What's Steph do for a living?" Siz had been trying for years to find a chef to take him on. Texan Randy Emerson, one of the assistant cooks, was now training to be his replacement.

"Construction."

"Seems like he should be able to find a job there. All they do in Miami is build."

"That's what I said, but he doesn't want to move. He's lived in Kansas all his life and refuses to care that I may never get a chance like this again."

Rocky walked over to the sink and washed her hands. Siz was like the nephew she'd never had and she didn't enjoy seeing him upset. "What about a long-distance relationship?"

"He shot that down, too. Either I stay or we're done."

"That sounds kind of harsh. How long have you two been together?"

"Almost six months, and I really thought he was the one. Guess not." Siz then asked, "What would you do, Rock?"

She shrugged. "No idea. I'm still trying to get used to the idea of being in love with Jack enough to marry him next month, so I'm probably not the person you should be looking to for advice. Reverend Paula's good at this kind of thing, maybe talk to her."

"Maybe."

Reverend Paula Grant had degrees in theology and child psychology. When people had problems, she was the town's go-to person. She was both patient and wise. Over the past few years, Rocky had talked to her a lot about everything from losing her mom as a child to making peace with herself about being worthy of Jack James's love. Rocky wasn't totally convinced marriage was right for her, but Reverend Paula had helped her get comfortable enough with the idea to admit how much she did love Jack, and to say yes to his proposal. Now, she had to find the courage to walk down the aisle. "I do think that if he truly loved you, he'd want the best for you."

"I told him that."

"And his response?"

"That I'm just thinking about myself."

"Have you talked to your parents about it?"

He began cutting veggies for the omelets so popular with the breakfast crowd. "I have. My mom says go to Miami whether he wants me to or not. She's never liked Stephen to begin with—says he's needy and manipulative. Dad agrees with her. He said I could probably find somebody in Miami who really cares for me and isn't ashamed of it."

"What's he mean by that?"

"Stephen's still in the closet. Doesn't want his parents to know he's gay."

"Oh, Siz." She found that so disappointing.

"I know, Rock. I know. It's complicated." For a few silent moments, he cut onions, then said, "Don't worry. I'll figure it out."

Rocky hoped so. Siz was young, intelligent, and

talented, not only in the kitchen but musically as well. His jazz band Bloody Kansas played at the Dog monthly. In a vibrant and diverse city like Miami he'd come into his own, but not if bullied into giving up his dreams. "I'm going to open up. Make an appointment to see Reverend Paula. I'm sure she'll be able to help you figure this out."

"Okay."

From his lackluster tone, she wasn't sure he would follow through, but Rocky was convinced that if anyone could help him it was Paula. Out in the dining room, she stopped a moment to say good morning to the Dog's other co-owner, Malachi July. He was in his mid-sixties, a retired county veterinarian, and had ten years of sobriety under his belt. He was also the son of town matriarch Tamar July and was dating town owner Bernadine Brown. When Rocky's dad passed away two and a half decades ago, Mal was among those who'd stepped up to fill the hole in her life.

"Morning, Rock. The two new cooks start today?"

"Yes, and we need them badly." Because of Siz's amazing cooking skills diners were flocking to the Dog like the staff was handing out winning lotto tickets. Randy was a great help but more bodies were needed.

"You could've given me an apron to help out."

She snorted. "Yeah right." Mal oversaw the books, seating, and greeting, but was not allowed in the kitchen. Back in the diner's early days, he'd almost burned the place down and now wasn't allowed to cook even an egg. Although he did help out pouring coffee.

"Hater," he said with a mock sneer.

"And proud to be."

He went to his office and she went back to making sure the dining room was ready.

The breakfast crowd began arriving a short while later. As always, the place was packed with locals, construction crews, folks who lived in neighboring towns like Franklin, and everyone else looking for a good meal. The diner's candy-apple-red jukebox, recently named Gina after songstress Regina Belle, was offering the sweet jazzy sounds of Boney James's sax, which perfectly complemented the morning vibe. Always one to help her young waitstaff, Rocky carried a tray loaded down with plates over to a table of carpenters. Out of the corner of her eye, Rocky saw her fiancé Jack James enter.

Mal, who'd come out of the office to help, caught her look. "You got yourself a good man in him, Rock."

Unable to take her eyes off Jack, she nodded. "I know. Let's just hope I don't screw it up."

"Stop that," he said firmly. "Just go with your heart and you'll be fine."

Henry Adams had no secrets. Everyone knew how antsy she was about this whole marriage thing. Jack loved her and she definitely loved him, but she continued to believe he could do much better than a motorcycle-loving chick like herself who preferred riding leathers over fancy dresses and couldn't let go of the fear that the mental illness that claimed her mother would suddenly rise from within and take her, too.

But each and every time his eyes met hers like now, his smile seemed to vanquish her inner demons and fears, and all she could see was happiness. "Will you get the order from booth number four so I can go say good morning?"

"Sure can."

Arriving at Jack's booth, she poured coffee into his cup. "Morning, Professor. How are you?"

"Always better when I see you."

Jack was a dark-haired, dark-eyed, gorgeous male who flirted better than anyone she'd ever met. "Are we still on for the movie tonight?" he asked.

"Yes." Every Friday night Henry Adams showed movies in the recreation center's auditorium and people of all ages came from miles around to attend the family friendly event. "*Jurassic Park* is one of my all-time favorites."

"Mine, too."

Rocky realized she was staring at him like something she wanted to spend a lifetime savoring. As if reading her mind, he chuckled,

"You should probably take my order before someone yells at us to get a room."

Embarrassment heated her cheeks and she dropped her gaze. When she raised it again his eyes sparkled with humor and she said, "You're right. I'll get your order out asap."

"Thanks." But before she got too far, he caught her hand.

She stopped.

"I love you," he said.

Wondering how she'd make it to the kitchen on water-filled knees, she gave him a nod and tried not to fall down on her way to put in his order.

Over in Henry Adams's small subdivision, Gemma Dahl's twelve-year-old grandson, Wyatt, was in bed still asleep when she settled into her car for the drive to Clark's, the grocery store where she worked as a cashier. The sun was up and the day promised to be bright and beautiful after last night's storms. Turning the key in the ignition made the *need gas* light flash on. Irritated and kicking herself for not dealing with this the day before, she considered walking. The store was close enough for her to get there on time, but she didn't feel like it, so instead, she backed out of the garage to drive the short distance to the gas station.

Gemma and her grandson had been living in Henry Adams for almost a year, but she'd been born and raised in the neighboring town of Franklin. Memories of her life there and afterward were bittersweet. Pregnant at sixteen. Shipped off in disgrace to an aunt in Chicago. Raising her daughter Gabby alone on the city's rough South Side. Watching her daughter become a pregnant teen, too. The joy of holding baby Wyatt for the first time and then heartbreak as she stood with him at Lieutenant Gabrielle Dahl's grave at Arlington National Cemetery after an IED took her life during her second tour in Afghanistan.

Now, at forty plus, she was back in Kansas. She had a good job and Wyatt had a future that didn't include daily beatdowns from the South Side gangs he'd refused to join. In Henry Adams, there was support for a woman starting over like herself, strong male role models for Wyatt to emulate and look up to, and friends for him with goals as lofty as his own. Problems remained, however, and one stood behind the counter when she went in to pay for her gas.

"Well, if it isn't Hester. Where's your scarlet letter?"

Gemma met the mocking eyes of Astrid Franklin Wiggins and wanted to slap the smirk off her face. Instead, she tossed back coolly, "Where's your bridle, Seabiscuit?"

Astrid flinched. A woman in line behind Gemma snorted. Astrid's wealthy family founded

Franklin. In middle school her long face and horselike teeth earned her the disparaging nickname Seabiscuit. Back then she and her clique of *mean girls* savaged Gemma and other less fortunate kids like wolves on elk. Recently however, as mayor of Franklin, she'd made the mistake of taking on Henry Adams and Bernadine Brown. When the dust settled, Astrid went from a fur-wearing, big-house-living, rich witch to residing in a trailer park and working behind the counter at her family's gas station for minimum wage. "Any other questions for me?" Gemma asked.

Astrid's red, tight-lipped face said no. Gemma tossed the twenty she owed on the counter. "Have a nice day," she lied, and walked out.

Only after she'd driven away did she acknowledge her hurt and fury. Being sixteen and pregnant by the married Owen Welke became even more horrifying once her pregnancy began showing and the kids at school figured it out. Having to read Hawthorne's *Scarlet Letter* in English class and be called Hester behind her back, or in Astrid's case to her face, had been so painfully humiliating she'd been glad when her parents sent her to Chicago. Her parents were both dead now and went to their graves still ashamed. Her only shame lay in being so naïve as to believe Owen would leave his wife and child for her. She heard he'd left Franklin shortly after she did but she didn't know or care where he lived now. Last year, when she moved back to Franklin with Wyatt, she'd initially rented an apartment but everywhere she went whispers followed. *Tramp. Whore. Homewrecker.* Not wanting her grandson subjected to the ugliness, she inquired about living in Henry Adams because she'd heard about its excellent new school and she wanted Wyatt to have the best. It turned out to be a smart move. Ms. Brown was an angel. She had no problem with Gemma and Wyatt not being African American, and even helped her find a home that she was renting to buy, but she wondered if people in her hometown would ever see her as anything other than a pregnant unwed teenager. In spite of their opinions, she was proud of the life she'd carved out for herself and Wyatt, and for putting that witch Astrid in her place. Hopefully, the next time their paths crossed, Seabiscuit would think twice before opening her mouth.

Lucas Herman opened his eyes and saw the sun above him. His back felt wet. He vaguely realized it was because he was lying in a muddy field, but he didn't know why or where he was. He sat up slowly and his head hurt so badly he dropped it for a minute hoping the pain would stop. Raising it again he looked around and saw debris scattered around him: tree limbs, splintered wood, shingles, coiled wire, a mangled STOP sign. There was even a white bathtub. About fifty feet away stood what was left of a small house. The walls were caved in and it had no roof. His roaring headache kept him from thinking clearly, so he closed his eyes again and tried to remember how he'd come to be where he was. Then it all rushed back. Heart racing, he looked at the house again. *Uncle Jake!* He spun his attention to the busted-up SUV a few yards away. There was a huge tree lying on top of it. Stumbling to his feet he screamed, "Jazzy!"

Head throbbing, he ran to the SUV, tripping over wood and limbs. "Jazzy!" The tree's big leafy branches covered the entire driver's side. Peering through the foliage he saw that the door was gone but the tree's trunk and branches blocked access to the inside.

"Lucas!" his sister screamed.

Thankful she was alive, he ran around to the passenger side and looked in through the cracked muddy window. Her clothes were soaked, there was blood on her face, and when she saw him she began to cry. Frantic, he pulled on the handle but the door was so buckled and damaged it wouldn't budge. "Hold on! I'll be right back."

Visually searching the piles of debris, he spotted bricks. Grabbing one he hurried back and shouted, "Cover your face so the glass won't get in your eyes."

Using his arm to shield his own, he smashed the brick into the window again and again until it shattered enough to make a hole large enough for her to maybe climb through. Jagged pieces remained though, framing the opening like a shark's gaping mouth. Removing his tee shirt, he folded it a few times and laid it over the bottom of the window. It didn't go all the way across but he hoped it created enough of a cushion to keep her from getting too badly cut. She scooted over, carefully avoiding the sharp shards on the seat, and stood up as much as the caved in roof would allow. He reached in and grabbed her around the waist. "Try and lift your knees real high."

As he pulled her through her knees and legs grazed the points of glass beneath his shirt and she cried out in pain, but he managed to ease her to her feet. Once she was standing, he held onto her like she was made from gold and she held him just as tightly. They cried together for a long minute while he prayed silently to God and their dead parents for help. He leaned back and looked down at her. "You okay?"

She wiped her dirty face and nodded. She had cuts on her hands and arms. Little rivulets of blood trickled down her knees and the front of her legs below her black-and-pink polka-dot shorts.

"Do you hurt anywhere else?" he asked.

She shook her head no. "What about you?"

"Got a ginormous headache." He'd never had a concussion but the last thing he remembered before blacking out was something crashing into his head, so he figured that might be what was wrong. He turned his attention to the remnants of the house. He already knew Uncle Jake was dead, either inside or close by and his heart twisted into knots.

"Uncle Jake's dead, isn't he?" she asked in a tiny voice.

"Yeah, probably." No sense in lying to her. He didn't know what lay ahead but they were alive and together so that helped him not be so messed up. "Do you want to stay here while I go check or come, too?"

"No. I'm going with you."

He nodded. Since the death of their parents they'd been forced to deal with stuff no kids should have to endure. He wished for a time machine so they could go back to the life they used to have but . . . He took her hand.

They crossed the field of debris and found Jake lying facedown beneath a large section of the roof.

She whispered, "What do we do now?"

"Probably see if we can find his phone in the car and call 911."

Lucas wondered what life might have been like with Uncle Jake had they made it to California.

Filled with sadness, he forced his mind away from what would never be and walked with Jaz over to the SUV. They looked through the window but didn't see the phone. The interior was soaked from all the rain so even if they did find it, he figured it probably wouldn't work. But he climbed back in through the hole he'd made earlier, cutting his arms and legs in the process. After a bit of searching he found it beneath the front seat. It was dead. *Of course,* he said to himself.

He climbed back out. Using his shirt to wipe the blood off his legs, hands, and arms he put it back on. The few changes of clothing they owned were in trash bags in the trunk, but the keys were nowhere to be found. He looked out at the road running by the field they were in. "Let's start walking. Maybe we can get some-body to stop and call 911 for us."

"I don't want to go back to foster care."

Her soft plea put a lump in his throat. "I know. Me neither."

Gemma was driving and singing to Adele at the top of her lungs when she spotted two kids, a boy and a girl walking hand in hand up ahead along the side of the road. The boy turned and upon seeing her car began waving frantically as if attempting to flag her down. Surprised, she slowed. When she stopped, they stood back as if uncertain but it was the sight of the dirt and blood covering them and their clothing that widened her eyes. Checking her mirror to make sure there was no oncoming traffic, she got out.

The boy appeared on the verge of tears but said firmly, "We need help. Can you call 911, please?"

Taking in their faces and bloodied and muddy clothes again, she asked, "What happened?"

He replied in an emotion-filled whisper, "We got caught in a storm last night. Our uncle is dead and we don't have any place to go."

Her heart broke. Tears stung her eyes. "I'll call 911. You come on and get in the car. I know I'm a stranger but I promise I'll take care of everything. Okay?"

The boy nodded and dashed away the tears on his cheeks. The little girl just looked incredibly sad.

"What're your names?"

"I'm Lucas Herman. This is my sister Jasmine."

"My name's Gemma Dahl. Come, get in."

Once the two were in the backseat, she took out her phone.

Two minutes later, Gemma was talking to County Sheriff Will Dalton. She explained what little she knew of the situation and where she was. He promised to send a car immediately. She thanked him and then ended the call. "Help's on the way," she told the children. "I have some water in the trunk, do you want something to drink?"

They shook their heads no. She wished she had a first aid kit to take care of their cuts, but assumed the officer would.

Jasmine asked, "Will the police take us back to foster care?"

Gemma paused, eyed their bleak faces, and wondered what their story was. She answered truthfully, "I don't know, honey."

"Can we go home with you, please?" Jasmine asked.

Gemma glanced between them. Lucas was staring out the window as if he'd been turned to stone. Jasmine, whose face was framed by a soft cloud of natural hair that had shriveled from the ordeal, had a plea in her eyes that tugged at Gemma's heart so keenly, she almost said yes. However, she knew the decision was beyond her control. "We'll see what the sheriff says."

"You don't have to take us in," Lucas said quietly. "You probably have kids of your own."

"Just my grandson, Wyatt. He's about your age." She wanted to pull him into her arms and let him cry. It was obvious they'd been through a lot. "While we wait, how about you tell me what happened."

They took turns telling her about the storm, the death of their parents, their stint in foster care, and the ill-fated adoption by the man whose body they said lay outside a house back down the road. Once they were done, all she could think was, things happen for a reason, and she knew as sure as she knew her name that she'd been sent to find these children—she felt it in her bones. And with that she was determined to take them home and ensure that at some point soon they'd feel safe enough to smile again.

A county sheriff's vehicle pulled up and Gemma was surprised to see Sheriff Dalton himself step out. With him was a young African American female deputy Gemma had never met. When he reached the car, he leaned down and peered in through her lowered window. He was a big man and the kids drew back sharply. "Sheriff Dalton's a friend," she said, hoping to reassure them. "He's one of the good guys."

Will seemed pleased by that and gave her a silent nod of thanks. "Hi kids. I'm County Sheriff Will Dalton and this is Deputy Davida Ransom."

The deputy said, "Hi you two."

The kids gave both officers tentative nods of greeting.

Will asked them a few of the same questions Gemma had earlier. Once satisfied with their responses, he said. "I'm so sorry you're having to go through this. I'm going to have Ms. Gemma follow me back to where you said your Uncle Jake is. Do you think you can find the place again?"

Lucas said, "Yes, sir."

"Okay. It shouldn't take us long to get things settled there."

Jasmine said, "Then can we go home with Ms. Gemma?"

Before the sheriff could respond, Deputy Ransom spoke up. "Unfortunately, no. When we're done, you'll ride back with us. A social worker from Child Services will take care of you from there."

Gemma saw Will's lips thin for a second as if the deputy had spoken out of turn, but he kept whatever he was thinking to himself. Instead, he asked Gemma, "Does that sit right with you, Ms. Dahl?"

"Truthfully, no. I'd rather take them home. They've been through enough for the moment. They need to get cleaned up, fed, and have a doctor check them out. I want to talk to Ms. Brown about their situation, too."

Ransom opened her mouth, but a pointed look from her boss shut her down immediately. He said to Gemma, "I agree with you. It could be hours before a caseworker shows up. Let's see what Ms. Brown can work out."

Ransom seemed shocked. "Sheriff, the law—"

"I know the law, Deputy, been handling it since you were probably in middle school. Ms. Brown knows the law, too, and if anybody can work the system so these kids can settle in with

34

Ms. Dahl, it's her. Now, how about we go see to their uncle so they can be on their way."

She nodded tersely.

He told Gemma, "We'll follow you. I'll call Ms. Brown on the way."

Gemma turned her car around so she could lead the sheriff, and Lucas asked her, "Does that mean we're going home with you?"

"At least for now. Is that okay with you?"

Eyes glistening, he gave her a quick nod. "Yes. Thank you."

She checked out Jasmine in the mirror. "That okay with you, Jasmine?"

She responded with a quiet, "Yes, ma'am. Real okay."

"Then let's help the sheriff take care of your uncle."

Once the sheriff finished his tasks and the county coroner was called to transport Mr. Gleason's remains, a crowbar was used to open the SUV's trunk to retrieve the trash bags holding the children's clothing.

Gemma thought it sad that it was all they owned in the world, then reminded herself it could be worse. The children could have lost their lives in the storm too, and be riding with their uncle to the morgue, leaving the bags to serve as the only testaments to their having lived at all.

CHAPTER
2

Gemma pulled into her driveway and cut the engine. The kids sat in silence behind her.

"Is this where you live?" Jasmine asked.

"Yes, so how about we get out and go inside."

They grabbed their bags and followed her up the steps and inside. The town's pediatrician, Dr. Reginald Garland, was in the living room talking with her grandson, Wyatt.

"Bernadine called me," Doc Reg said, explaining his presence.

"Thanks for coming." She saw Wyatt giving Lucas and Jasmine a silent once-over. He was always so poker-faced, she sometimes had difficulty knowing what he was thinking. Setting concerns about his reaction aside for the moment, she made the introductions. "Dr. Garland and Wyatt. This is Lucas Herman and his sister Jasmine."

Wyatt nodded in their direction but didn't approach.

Dr. Garland extended his hand first to Lucas and then his sister. "Everybody calls me Doc Reg. Glad to meet you. I want to take a look at you and ask you some questions about how you feel physically. Is that okay?"

They gave him tight nods.

He checked them over in turn, asking about the accident and if they had any pain. "How'd you get these cuts on your legs, Jasmine?"

Lucas spoke up. "It was my fault, sir. I had to break the window to get her out of the car. I tried to make a cushion out of my shirt, but she still got cut when I pulled her out."

"Using your shirt was a great idea, son. Without it, the cuts would probably be a lot worse. Good thinking."

Gemma couldn't tell whether that absolved the guilty feelings Lucas apparently had, but he seemed relieved.

Jasmine said, "Lucas cut his arms and legs on the windows too, when he crawled back in to look for Uncle Jake's cell phone."

Garland surveyed the scrapes and cuts. "You won't need any stitches, but I want you both to take a nice hot shower and wash the cuts out as best you can. I'll leave Ms. Gemma some ointment for you to apply so they don't get infected."

Lucas volunteered, "I think I might have a concussion, too," and told him about his headache and the probable cause.

Reggie checked his pupils with a small penlight. "Ms. Gemma said you two were walking along the highway. Any trouble with your balance?"

"No, sir."

After inspecting the spot where Lucas had been hit in the head, Reg put his instruments back into his bag. "I think you might be right about the concussion but it appears to be mild. If the headache persists we'll do some tests." He looked between them. "I'm sorry for you loss. Ms. Gemma will take good care of you. I'll come by tomorrow and check on you. In the meantime, get those showers, something to eat, and then rest up."

Gemma was pleased with how thorough and gentle he'd been. "Thanks, Reg."

"You're welcome. See you tomorrow."

After his departure, she was about to take them upstairs when the doorbell rang.

"I'll get it," Wyatt said. He returned with Bernadine.

Gemma introduced her to the children as the town's owner, and Bernadine said, "Pleased to meet you, Lucas and Jasmine. Wish it was under better circumstances. This being such a small town, word's already spread about you being here and our kids are anxious to meet you but I told them to let you settle in first."

Jasmine asked, "How many kids live here?"

"Nine," Wyatt said.

"That's all?"

Wyatt shrugged. "It's Henry Adams. Not Chicago."

Bernadine shot him a small smile.

Jasmine asked warily, "Does this mean we get to stay here?"

"For the time being."

"Good," Jasmine said firmly. "We don't want to go back to foster care."

Gemma got the impression that their foster care experience had not been a good one. She knew from the foster parents who'd lived in her building back in Chicago that many were wonderful people and it saddened her that these kids seemed to hold bitter memories.

Bernadine said to Jasmine, "We'll talk about what might happen next in a day or two. In the meantime, welcome to Henry Adams." And in a soft voice added, "I'm very sorry for your loss."

"Thank you," Lucas replied.

"I'll see you soon."

Gemma walked her to the door and out to the porch.

Looking concerned, Bernadine said, "Poor babies, there's no telling what might have happened to them had you not been driving by."

Gemma agreed. "This might sound weird but I feel like I was supposed to find them. Does that make any sense?"

"Yes. God works in mysterious ways."

"But I've never been a religious person."

Bernadine gave her a shrug. "Doesn't matter. God still gets it done. So, tell me. If you think you were meant to find them, do you want them to stay with you if I can arrange it?"

"My heart says yes, but, I'd like to talk to Wyatt about it first. This will affect him, too."

Bernadine nodded understandingly.

"To become a foster parent, I'll need to be certified, won't I?"

"Yes, but because of all the other fostering we've done here, we might be able to put you on a fast track. The state will want to do a background check and schedule a visit to make sure your house is safe and that you have adequate space. Which you have of course."

The house had four bedrooms so that wouldn't be an issue, and she had smoke detectors in case of a fire. She had no idea what else might be needed, but she'd do whatever else was required. "Thanks for sending the sheriff and Reg. Let me go back in and get them washed up and fed. Reggie wants them to rest up. They've had quite a day."

"I'll start making calls on their behalf, I'll also give Judge Amy Davis a call and let her know what's going on, just in case we need judicial assistance while we work things out. I'm heading back to my office. Call me if you need any-thing."

Back inside Gemma found the three young people still standing in the same places. The

41

silence felt awkward. "Lucas and Jasmine, let me show you where you can shower and sleep. Wyatt, I'll be right back."

He didn't respond but watched their ascent intently. Yes, she needed to speak with him. If he didn't want the Herman kids to stay it would present a problem.

She led them down the hallway to one of the unused bedrooms. Lucas glanced around the interior. "I don't want Jazzy to be by herself so is it okay if we sleep in the same room?"

She mentally applauded his protectiveness. After all they were in a strange place. "Sure. That's not a problem."

"I can sleep on the floor."

"That won't be necessary. We'll drag the mattress off the bed in the other room. You can use the shower in here," she told him. "And your sister can use mine."

His trash bag in hand, he went into the bathroom while she led Jasmine across the hall to her bedroom with its connected shower.

Gemma asked her, "Will you be okay in here alone?"

"Yes, I think so."

"Towels are here and remember to wash those cuts good."

"I will. Can I wash my hair? It feels dirty."

"Sure. There's shampoo right there. I don't have any hair dressing for you, but I can get some from Ms. Bernadine. Would that be okay? She just lives across the street."

"I have a little bit but I'll need some more."

"Can you do your own hair?"

"Yes, when it's in a fro like this, but I can't do cornrows. I have my own comb and brush." Jasmine then eyed her. "Can you do cornrows?"

"Yes."

"Really?"

Gemma smiled. "Yes, I used to do the hair of the two girls who lived upstairs from me when I lived in Chicago. They were about your age."

"You're really nice."

"Thanks Jasmine. You're pretty nice yourself."

That earned Gemma the first smile and her heart swelled. "You and Lucas come down when you're done."

On her way back to where Wyatt was waiting, she gave Bernadine a quick call about the hair dressing. She also called her job to let store manager Gary Clark know why she hadn't shown up. After verbally applauding her for rescuing the kids, he told her to take the rest of the day off to get them settled in. Thanking him and knowing she was going to catch grief from the assistant manager Alma House because of Gary's largesse, she put Alma out of her mind for the moment and stuck her phone in the side pocket of her black slacks.

In the kitchen, she dropped into a chair. Wyatt

watched her silently before remarking, "They look pretty messed up."

"They've had it rough." Because he hadn't been privy to all the details, she shared what she knew of their story.

His dark eyes widened. "The guy who adopted them was killed in the tornado last night?"

"Yes."

"That sucks. Are they going to stay with us?"

"I'd like them to if Ms. Bernadine can arrange it. How would you feel about that?"

"Do they have any other place else to go?"

"For now, no."

He shrugged. "Then they should stay here."

"You don't mind?"

"No, Gram. Will they stay, like permanently?"

"That I don't know. We'll have to wait and see if the uncle's wife still wants to go through with the adoption and if not what the court and social services say. Would you mind if they did?"

He shrugged. "I guess I'm okay with it as long as they don't turn out to be jerks. Gets lonely being the only kid here sometimes."

She found that telling. He rarely shared his feelings. "Miss your Chicago crew?"

"Yeah. I was never by myself there, or at least not during the daytime."

There were eight other children his age in their housing complex and they were all close. "You have friends here."

"I do, but we're not as tight."

"We've been here less than a year, Wyatt. That may change."

"I know but they already have their alliances. I need my own. Especially now with Eli moving to Cali." Eli was the son of teacher Jack James. He'd taken Wyatt under his wing a few months ago, and would be heading to California to attend community college. She knew Wyatt would miss him a lot.

"Can I ask you something?"

"Sure."

"Are you happy here? Should we have picked another place to live?"

"No, this is fine. The people are nice. I have a good school. Mr. James is an awesome teacher and the kids let me be myself. I don't want to move again if that's what you're thinking about."

"I'm not."

"Good. It's okay by me if we add Lucas and Jasmine to our crew."

"Okay. Just needed to get your opinion. After they lost their parents they were put in different foster homes and they just got back together. Be nice if they didn't have to be separated again."

"I don't have to share my room, do I?"

"Not if you don't want to. We have two extras."

"I don't want to."

"Nothing wrong with you stating that up front." She was glad they were having this talk.

He added. "The room I had in Chicago would fit into my closet now. I like having space."

"So do I." Their tiny two-bedroom place in Chicago served them well but this gorgeous home with its four bedrooms, beautiful kitchen, and the rest was more than she ever imagined living in, let alone having the opportunity to purchase.

The doorbell rang.

"I'll get it," Wyatt offered.

Gemma quickly turned her mind to dinner. Her guests probably hadn't eaten since yesterday and were for sure starving. She was eyeing the contents of the fridge when he returned with Crystal, Bernadine's eighteen-year-old daughter. "Ms. Bernadine said you needed something for the little girl's hair."

"I do."

"She can use this. Do you want me to help her with it?"

"No, she says she can do it herself. She has a fro now, but I can do braids if she needs me to." Seeing the obvious skepticism on Crystal's face, Gemma told her what she'd told Jasmine.

"The girls were Black?"

Gemma saw Wyatt smile.

"Yes. Their mother Audrey had to be at work at six a.m. so I did their hair before they went to school."

The skepticism was replaced by approval. "Okay," Crystal said, grinning, and handed her the jar of dressing.

Gemma added, "I'll make her an appointment with Kelly for later this week, though. She could use a little pampering. I'll have Mr. Curry give her brother a haircut, too."

"Mom told me a little bit about what happened. Hope they get to stay. Anything else I can do?"

"Yes. If I call in an order to the Dog can you go pick it up?"

"Sure."

Gemma made the call and Crystal said, "Be back as soon as I can."

"Thanks, Crystal."

"No problem. This way when I bring the food back I can meet them." She was the town's big sister and although sometimes known for putting the fear of God in the other kids, her heart was in the right place.

After leaving the shower and drying off, Lucas looked through the bag holding his clothes for something clean to wear. He knew he should be thankful to have anything to put on, but all the clothing he'd worn for the past two years had been worn first by someone else and he was so sick of hand-me-downs. Back before his parents died everything he and Jaz owned, from clothes, to toys, to the shoes on their feet, had been brand new. Dressed, he checked himself out in the oval mirror hanging on the wall. Growing up he was often told how much he resembled his parents. He supposedly had his dad's chin and mouth and his mom's eyes and coloring, but all he saw now was just a sad-faced ten-year-old boy beat down by life. Death had taken his parents and Uncle Jake and now he and his sister were in the house of strangers. Admittedly, Ms. Dahl was nice, as was everybody else they'd met so far, but he was so tired of being sad and scared of what might happen next. He wanted to hear his dad's big laugh, and missed the way his mom would sometimes hug him for no reason, even though at the time he found it embarrassing. He missed his room, their dog Bowser, the family camping trips, and seeing his dad all dressed up in his suit and tie when he left the house in the mornings to go off to work. Lucas thought back on the friends he'd had in his subdivision and at school, his teachers, and the members of his soccer team. He wondered if they ever thought about him. Why was all this bad stuff happening? Was he being punished for something? If he prayed and told God he was really sorry, would it stop? The boy in the mirror had tears in his eyes again and he wiped them away. *This is so hard,* he cried inside, but he needed to man up and be strong for his little sister.

He walked down the hall to the room where she

was and knocked on the door. "Jaz. You okay in there."

"Yes."

The door opened and she looked up at him. She had on a red tee and a pair of green shorts. Her hair was wet but looked better. She smoothed her hand over it. "Miss Gemma said she'd get me some more stuff for my hair."

"How do you feel?"

Instead of answering she asked, "How do you feel?"

"Okay, I guess. Head still hurts but not as much. Did you put the medicine on your cuts?"

"I did," she said, then added in a soft voice, "I wish Mama and Daddy were here."

"I know." Grief bubbled up in his chest so he changed the subject. "Ms. Gemma's nice."

Jaz nodded. "Do you think Aunt Leslie will still want to adopt us?"

She was Uncle Jake's wife. "I don't know."

"If she doesn't, I want to stay here."

Lucas wasn't sure what he wanted other than to have their old lives back, but that wasn't happening. He held out his hand. Together they walked to the stairs.

In her office in the red architectural beauty of a building the locals dubbed the Power Plant, town owner Bernadine Brown sat at her desk thinking about Lucas and Jasmine Herman.

Sending Crystal to Gemma's with hair dressing had been an easy task, but she sensed going forward might be more concerning. Both children looked incredibly sad and had good reason to. One minute they'd been on their way to a new life in California, only to have it cruelly snatched away and cast adrift once again.

Lily Fontaine July, Bernadine's right hand and the wife of town mayor Trent July, stuck her head in the door. "How are the children?"

"Whole, at least physically. Reg checked them out."

"Such a sad story."

"I know. Hopefully things work out so we can give them some good news soon. They've had enough bad. Will Dalton is going to call the uncle's wife to see where she stands on the adoption. If she's still willing, I'll have Katy fly them there as soon as they get rested up." Katy was the pilot of Bernadine's personal jet.

"Does Will know if the kids and the wife are close?"

She shook her head. "But we'll keep a good thought."

"Okay. Shifting gears. The pool people just conducted their final water quality tests so we're good to go. The Astrid Wiggins Memorial Pool can officially be opened this afternoon."

That made Bernadine smile. The opening had been highly anticipated. There'd be a ribbon cutting ceremony, a short speech from Mayor Trent July, and after that the fun would begin. She then thought about town nemesis Astrid Wiggins. "When she finds out we named the pool after her, smoke will be pouring from her ears."

"You told her we would."

"I'm sure she didn't believe me, though." Bernadine couldn't think of a better way to reward a bigot than to name something after her in a town founded by freed slaves. Astrid would undoubtedly gnash her horsey teeth and curse them up and down, but she'd be too busy ringing up diesel and jerky to do anything else.

Lily's voice cut into her thoughts. "I still think the sign on the pool gate should read: 'The Astrid Wiggins Memorial Pool. Named for her because she hates Henry Adams and everyone in it.'"

Bernadine chuckled. "I do too, but Reverend Paula talking us out of that was probably a good thing."

"I suppose," Lily agreed grudgingly.

"Does your hubby have his speech ready?"

"Yes. All three minutes of it."

"Good. I can always count on him to be short and sweet."

"And it's going to be real sweet having him all to myself while the boys are gone."

"When are they leaving?" Lily and Trent were adoptive parents to two sons—eleven-year-old Devon and fifteen-year-old Amari.

"Both leave Sunday. Devon's going to Mississippi to spend a week with his grandmother's friend, Ms. Myrtle."

"Will he see his mom while he's there?"

"Not sure. I told Ms. Myrtle to play it by ear. If he wants to go, she said she'd arrange it."

Devon's mother, Rosalie, was developmentally challenged and had resided in a state facility most of her life. Devon's birth was the result of her being sexually assaulted by a still-unknown man who took advantage of her childlike state.

"And when does Amari leave?"

"Same day. He'll be gone for two weeks, though. He's spending the first week on the Lakota Sioux reservation with his grandmother Judith Windsong, and then who knows where he and Griffin will take off to. Griffin's promised me and Trent that Amari will wear a helmet, but I'm still scared to death at the thought of him being on the back of Griffin's motorcycle."

Griffin July was Amari's biological dad and Trent's cousin, and now that Bernadine knew Amari's vacation plans she was going to be worried about him being on the bike, too. "Your boys will be gone. Preston's going down to Florida to hang with his mom, Margaret, at NASA. Gary's girls will be visiting their mom, Colleen. Ronnie and Zoey are touring South America and South Africa, and Alfonso and Maria Acosta are off to Mexico with Abuela

Anna to hang out with family. It's going to be pretty quiet around here with all the kids gone."

"We hope. This is Henry Adams after all."

"True." In the five years since purchasing the town off eBay, there'd been enough drama for a town three times its size.

Trent appeared in the doorway. "How are the new kids, Bernadine?"

"Doing good. Gemma has them at her house."

"If they need anything let me know. I'll stop in to see them later. Pool ceremony in one hour."

Bernadine replied, "We'll meet you there."

He winked at his wife and disappeared. Bernadine was amused by the dreamy look on Lily's face. They'd been madly in love since high school. "I assume you and Mr. Mayor have big plans for being home alone."

Lily grinned.

"Enjoy it."

"Oh, we will. Don't worry."

Laughing, Lily exited and Bernadine turned to her laptop to send Will Dalton an e-mail with hopes he had good news concerning the Herman kids.

CHAPTER
3

On her way into town for lunch and the pool opening festivities, Tamar was driving along July Road in her ancient truck, Olivia. Loving the power in the olive-green Ford, she gleefully hit the curve doing eighty-five miles per hour. She was well known for her need for speed but upon seeing a brown county squad car pull out behind her, its bubble flashing, she let out a sigh, downshifted, and eased to a stop on the gravel shoulder to wait. She didn't expect more than a warning. After all, the county deputies knew she drove like an Indy qualifier. Using her rearview mirror to see which one it might be, her jaw dropped at the sight of an unfamiliar African American female in the familiar brown uniform and hat. There were only three men of color under County Sheriff Will Dalton's command, but when had this woman been hired, and why hadn't Tamar been informed?

The woman had clear dark skin, and although tall, appeared to be too young to be an officer of the law. She leaned down and said through Olivia's lowered window, "Good afternoon, ma'am. License and registration please."

Unaccustomed to being asked to show her

55

JAMES RIVER VALLEY
LIBRARY SYSTEM
105 3RD ST SE
JAMESTOWN ND 58401

papers, Tamar swallowed her pique, leaned over, and withdrew the documents from the glove box. "You're new here."

"Yes, ma'am. Deputy Davida Ransom." She took a moment to compare Tamar's face to the photo on the license, checked the registration, and passed them back. "Do you know what the speed limit is on this road, Ms. July."

"Since it's named after my family, of course I do."

The woman paused.

Tamar asked, "When did Will hire you?"

This time she studied Tamar intently. "A week ago."

"And you're from, where?"

"Denver."

"Welcome to Kansas, Deputy Ransom. My family has lived in Henry Adams over a hundred years."

"Nice to know, but it doesn't give you the right to endanger yourself and others by speeding."

Tamar bristled. She knew the young woman was just doing her job but that didn't soothe her irritation when the deputy handed her a speeding ticket.

Ransom said, "I wrote it for five miles over the limit as opposed to the fifteen you were actually doing."

Tamar eyed her coolly but the woman appeared unfazed.

"Slow down, Ms. July. Thanks for the welcome. Nice meeting you."

Tamar lied, "Same here."

Ransom touched her hat respectfully, walked back to her vehicle, and drove off in the opposite direction.

Seething, Tamar steered Olivia back onto the road, and just to show how she felt about being ticketed for the first time in her life, she floored Olivia the rest of the way into town.

The Dog's jukebox was blaring "Mustang Sally" by Wilson Pickett when she entered. The long line of people waiting to be seated ahead of her only added to her mood so she pulled rank as resident matriarch and caught Rocky's eye. The set of her jaw must have let Rocky know she was not to be fooled with today, so she came over and took her to a booth in the back. Without being told, Rocky grabbed a carafe of coffee and poured the steaming brew into Tamar's waiting cup. "You look like you want to shoot some-body."

"I just got a speeding ticket."

Rocky was smart enough to keep her smile hidden. "And who had the audacity to do that?"

"A new deputy named Davida Ransom."

"Guess she doesn't know you double for Danica Patrick around here, huh?"

The black hawkeyes gave Rocky a hard stare, which left her as unfazed as Deputy Ransom.

Tamar exhaled a breath of frustration. "I've never been ticketed in my life."

"We've been telling you for years to slow down. Deputy Ransom just earned herself a free lunch. You drive entirely too fast. All the time."

The jaw tightened further. "I'll have my usual," Tamar said tersely.

Rocky's grin played on her lips as she left Tamar sugaring her coffee.

On her way to put in Tamar's order Rocky was stopped by Mal.

"Tamar looks like she's spitting nails."

"She is. Got a speeding ticket from a new deputy."

His face widened with surprise. "Really? What's the deputy's name?"

"Davida Ransom."

"If Will comes in for lunch, I'll let him know Deputy Ransom gets a meal on the house. Maybe now she'll slow down."

"Great minds think alike."

After lunch, having almost gotten over her annoying encounter with Deputy Davida Ransom, Tamar allowed herself to enjoy the festive atmosphere and the people waiting for the pool's opening ceremony. There were balloons, hot dogs cooking under the watchful eye of town grill masters Clay Dobbs and his buddy Bing Shepard, bags of chips, and soft drinks nestled in colorful ice-filled tubs. The fenced-in pool was behind the rec center, and the area around it was packed with people laughing and conversing. The Henry Adams kids, from Eli and Crystal down to Kelly and Bobby Douglas's toddler twins, were decked out in new swim gear and chomping at the bit to jump in. Preston and Amari were doing their best not to ogle the lifeguard, a tall curvy brown-skinned beauty named Simone Vale, and failing badly. Preston's girlfriend, Leah, noting the interest, was glaring so icily their way, Tamar was surprised the pool's water hadn't frozen over. Bernadine let it be known that everyone in the area was welcome to enjoy the new pool, so there was a large group of people and children from neighboring Franklin.

"I hear you got a ticket this morning."

Tamar fixed a leveling stare on Marie Jefferson. Never without her signature cat-eye glasses, she'd served as the town's only teacher until retiring a few years ago. She was now school superintendent and her family had been in Henry Adams even longer than the Julys.

"Stop giving me the evil eye," Marie said in response to Tamar's look. "Everybody knows you drive too fast. Glad the new deputy had the guts to write you up."

Wondering how much more of this she'd have to put up with, Tamar turned away and focused on barber and former Henry Adams mayor Riley

Curry. Dressed in a new version of his old black suit, complete with a fake red carnation on his lapel, he was skinning and grinning his way through the crowd.

Marie asked, "Why is Riley decked out like he's been asked to speak?"

"Who knows." After finding himself destitute and homeless last month, he'd supposedly turned over a new leaf, but many in town, Tamar included, remained skeptical. "His talking about running for mayor this fall means he's as delusional as ever."

"Nobody's going to vote for him," Marie stated flatly, "but two thumbs up on this pool. For Henry Adams to have gone from being destitute to having this gorgeous pool is amazing. The Dusters would be so proud."

Tamar agreed. The founders certainly wouldn't recognize the place. They'd lived in dugouts that first winter back in 1879 and the only structures aboveground were the pipes of the stoves that kept them warm. "Who's that with the purple hair?" she asked Marie.

"Candy Stevens. She's the new butcher over at Gary's store."

Tamar had no problems with her hair; Siz changed his hair color seemingly daily. What bothered her was her unfamiliar face. First Deputy Ransom and now a new butcher. Since when did folks come to town and not introduce themselves. "Any other new folks I should know about?"

Marie appeared confused by the question and the tone. "I'm not sure, Tamar."

"As the matriarch, I'm supposed to know everyone."

"Place is growing. Those days might be over."

Tamar didn't like the sound of that. What use was a matriarch if no one respected her enough to at least pretend to honor her position?

"Do you want me to bring Candy over so you two can meet?"

"No."

Marie studied her closely. "You okay?"

"Does it matter?"

"Yes."

Tamar huffed out an impatient breath. "Trent needs to hurry up and get this show on the road. It's hot standing out in this sun." She ignored the concern on Marie's face and concentrated on Trent now stepping up to the blue satin ribbon to get things underway.

As always, his remarks were short, and when he finished he turned the mic over to Lyman Proctor, Franklin's newly appointed town supervisor. He offered a few words thanking Bernadine and the people of Henry Adams for including the residents of Franklin in the grand opening.

Trent stepped to the mic again. "And now, I'd

like to invite my son Amari July to the ribbon."

The surprise on Amari's face generated smiles and chuckles.

Trent continued. "If I remember correctly, building a town pool was his idea, so we want him to cut the ribbon."

Appearing both proud and embarrassed, Amari took the scissors and made the cut. Applause and cheers filled the air and Trent called out, "The Astrid Wiggins Memorial Pool is now open. Let the swimming begin!"

There were races, cannonball contests off the diving board, and dodgeball games played with beach balls. Soon after, a pool-wide game of Marco Polo broke out.

Tamar watched the fun for a while then walked the short distance to the rec center. Inside, the air-conditioning felt good after being out in the heat of the day. She entered the office she and her volunteers used as the base of operations for everything from prepping for the Friday Night Movies to conducting the yearly tornado drills and sat at her desk. Marie's words came back: *Those days might be over.* Were they, she wondered? Would progress pave over all she'd done to preserve the history and soul of Henry Adams, like the old dirt roads had been? Would there come a day when the names of their ancestors like Mayor Olivia July and schoolteacher Cara Lee Jefferson were forgotten?

A chill spread through her. In truth, she knew it was a possibility because it had happened before. When the town was at its nadir, the handful of residents that remained, including herself, were so focused on surviving they'd stopped celebrating August First, once its most honored tradition. The old photo albums passed down to her by her father, Trenton, had lain in her bedroom closet all but forgotten. Then Bernadine and the families arrived, reinfusing Henry Adams with life and vitality. Amari personally revived the August First parade, and the day, originally celebrated by nineteenth-century abolitionists to honor Britain's decision to end slavery in the West Indies, became special again.

"What are you doing in here by yourself? You okay?"

She glanced up to see her grandson the mayor in the doorway. "Yes. Just doing some old lady thinking."

He came in and sat down. "Heard you got a ticket."

"Is there anyone who hasn't heard?"

"Probably not. Small town you know."

She rolled her eyes. For all his gentle ribbing, she loved him madly.

He asked, "So what kind of old lady thinking? Anything a young pup like myself can help with?"

"No. Just thinking about time passing and the change it's bringing. Nothing earth-shattering."

He studied her. He knew her better than anyone except maybe her BFF Mable Lane. "You sure?" he asked.

"Positive, so go on back and run your town. I have things to do."

He stood but she noted his reluctance. "I'm fine, Trent. Really."

"All right. If I find out you're holding out on me, I'm putting you in time out."

"Bye."

His smile met hers and he departed, leaving her alone with her melancholy thoughts. She didn't wallow for long, though. The Friday Night Movies were on tap for later, so she stood and went to work.

After enjoying the Friday Night Movie at the rec center, Rocky cuddled next to Jack while he drove them back to her place. "Did you like the movie?" she asked.

"I did."

She peered up into his shadow-covered face. "Are you telling the truth, Professor?"

"I am. I've always liked *Jurassic Park*."

"But?"

He grinned. "You're not supposed to know me that well, Rock."

"If we're getting married, I should know a little bit about you, don't you think?"

"Yes."

"So, spill it."

"I'd like a serious movie sometimes."

"Like what?"

"Oh, I don't know." He quieted a moment as if thinking. "Ever seen *Lion in Winter?*"

"No. Who's in it?"

"Katharine Hepburn and Peter O'Toole."

"Ah, the African Queen and Lawrence of Arabia. What's it about?"

So, he told her about the movie's fictional take on the intrigue surrounding the marriage of O'Toole's character Henry the Second and Hepburn's Eleanor of Aquitaine. Rocky found herself fascinated. "So, Eleanor had one of their kids start a rebellion against his dad, the King—her husband. And he put her in prison?"

"Yes."

"She was that much of a badass?"

He nodded. "She rode on one of the Crusades, too."

"Sounds like my kind of woman."

He laughed and Rocky admitted to enjoying the sound of it as much as she did him. "How about we have our own movie night then?" she asked.

"Great idea. Can we have snacks?"

"Yes, Professor, as long as you don't pick a

movie that puts me to sleep. How about we add *Seven Beauties* to our list, too?"

He stared her way.

She smiled. "What's the matter? Shocked you, did I?"

"No offense intended, but yes."

"Just because I've seen *Mad Max* a thousand times, doesn't mean I can't enjoy a *film,*" she said in a mock haughty tone. "Lina Wertmüller was the first female director nominated for an Oscar. I liked her *Swept Away,* too."

"Where'd you see them?"

His still-stunned tone was amusing. "Marie rented them back in the day."

"I'm impressed."

"There's more to me than motorcycles and leather, my dear Professor."

"I like the motorcycles and leather."

She swore he waggled his eyebrows, so she tossed out, "Down boy, before we hit something."

He laughed and she snuggled closer.

When they reached her trailer, they sat in the quiet interior of his truck. Rocky wondered if she'd ever get used to being in love. "I got a call from your mom today," she told him.

"Has she booked Buckingham Palace for our wedding and invited the Queen?"

"Not as far as I know." His mother had been giving them fits about wanting in on the wedding plans. "She said she has a few more people she needs to invite and wants me to say yes, they can come."

"No," he said firmly. "She's invited way too many people as it is. Most of whom I don't even know."

"That was my reaction too, but I wanted to get your opinion first."

"Do you want me to talk to her?"

"No. She and I need to come to an understanding about who runs what, and that will never get straight if I pass everything off to you. I like your mother, probably a lot more than she does me—"

"Rock, she—"

"I'm being real here, Jack. She tolerates me at best, and I'm okay with that. It's the price I'm willing to pay to be around your fabulous dad."

"He is the bonus."

"Yes, he is, but they come as a package, so I'm being respectful. They're elders after all, and your parents, but she's trying to take advantage of that." Since learning about the wedding, Stella James had pushed to have a say in where they got married, who married them, the date, the time, the service, and the menu at the reception. "The only thing she hasn't wanted to take charge of is the music."

"That's because she's tone deaf," he replied,

and placed a supportive kiss on her brow. "How mad are you?"

"Not very, but if she keeps poking the bear I may have to eat her."

"She probably tastes really good with mustard."

Rocky enjoyed his sense of humor, too. "You want to come in?"

"Will there be leather involved?"

She laughed. "Get out of the truck, crazy man."

Inside, Jack marveled at the beauty of her place as he always did. The eclectic furniture, a mix of secondhand-store and flea-market finds, melded nicely with others made of expensive exotic woods. Vibrant, gallery-quality artwork covered the walls. One piece in particular, a large blue-themed watercolor painted by Crystal of the leather-wearing Rock astride her Black Shadow motorcycle, was his favorite. Crystal had somehow managed to capture her fierceness and her vulnerability. He didn't know where Rock would place all her furniture and art when she moved into his place but he planned to sit back and enjoy them enlivening his very vanilla home. After losing his wife Eva to cancer five years ago, he was sure he'd never love again, but the moment he set eyes on Rochelle *call me Rocky* Dancer, after moving to Henry Adams, he was a goner. Bets were placed all over town as to whether she'd give him the time of day, and he and everyone else was convinced she wouldn't. But he'd been persistent, not in a stalking way but in a way that gave her space. Eventually she'd lowered her shields, and then her heart, and now they were planning to marry around Labor Day, if she didn't jump on her Black Shadow and roar off into the sunset.

The thought of that was chilling. He wanted to believe she'd show up at the church but there was no guarantee. She was an extraordinary woman who played the flute, restored classic motorcycles, and had more tools than most men. She also had a passion for cooking and sports. On the inside, however, she was like a wary child peering out of the shadows. With her family history, he understood why. So, he loved her gently, hoping to fill those spaces with feelings of softness, safety, and reassurance.

"You want coffee?" she asked from the kitchen.

"Sure."

Although she refused to drink decaf, he did, and she began purchasing it for him soon after their first date. It pleased him because it meant she valued his place in her life.

Coffee mugs in hand, they walked back to the living room and took seats on her buttery soft, navy-blue leather sofa. He draped an arm over the back and she rested her head against his shoulder and asked, "So, have you decided where we're going on our honeymoon?"

69

"Have you?"

"Is that what you teach your students? Answer a question with a question?"

His smile showed above the rim of his cup. "How about Hawaii?"

"How about New York City?"

"Really?"

"Always wanted to go there. See some shows. Times Square. Lady Liberty. Take the subway."

"Then let's do that."

She angled away and met his eyes. "Really?"

"Rock, if you wanted to visit a garbage dump in Kokomo, I'd do my best to get you there. I want our marriage to make you happy."

"You're sweet, do you know that?"

"So you keep saying."

"Did Eva say that, too?"

It always surprised him when she brought up his late wife's name. "Yes, she did."

She viewed him silently for a few moments. "Does my asking about her make you uncomfortable?"

"Sometimes, because I'm never sure why you do."

Again, the silent study before she explained, "Because she loved you and I know you loved her. I don't ever want you to feel you have to erase her from your memory or your heart because we're together."

Her words touched him so intensely, tears stung the corners of his eyes.

She whispered, "Okay, Professor?"

He hugged her tightly. "Okay, Rock." He considered himself the luckiest man in the world to have been loved by two different but similarly amazing women. "I love you, Rochelle Dancer."

She stood and took his hand. "Good thing because now comes the part with the leather you like so much."

Grinning, he let her lead him into the bedroom.

CHAPTER
4

As Tamar sat on her front porch sipping coffee in the early Saturday morning quiet, she was determined to ignore the date on the calendar because of the painful memory the day held. Instead, she watched Jack's pickup drive by her place, heading out to July Road, and smiled knowingly. Rocky's trailer, along with ones occupied by Reverend Paula and the Acosta family, sat on the back of her land, so she assumed he'd spent the night there. She didn't judge. Rocky was owed some happiness after all she lived through, and Tamar thought Jack the perfect choice. However, having known Rocky since she was born, Tamar prayed she didn't get cold feet and break Jack's heart.

The next truck she saw heading out to the road had Reverend Paula Grant behind the wheel and Paula's seventeen-year-old cousin Robyn riding shotgun. Paula tooted the horn as they drove past and Tamar waved. The good reverend was also one of the blessings of the new and improved Henry Adams. Her work with the town's kids and with Rocky earned her a special place in Tamar's heart. She worried about the incredibly shy Robyn, though. Considering the girl had grown up under the abusive hand of her recently incarcerated grandmother, Della, it was no wonder the teen barely spoke a word. Della's trial for the murder of Robyn's mother would be taking place in the fall. Tamar had yet to hear a more tragic and twisted tale.

Intending to go inside and warm up her coffee, she stood, then paused upon seeing a black town car slowly making its way up the dirt road to the house. For a moment, she thought it might be T. C. Barbour, Bernadine's driver, who'd recently married longtime resident Genevieve Gibbs, but as the car drew near, she realized it was a different model and that the driver was White. Curious, she waited. After it stopped, the chauffeur stepped out. Clad in a smart black suit he gave her a polite nod before hastily moving to open the car's back door, and her best friend, Mable Lane, stepped out. Tamar was pleased to see her even though the reason she'd come had to do with the date on the calendar she'd been determined to ignore. Moving slowly on her cane, Mable was dressed in her signature cashmere twinset, green today, and a nice pair of slacks. "Morning Tam. What're we drinking?"

Tamar smiled. "Coffee for now, May."

"That'll do. We can break out the hard stuff later. Do you still hate the bastard?"

"I do."

"Good. Happy Anniversary. Let's hope Joel Newton is enjoying hell."

At ninety-two years of age, Mable Franklin Lane was as outrageous as ever and Tamar loved her with every beat of her heart. Joel Newton was the bigamist who'd broken Tamar's heart on this date, over sixty years ago.

Inside, they sat across from each other at the kitchen table and sipped the brew in their cups. "When did you get in?" Tamar asked.

"Last night. Flew back here to meet with a consultant Lyman's hired to try and get Franklin back on its feet." She quieted for a moment before asking, "Did you ever think we'd live this long?"

Tamar shook her head. "Not really." And she hadn't, even though the Julys were known to be long-lived.

"Yet here we are, the oldest hens in the pen."

They'd been childhood friends at a time when segregation and Jim Crow ruled the nation, yet their mothers hadn't tried to keep them apart. They'd met in school at age six. In spite of the teacher doing his part for Jim Crow by relegating Tam and her brother Thaddeus to seats in the back of the classroom, the girls formed an instant connection.

"How's life been treating you?" Mable asked.

"I'm okay. Feeling my age, though, I suppose."

"Meaning?"

Tamar shrugged. "Just wondering if I've outlived my usefulness." And because she'd always been able to tell Mable anything, she confessed her reaction to Marie's remarks about the old days being gone. "I'm the matriarch, dammit. When did that stop being important?"

"I don't think it has, Tam. Marie's right about Henry Adams's growth, though. Bernadine has done some amazing things. Would you rather go back to the days when the town was dying?"

"Of course not."

"Then decide what's more important. A living and growing Henry Adams or your ego?"

Tamar's lips thinned.

"Hey. We've been joined at the hip since we were six and we've always told each other the truth. We're way too old to start lying about things at this point."

Tamar sighed.

Mable said, "Think about it this way, Tammy. You've kept the Dusters' dreams alive into the twenty-first century. You've made sure the history has been passed down. When God decides to call you home, you'll be leaving behind a damn fine legacy, my friend. Me? I'm leaving behind Astrid."

They laughed at that.

Tamar thought back on all the turmoil Astrid caused: the kidnapping of poor Tommy Stewart, the fights she picked with Bernadine, the riot that caused so much damage to the rec center. "You were right to replace her with Lyman Proctor. Trent says he's doing a great job."

"He is. When I moved to Miami fifteen years ago, I was feeling a bit like you are now. I'd had the stroke and was questioning my own usefulness. Never thought I'd have to fly in like Wonder Woman to save my town from my greedy, boneheaded granddaughter."

"I hear she's not happy working at the gas station, or living in the trailer park."

"No, she isn't, but the alternative was making license plates in prison. Speaking of family, how's Thad?" Mable asked.

Tamar shrugged and thought about her brother. "Okay. Since Trent and Lily's wedding I talk to him more than I used to." The aforementioned Joel Newton had been a friend of her brother's, and Tamar held Thad directly responsible for the disaster Newton brought into her life because he neglected to tell her that Joel was married. "I thought we'd worked things out until the morning he and his wild clan left and I found Olivia turned upside down and stripped of her tires."

"It's good you two are speaking again, regardless of Olivia."

Tamar had her doubts, but didn't argue.

"I talked to him recently," Mable said. "And he explained his reasoning. He didn't want to tell you about Joel because he knew it would break your heart. He didn't know what to do."

"So instead he let me get gussied up for the wedding and be humiliated in front of the entire town when Joel's wife stood up during the vows and screamed he was already married to her." It was the most horrible day of Tamar's life. Then to find out a month later that she was pregnant . . . "It was the smug smile on his face when he slunk out of my parents' yard with his wife that I'll never forget. Or forgive."

"I know. Could be worse, though. He could've turned out to be a Klansman like the asshat I married."

Tamar chuckled softly. "We sure could pick them."

Mable shook her head and raised her cup. "To better choices in the next life."

"Amen. How long will you be around?"

"I'm meeting the consultant Lyman's hired on Monday, and if all goes well, I'll be flying back home on Wednesday. I need to see my other grandkids in Franklin while I'm here too, to make sure Astrid isn't giving them grief."

"Do you want to come for dinner before you leave?"

"Most certainly."

Tamar walked her out to the porch. They shared a strong hug.

"You matter," Mable whispered. "Never doubt that."

Watching her drive away, Tamar was thankful for their friendship, and wondered how much longer they'd have before the ancestors called them home.

Walking into Clark's grocery store for her shift, Gemma was glad Wyatt would be taking Lucas and Jasmine with him to Pizza Saturday at Leah and Tiffany's house, a monthly kids' gathering instituted by their uncle T. C. Barbour. Because she'd had to take off from work the day before, not coming in again was impossible. She'd been worried how the kids would spend the day but thanks to T. C. Barbour that wasn't an issue. Her mood was dragged down when she entered the employee lounge and saw assistant store manager Alma House, aka Sergeant Ma'am, a no-nonsense, by-the-book former Army sergeant. She'd been dubbed Sgt. Ma'am by Amari July, a member of the night crew, the son of the mayor, and also the town's unofficial head of nickname-bestowing. Standing with Alma was her mini me, head cashier Sybil "Rhymes with Witch" Martin.

"Gemma," Alma said, glancing at the watch on her wrist.

"Alma. Sybil."

"Ten more minutes and you would've been late."

Gemma sighed internally at the ridiculousness of the statement. "Good thing I'm here now, then."

"Yes, it is." The woman had the coldest gray eyes Gemma had ever seen. "Mr. Clark says you're taking night classes."

"I am."

"In what?"

"Business."

Sybil snorted disdainfully.

Gemma held on to her temper.

"Don't think you'll be given any rescheduling considerations."

"I haven't asked for any." Not wanting this to play out any longer than necessary, Gemma added, "I need to punch in."

"You do that."

Walking away, she felt Alma's glare burning a hole in her back. She knew the woman disliked her but didn't know the reason. Alma originally hailed from Franklin too, but she was a good ten years older than Gemma's forty-five, and Gemma had never met Alma before working at the store. She assumed Sgt. Ma'am must know about her past and if that was the case so be it. Gemma refused to allow it to dampen her enthusiasm for her job or wanting to improve her life by going back to school.

After clocking in, she took the long way to the

front of the store in order to say good morning to her fellow employees: Candy Stevens, the recently hired butcher who was all of twenty-two years old and had bright purple hair, and Otto Newsome, the short, balding head of produce who always asked after Wyatt. She waved and smiled at manager Gary Clark, the baggers, stockers, and the other cashiers, particularly, her partner in crime, Edith Greenwood, a sixty-year-old firecracker who'd taken Gemma under her wing the day she was hired and was raising a grandchild of her own. She also gave a wave to Colonel Barrett Payne, the head of the store's security, a former Marine, and one of her neighbors. But Gemma gave the dairy department a wide berth. Wilson Hughes headed up that department. Like Gemma he was in his mid-forties. Unlike her, he was obsessed with Elvis. In fact, when he wasn't stocking milk and cheese, he moonlighted as an Elvis impersonator. He was tall, had dark, Elvis-styled hair, and was supposedly a big hit when he performed. There were those who found him attractive but he was a bit too smarmy for her taste. He was what her friends back in Chicago called a legend in his own mind and she supposed that was the reason he refused to believe Gemma didn't want to go out with him. The first time he asked, she politely turned him down. He responded by giving her his patented oily smile and said in a bad imitation of Elvis's voice, "Come on, baby, let the King treat you like a queen."

She was not impressed. In the months since, he continued to press his case. Edith said he was going to keep at it until he wore her down, but hell would freeze over first. Gemma had no room in her life for a dollar-store Elvis prone to seedy blue suede shoes and dingy white jumpsuits. Hoping to get through the day without him crooning "Love Me Tender" whenever she walked by, she joined the other cashiers.

Ringing up the purchases of her first customer, a lady from Franklin, Gemma made small talk with her as she scanned and bagged each item.

The woman said, "I really like coming here. All the cashiers are so nice."

Gemma slid a package of frozen broccoli over the scanner. "That's good to hear."

"At some places the cashiers act like they're doing you a favor just saying hello."

"We try and be friendly and efficient because no one wants to be in line all day."

"You all do a good job."

Gemma rang up the final item, a jar of hand cream, and waited while the customer went through the motions with her debit card. Once done, the customer gave Gemma a smile. "See you next time."

On Saturday afternoons, the store was always crowded, and this day was no exception. All six lanes were packed and she and the other cashiers were doing their best to keep up. When she glanced at the people waiting in her line and spotted Mrs. Ora Beadle, Gemma sighed. Mrs. Beadle was an elderly lady known for picking up two bottles of wine, drinking one while she shopped, stashing it in the restroom when it was empty, and insisting she only had the unopened one when it came time to check out. Because she was a repeat offender, the moment she entered the store, security went on alert. With a bevy of high-tech cameras powerful enough to read the face of a twenty-dollar bill, it was easy to view her guzzling her way through the aisles. Since Gemma was hired, Mrs. Beadle had been escorted from the store by deputies at least five times, always loudly and drunkenly proclaiming her innocence and threatening to sue the store and the county for false arrest.

There were three people ahead of Mrs. Beadle in line and as Gemma greeted the next customer a member of the store's security team approached the white-haired, blue-eyed Mrs. Beadle and Gemma assumed she'd been busted again. He spoke to her quietly only to be told, "How dare you accuse me!" Her words were slurred, her voice loud. "This is senior citizen profiling and I will not put up with it one more minute."

A buzz went through the people waiting to check out. Then the deputies showed up. She was still shouting her innocence when they led her out to the patrol car.

At lunch, Gemma sat with Edith at a table in the employees' lounge and they chuckled over Mrs. Beadle. "I had Beadle, you had Pettigrew."

Edith shook her head. "Wallace Pettigrew."

His claim to fame was his attempts to pass off old coupons and bottle slips he'd dug out of the store's trash cans as new. "Mr. Clark keeps telling him to stop going through the trash. If he cuts himself on a piece of broken glass the store will be liable."

Gemma didn't understand the man's thinking at all. "And it's not like he's going to run up on a coupon that's any good."

Butcher Candy Stevens came over. "Can I sit with y'all?"

Gemma liked the new lady butcher and her Georgia accent. "Sure, join us."

She took a seat. Opening a small red cloth tote, she took out a wrapped sandwich and a small container of yogurt. She looked over at Gemma. "What is this I'm hearing about you finding two kids yesterday?"

As always there were no secrets in Henry Adams, so Gemma told her the story.

"Oh, that's so sad. You were a blessing."

"I'm hoping to foster them."

"Awesome."

"State's not going to allow it."

They all looked up. The negative opinion came from Elvis impersonator Wilson Hughes. He had on his required white grocery coat and a pair of blue suede shoes shiny from age and wear. His pompadour was styled to the max.

Gemma asked, "And you think that, why?"

"Racial. You're White and they're not from what I heard."

Edith said, "That's not going to make a difference."

He sat down even though he'd neither asked permission nor been invited. "Sure it will. Blacks foster Blacks. Whites foster Whites. The Social Services people are going to give you the whole song and dance about you being unable to bring them up with their culture—whatever that means," he said dismissively.

Edith, who bore a startling resemblance to the late great Ella Fitzgerald, said, "That might have been the way things were in the past, but times have changed, even here in Kansas."

Wilson bit into his sandwich. "I know you think you know, but you don't."

Gemma thought he was full of crap, but didn't argue because he considered himself an authority on everything.

He added, "And you know Gem-Gem, it's

going to be even harder for you to find a man with those two kids in your life. Lot of men around here don't like the whole race mixing thing."

Gemma hated his nickname for her. "Does that include you?" she asked coolly.

He shrugged. "Maybe."

"Then I'll make sure to adopt them."

He smiled smugly. "You know you could do worse than this hunka hunka burning love."

"I doubt that."

Then he sang, *"Don't be cruel to a heart that's true."*

Candy rolled her eyes. Edith shook her head.

He looked into Gemma's angry eyes, gave her a grin, and winked. "I'm going to wear you down eventually."

"Not a chance, but if you sing one more lyric or call me Gem-Gem again, I'll be filing sexual harassment charges."

That got his attention. "Really?"

"Really. I'm tired of you, Wilson. Sick and tired."

"But, baby, just trying to show you how much I care."

She sat silently.

He took a draw on the straw in his drink. "So, what are you, some kind of lesbian?"

Candy said, "Nope, that's me."

He spit out his drink and began coughing.

Candy grinned. Edith gave her a high five.

Gemma said, "You might want to stick with the women you meet at the state fair, Wilson. They're more your speed. The rest of us aren't feeling you." She'd wanted to tell him before to stop harassing her but thought he'd get the message from her no-nonsense responses, but apparently, he wasn't bright enough for that. Now that she'd officially warned him and had witnesses, she hoped he'd focus his interests elsewhere. There were rumors that he and Head Cashier Sybil Martin were on-and-off bed buddies, but she didn't care enough about either of them to be interested in the truth.

And as if cued, Sybil walked over to the table. In a frosty voice, she said, "Gemma, I need to speak to you. Privately."

Wondering what this was about, she stood and followed Sybil out into the hall.

Gemma asked, "Is there a problem?"

"Yes. Alma and I have noticed that you spend too much time talking with your customers."

"Have you been timing me?"

She paused, turned red, and stuttered, "Yes—yes we have."

A lie, Gemma guessed. "Can I see the stats that compare my interactions with the other cashiers'?"

"That's privileged information," she replied hastily.

"Then I'll file a FOIA request to get it."

Sybil looked like a deer caught in headlights. Gemma didn't know if she could file a FOIA request or not but she was pretty certain Sybil had no idea what the Freedom of Information Act was. She asked calmly, "Does Mr. Clark know about this so-called timing you and Alma are doing?"

"That's none of your business."

"I think the answer is no."

"Just do your job if you want to keep your job."

Gemma folded her arms, studied the hostility on the other woman's face, and asked, "What have I ever done to you or Alma that makes you want to make up a reason to fire me?"

"Just do your job!" she snapped and strode off.

When Gemma stepped back into the lounge, Edith looked concerned. "What was that about?"

Thankful that Wilson was no longer at the table, Gemma explained what happened.

Edith and Candy looked surprised.

"I'll bet you dollars to donuts, Mr. Clark doesn't know a thing about this," Edith said.

"That was my feeling, too. But what did I ever do to them?"

Candy said, "Maybe it's because everyone in the store really likes you. Nobody can stand either of them, especially Alma."

Gemma didn't know what was going on and she didn't want to go crying to Gary about the incident unless it became necessary. "Edith, do I spend more time talking to the customers than I should?"

"No, honey, you don't. Believe me."

Edith had been a cashier for years so Gemma trusted her take, but she was also a friend. "Okay, let me get back to work before I'm accused of taking too long a lunch." As she gathered up her things and headed to her lane, she wanted to know what she'd done to Alma to warrant this drama. She was sure Alma had been the source. Sybil was only the messenger.

CHAPTER
5

"Today's Pizza Saturday with Uncle T.C. Do you and Jasmine want to go?"

Lucas glanced up from his bowl of cereal and eyed Wyatt seated across the table from him. "What's Pizza Saturday?"

Wyatt explained, "All the kids in town get together at Leah and Tiffany's house one Saturday a month and we make homemade pizza with their uncle T.C. It's a lot of fun and you'll get a chance to meet everybody before they split tomorrow."

"Where are they going?" Jasmine asked.

"Amari, Devon, and Brain are adopted so they're going to see their bio fams. Leah and Tiff's parents are divorced, so they're heading to their mom's place in Atlanta. Alfonso and his sister Maria are going to Mexico to visit relatives."

Lucas looked at Jasmine, who shrugged in reply. "I guess so."

"Good. Uncle T.C. is a boss."

"Does your grandmother know we're going?" Jasmine asked. Ms. Gemma was at work.

"Yes. She and I talked about it last night after you two went to bed."

"Is it at one of the houses across the street?" Lucas asked.

"No. It's a little way away. Eli said he'll drive us and bring us back."

"Who's he?"

"One of the older kids. He has his own car. He taught me how to ride a skateboard. He'll be leaving for college next month."

Lucas noted the sadness in Wyatt's tone when he spoke of Eli going away and guessed he was important to Wyatt. "He a good friend?"

"Yes."

Lucas wondered if he'd ever have friends again but pushed the thought away.

Jasmine asked, "How many kids here are adopted?"

Wyatt counted off on his fingers. "Zoey, Brain, Amari, Devon, and Crystal. Five."

"Were they in foster care?"

"Yeah. They're all from different places and were already living in Henry Adams when Gram and I moved here last year. You won't get to meet Zoey, though. Her mom's a famous singer and they're on tour in South America. Zoey's bio dad is an English rocker."

Lucas wondered how long they'd been in foster care and if they'd hated it as much as he had.

Jasmine asked, "Are the other kids nice?"

Wyatt said, "Yeah. Nobody gives you attitude

or tries to make you feel bad. We're like cousins almost."

"Lucas and I were in homes where the kids were really mean. They took all of Lucas's clothes."

"They did?" Wyatt asked.

Lucas nodded. It was another thing he didn't want to think about but the memory rose anyway. He hadn't been raised to fight, so when the two other boys in the foster home started going through his stuff on his first day, they'd laughed at his pitiful efforts to defend himself. Pushed him down, called him names, and took his clothes, shoes, watch, and everything else he'd brought with him from home. He was left with only the clothes on his back. When he told the foster mother, she shrugged and said, "This is how life works, little rich boy. Man up."

When the memory faded, he came back to the present and found Wyatt watching him intently. As if having seen the scene played out, Wyatt said, "You and your sister will be okay here. Promise."

After the sadness of the past two years, Lucas very much wanted to believe that. "How old are you?"

"Twelve. You?"

"Ten. Jaz is eight. What about the adults?"

"Real nice, too. We're like the whole town's kids. Wait until you meet the OG."

"Who's he?"

"His name is Malachi July and he owns the Dog—the town diner. He's the town grandfather."

Jasmine said, "Our grandfather didn't want us to live with him after our parents died."

"Why not?"

"Said he was too old to be raising little kids."

"Wow," Wyatt said softly, looking between them. "So he let you go into the system?"

Lucas nodded. It was the first of many heartbreaks to come.

"That's pretty wack. Do you have a grandmother?"

"No."

"Well, you're here now, and if Ms. Bernadine gets her way, you'll be here forever."

Lucas asked, "You're okay with us living here?"

"Yeah. I'm okay."

Because Wyatt sounded so sincere, Lucas replied, "Then I'm okay with it, too. How about you, Jaz?"

She smiled. "Me, too."

When it came time to leave the house, they poured into Eli James's old car. After Wyatt made the introductions, they drove off. From the backseat, Lucas listened to Wyatt and Eli's conversation, most of which centered on Eli's going away to school. At one point, Eli asked Lucas if he knew how to ride a skateboard.

When Lucas said yes, Wyatt pumped his fist like Tiger Woods.

"Do you have a board?" Wyatt asked.

Lucas shook his head. It too was taken from him at the foster home, even though neither of the two boys knew a thing about riding.

Wyatt said, "I'm sorry, that was a dumb thing to ask. Maybe we can get you a new one."

Eli said, "I'll see what I can do."

As they entered the house, Lucas wondered if Jaz was as nervous as he was about meeting the other kids. But he didn't have to worry; the first one to approach introduced himself as Amari July.

"I'm Lucas Herman."

Jaz said, "I'm Jasmine."

Lucas saw what appeared to be a sea of smiling faces turned their way. One of the faces belonged to Crystal, who they'd met the day before. She nodded in greeting and Lucas nodded back.

Amari said, "That's Preston Payne over there. We call him Brain."

"Hey, you two. Welcome to Henry Adams."

"The one with the round head is my little brother Devon."

"Shut up, Amari. Pleased to meet you."

He then introduced Alfonso Acosta and his sister Maria. Alfonso looked like Harry Potter. "Hola," he and his sister said in greeting.

Amari pointed out two girls. "That's Leah with the glasses, and the shorty is her sister Tiffany Adele. We all think her name sounds like a store in the mall." Tiffany laughed and stuck out her tongue at Amari in response.

Amari continued, "This is their house, and the big guy with the apron over there is Uncle T.C."

The tall dark-skinned man called out, "Good to meet you, Lucas and Jasmine. Glad to have you with us. Ever made pizza?"

They both shook their heads.

"Then you're in for a treat. Everybody get those hands washed so we can get started."

As they got to work, Lucas had to admit it was the most fun he'd had since the death of his parents. Jokes flew back and forth, people laughed and called each other out. He and Jasmine were grating mozzarella and parmesan cheese with Wyatt, who explained, "We switch jobs each month so nobody gets stuck doing the same thing every time."

Some of the kids, like Eli, were helping Uncle T.C. with the dough while others, like Devon and Brain, were cutting up toppings. Leah and Crystal were putting together the ingredients for the sauce. While they waited for the pizzas to cook, they played video games, watched baseball on TV, and talked about what they were going to do while they were gone. Lucas was surprised to learn that the grandmother Amari was going to visit lived on a Sioux reservation in South Dakota, and that Brain was going to Florida to hang with his mom, who worked for NASA.

And then the pizzas were finally out of the oven and Lucas was chomping down on the best pizza he'd ever eaten.

"This is so good," Jaz said.

Lucas couldn't believe they'd made their own pizza. "It is."

Amari said, "You and Jasmine are going to like it here."

Leah teased, "Not if you keep talking with your mouth full. Yuck, you!"

Amari rolled his eyes.

Brain said, "When we first got here it was kind of slow, but it was better than where we were."

Wyatt said, "Lucas got all his stuff taken by the other kids at the foster home."

"Damn," Brain said.

Lucas wished Wyatt had kept that information to himself, but Amari said in bitter tones, "The wonderful world of foster care."

Brain added, "My foster mother refused to buy me an inhaler. I had to set the house on fire so Social Services would move me to another place."

And for the next few minutes, Amari and Brain shared their terrible experiences as wards of the state. Lucas saw the sadness on the face of Uncle T.C. and guessed this was the first time he'd heard the stories.

And when they finished talking about their times in foster care, Amari said to Lucas and Jasmine, "Let's hope Ms. Bernadine can work it so you can stay because you'll get a lot of love here."

"And a lot of chores from Tamar," Tiffany tossed out from her seat next to Jasmine.

"That, too," Amari said.

Lucas had no idea who Tamar was or what kind of chores they meant, but he figured he'd find out if he and Jaz stayed.

Amari continued, "But you'll be safe here. No pee-stained mattresses, nobody dissing you or stealing your clothes. Nobody making you carry drugs to the crackheads down the block, like I had to do a couple of times. None of that. Folks here are great. I even learned to read here."

Lucas wondered if he'd ever be as open about what he'd lived through as these kids.

Brain added, "We're all leaving here tomorrow but we'll be back in two weeks. Until then, W. W. Dahl, you're running the show. Take care of our new crew members."

Wyatt grinned. "Gotcha."

Crystal loudly cleared her throat. "Am I invisible?" But she was smiling. "Lucas and

98

Jaz, I'm in charge here. Always. But if you run into something Dubs there can't handle, let me know."

Lucas nodded, as did his sister. He made a mental note to remember to ask Wyatt why he was called W.W. and Dubs.

When Eli announced he had to go to work, Lucas sadly thought he and Wyatt and Jasmine would have to leave, but Uncle T.C. said, "If you kids want to stay a bit longer I can run you home when you're ready."

Lucas looked to Wyatt, who asked, "Do you want to stay?"

Lucas nodded eagerly.

Her shift over, an exhausted Gemma was just about to turn the key in the ignition when a text came through. It was from Bernadine. *Stop by on your way home. Herman kids' info.* Texting back an OK, Gemma dashed off a text to Wyatt to let him know she'd be making a stop before coming home. He texted back that he and the Herman kids were still at Leah's and that Mr. Barbour would be giving them a ride home. Once again thankful for Genevieve's new husband, T.C., Gemma drove to the Power Plant.

"So," Bernadine began after Gemma took a seat in her office. "I spoke with Mr. Gleason's wife. I told her the kids were here, gave her our condolences, and apologized for intruding on her grief."

"She must be devastated by the death of her husband."

"She is and doesn't want to go through with the adoption. I asked her if she might want to wait until she feels better to make the decision. She said no and that if he hadn't been driving those children he'd still be alive. She's going to get with her lawyer asap."

Gemma had been wondering what the wife would do about Lucas and Jasmine. It never crossed her mind that they would be blamed for Jake Gleason's death. "They'll need to know."

"Yes."

Gemma sighed. One more blow to their fragile psyches and hearts. "Did you talk to Judge Davis?"

"I did and explained the circumstances. She's giving me temporary custody until we contact Social Services. She's been an angel to the kids in Henry Adams, and they have a special place in her heart, too. Off the record, she said, she'll do whatever she can to help."

"Good to know."

"I agree. But there's no telling what Social Services will do. They've been good to us over the years, too. In a perfect world, we'll get you certified as a foster parent and the kids will stay with you. I'll reach out to them Monday morning, first thing."

Gemma knew how imperfect the world could be, though—wasn't her daughter Gabby buried at Arlington National Cemetery? "Do you think they'll deny me because I'm not Black?"

"I will hurt someone if they do."

Gemma smiled. At least she knew where Bernadine stood. Not that she'd had any doubts. "Anything else?"

"How'd their first night go?"

"No problems that I know of. Lucas slept on the floor in his sister's room. I'm sure he was being protective. He's had to shoulder a lot for a ten-year-old."

"I can only imagine. Let's hope we can get this custody thing straightened out so he can go back to being a regular carefree youngster—as much as he can."

Gemma agreed. "I'm hoping they had fun making pizza with the kids and T.C."

"I'm sure they did. We need T.C. to come to a Ladies Auxiliary Meeting and teach us how to make scratch pizza, too. Why should the kids have all the fun?" The Auxiliary was made up of the town's female residents.

"I really appreciate your help on this, Bernadine."

"And I appreciate your open heart. I'll keep

you posted. Are you coming to Rocky's shower tomorrow?"

"No. I think I need to hang with the kids. I hope Rocky won't mind."

"I'm sure she won't."

At home, Gemma enjoyed listening to the spirited recap of the kids' pizza making adventure.

Jaz said, "The pizza was so awesome!"

They all laughed and Wyatt said, "Uncle T.C. said Lucas and I can help make the dough next time."

"Very good. Then you can come home and teach me."

"How was work?" Lucas asked.

The unexpected question surprised her. "Pretty good. Saturdays are always busy."

"Do you work tomorrow, too?"

"No. I have Sundays off."

Wyatt asked, "Can we spend the day at the pool and eat at the Dog?"

Gemma was watching her pennies but didn't think Wyatt's plan would put her in the poorhouse. "Sure. Lucas, can you and Jaz swim?"

He nodded. "We used to have a pool at home."

"Really?" Wyatt asked.

Jaz added, "Our parents taught us to swim when we were little."

Gemma noted the shadow that crossed Lucas's

features at the mention of their former life and the urge to pull him into her arms rose again. "We'll have to get you some swim gear."

"I have an extra pair of trunks Lucas can have," Wyatt offered. "You bought me two pairs, remember?"

She did and was pleased by his generosity. "Jaz, let me call around and see if I can find you a suit. Doc Reg's daughter Zoey might have an extra one."

"Her mom's the singer?"

"Yes."

"And I know Zoey won't mind," Wyatt told them. "She got a bunch of gold coins last year and gave everybody in town some."

"Gold coins?" Lucas asked.

Wyatt nodded. "Yeah. I'll tell you about it upstairs while we play *Minecraft*."

"What about me?" Jasmine asked.

Wyatt said, "You can play too if you want?"

She asked instead, "Do you play chess?"

Wyatt's brow furrowed with confusion as he studied her. "No."

Gemma was also surprised by the question. "You play chess, Jaz?"

"Yes, ma'am. My mom taught me. She was on the chess team in high school and college."

Wyatt said, "Brain and Amari play. I think Leah does, too. You can hook them up when they get back from vacation."

103

"Okay," she said, but her disappointment was obvious.

Gemma wondered if the Paynes had an extra chess set she could borrow? She'd ask him the next time she saw him at work and made a mental note to ask Gary, too.

The kids trooped upstairs to play their game and left Gemma downstairs pondering the future. Unlike many of the other kids in town, Lucas and Jasmine had apparently grown up in a wealthy, well-educated family. A part of her wondered how they'd deal with being potentially fostered by a lady who worked as a cashier in a grocery store, but another part didn't think that would matter if they felt safe and loved. She knew she needed to tell them Gleason's wife didn't want to go forward with the adoption, but she decided to postpone the news until later. They'd had such a good day, she wanted them to continue to enjoy it.

That night, just before bed, she knocked on the door of the room the Herman kids were sharing.

"Come in," Lucas called.

Dressed in a pair of threadbare pajamas, he was lying on his mattress bed on the floor, and Jaz, in pajamas too, was sitting on her bed. They were watching *The Princess Bride* on TV.

"I need to talk to you two about something."

Jaz picked up the remote and paused the movie. "Do we have to leave?"

Gemma sat on the edge of the bed. "No honey, but I have some sort of bad news."

Lucas sat up, tensed and wary.

"Your Uncle Jake's wife doesn't want to go ahead with the adoption."

"Oh," Jasmine said softly.

Lucas turned away but not before Gemma caught a glimpse of the bleakness in his eyes. Face still averted he asked bitterly, "So what happens now? We go back to foster care in Ohio?"

"Not necessarily. Ms. Bernadine is trying to work things out so I can be your foster parent."

Neither responded.

"I know things have been hard, but try and keep a good thought."

"Why?" Lucas demanded, his voice raw. "Nobody cares about us! Nobody wants us! I'll run away if I have to go back to foster care!" He leaned forward and sobbed. "Why did Mom and Dad have to die?"

Unchecked tears rolled down Jasmine's cheeks. She scooted off the bed and went to her brother. He put an arm around his sister and they both wept. Gemma did, too. She turned and saw Wyatt standing in the doorway. His eyes were wet. He held her gaze for a long moment then disappeared. She wondered if their grief reminded him of his own. He'd been Jasmine's age when they buried Gabby. Gemma put her head in her hands and drew in a shaky breath. Blowing it out, she went to the kids, took them both in her arms and held and rocked them while they cried out their pain.

Later, she knocked on Wyatt's door.

"Come in," he called.

He was lying on his back on the bed, his attention focused on the ceiling. His red eyes told all. "We have to help them, Gram."

She came in and sat beside him. "I know."

"We have a lot in common."

"Yes, you do."

He was silent for a few long moments and finally said in a soft voice, "I miss her a lot."

"Me, too."

Tears filled his eyes. "Why does stuff like this happen?"

"I wish I knew, babe, but all we can do is go on and hope the pain dulls at some point because I don't think it will ever go away."

He turned his face to her. "It still hurts."

"I know."

"But at least I have you. Lucas and Jaz don't have anybody."

"Ms. Bernadine and I will do everything we can for them. I promise."

"Eli said Reverend Paula lost her mom too

when she was a kid. He talks to her every now and then about how much he misses his mom. Do you think I can talk to her?"

"That might be a good idea. I'll call her and ask. Maybe she'll let me talk to her, too."

He focused on something only he could see and nodded distantly.

"Will you be okay?" she asked. At times like these she felt so inadequate.

"Yeah. I want Lucas and Jaz to be okay, too. Maybe Reverend Paula can help them, too."

"I'll ask her."

"Being here will be good for them."

"I agree."

He turned back to her. "Thanks, Gram."

"You're welcome." Leaning over she kissed his cheek. "Don't stay up too late. I love you."

"Love you, too."

She stood, gave her remarkable grandson a last look, and left him to his thoughts.

In her room alone, Gemma did something she hadn't done since Gabby's death. She prayed—for the Herman kids, for Wyatt, and for strength to do whatever it took to help the three make it through.

CHAPTER
6

Sunday morning, while some of the Henry Adams parents headed to the Hays airport to send their kids on vacation, other residents spent the morning in church. Gemma, wearing shades, a white tee, and loose blue shorts, sat on a lounge chair by the new pool while Wyatt and the Herman kids swam. Lucas and Jasmine hadn't been kidding about being able to swim. Both cut through the water, sleek as dolphins. Lucas even took a dive off the high board, under the watchful eyes of the lifeguard. Gemma tensed as he did so, but when he resurfaced smiling, she relaxed and went back to the book she'd brought along. She'd never learned to swim but encouraged Wyatt to take lessons at the local Chicago Boys and Girls Club, and he was at home in the water, too. There were several kids from Franklin in the pool and soon the air was filled with the calls of "Marco! Polo!" Gemma never knew the game's origin or its connection to the famed explorer, but the kids were having a blast. She envied the small group of parents in the water laughing and playing with them, and wondered if she could possibly learn to swim at the ripe old age of forty-five. Her speculating came to a screeching halt when Sybil

Martin came through the pool gate. Dressed in a frilly white cover-up over a very brief teal bikini, she was with a little boy wearing red trunks who Gemma assumed to be her son. Accompanying them and decked out in full, white jumpsuit Elvis regalia was Wilson Hughes. Behind her shades, Gemma sighed with irritation. Upon sighting Gemma, Sybil threw her nose in the air and chose a spot on the far side of the pool. Gemma hoped Wilson would do the same. Nope. Soon as he saw her he made a beeline straight for her, and she sighed again.

"Fancy meeting you here," he said.

"Nothing fancy about it. I live here." Everyone in and out of the water stopped what they were doing to stare. With the temperature hovering near ninety degrees, they were probably wondering how soon he'd succumb to heatstroke, she thought, taking in his attire.

"First time I've ever seen you in shorts."

Gemma wanted him gone. Sybil was glaring and Gemma understood. That he would be so disrespectful to the woman he was supposed to be with by trying to hit on someone else summed up just what a jerk he was. "Go away."

He grinned and left but called out to the people around, "I'm available for autographs. I sign The King's name just like him."

Jaws dropped.

Gemma's didn't.

Blessedly, her kids walked up, and Wyatt asked, "Can we go home now, then go eat at the Dog? We're hungry."

"Absolutely." After waiting for them to dry off and gather their belongings, she led them back to the car.

At the diner, Lucas stood in the long line and peered around at all the people sitting and talking, heard the music pumping, and watched the waiters flying around. More accustomed to fast food places that had drive-throughs, he wasn't sure what to make of the Dog and Cow.

Crystal, dressed like the waitstaff, walked up. "Hey there. Welcome to the Dog."

Not knowing she worked there, he found that surprising, too.

Ms. Gemma and Wyatt said "hi" to her.

"It'll be a few minutes before I can get you a seat," she replied. "Sorry."

"No problem," Ms. Gemma said.

Crystal left them to seat some of the people ahead of them in line.

Lucas saw only a few kids eating but remembered Amari and the others had left for vacation. The kids he saw weren't familiar so he assumed they lived elsewhere.

Wyatt came to stand beside him. "Kind of crazy in here, isn't it?"

Lucas nodded. "Is it always like this?"

"Yeah, but the food's awesome."

That was good to know.

A very tall lady wearing lots of silver bracelets walked over to them and said to Ms. Gemma, "Hi, Gemma. Are these the new children?"

Ms. Gemma smiled. "Yes. Lucas and Jasmine Herman, this is our town's matriarch, Tamar July."

"Hello, ma'am," Lucas said.

"Hi, ma'am," Jaz echoed.

"Glad to meet you. Welcome to Henry Adams."

"Thank you."

"I'm hoping you'll be with us long enough for us to know each other."

Lucas wasn't sure how to respond. He just kept seeing how tall she was and how silver her long hair was. Her face looked kind enough, but he'd heard some stories about her from Brain and the others that left him wary.

"I'm sure my great-grandson and his crew have told you I'm a dragon lady, but I'm not. Gemma and Wyatt, take care of them."

They responded in unison, "We will."

Lucas thought she must be important because she walked to the front of the line and was seated right away.

Jaz echoed his thoughts and whispered to Wyatt, "She doesn't have to wait in line?"

"No. She's Tamar," he said as if that was explanation enough.

"Oh."

A few minutes later, Crystal led them to a booth and a waitress came and brought them water and soft drinks. Lucas looked over the menu. The pictures made everything look really good. Ms. Gemma chose a salad and Lucas, Wyatt, and Jaz ordered burgers and fries. While they waited for their food, a lot of the adults came over to introduce themselves and to say hello. There was the OG the kids talked about liking so much, Bobby Douglas, a big tall dude with real cool tats on his arms; a lady named Ms. Genevieve, who was with Uncle T.C.; and two guys named Bing and Clay. They were all nice and welcomed them to the town, but Lucas was tired of smiling and just wanted to eat. When the food finally arrived, Wyatt was right. It was awesome. He was kind of liking Henry Adams, but he knew something would probably happen to mess up their stay, so he told himself not to think he'd be with Ms. Gemma and Wyatt for good.

"Wyatt, why do the kids call you Dubs and W.W.?"

Ms. Gemma grinned.

"Zoey and Devon have a band and I'm the manager. I call myself W. W. Dahl. Dubs is short for the letter W."

Lucas chuckled and went back to his burger.

Later that afternoon, the town's Ladies Auxiliary convened in Lily July's Lady Cave for Rocky's wedding shower. Trent built the addition for the space on the back of their home as a wedding gift for her, and it was where she retreated to escape all the testosterone exuded by a husband and two growing sons. It was also used by the Auxiliary for special occasions. The Cave had its own entrance so Rocky parked the Shadow and, carrying her helmet under her arm, turned the knob and went inside. The beautiful indigo-themed decorations stopped her cold. It was her favorite color and it was there in the balloons, tablecloth, napkins, cups, and in all the bags and presents stacked up by the big gray sectional. Her friends were wearing the color too in blouses, jeans, earrings, and bangles. Everywhere she looked the dark blue caught her eye. That they'd gone to so much trouble on her behalf made her eyes sting with tears.

"Don't you dare start bawling now," Lily admonished, ushering Rocky in. "There'll be plenty of opportunities for that later."

Rocky dashed away her tears. "I'm not crying."

Laughter greeted that and the party began.

None of the attendees liked the dumb games played at wedding showers so they talked and ate and laughed instead. There were bottles of Bernadine-supplied champagne and wine, and soft drinks for those who didn't imbibe.

"Have you decided what you're wearing?" Bernadine asked.

"No."

"Rock?" Marie cried. "The wedding is less than six weeks away. When are you going to decide?"

"When I come across something I like."

"Please tell us you've been looking at least," Sheila Payne said.

"Only if you want me to lie to you."

"Rock!" Marie cried again.

Rocky chuckled and bit into the shrimp on her fork. "I'll start looking soon. Promise."

That was met with humorous groans.

"I will. I'm looking for the perfect leather *ensemble*," she explained, employing a mock haughty tone for the last word. "Jack's mother Stella wants me to wear her wedding dress. She said we could let it out up top, but no. Not wearing her dress."

Bernadine said, "She's still pressuring you?"

"All day and all night."

Lily eyed her boss and cracked, "Sort of like the way you pressured me when Trent and I were planning our small, simple wedding."

Bernadine had the decency to look embarrassed. "I admit to going a bit overboard."

Lily rolled her eyes. "Says the woman who called the White House to see if they rented the place out for wedding receptions."

Laughter filled the room.

"Hush," Bernadine said, grinning over her champagne flute.

Marie said, "And thank God you aren't related to the Oklahoma Julys. They definitely made Trent and Lily's wedding memorable."

Tamar said, "They are not to be invited to anything here, ever again."

Rocky was glad to have these ladies in this new life of hers. In her old one, she didn't do females. The ones she knew outside of Tamar and Marie were barely tolerable. Because of her looks and figure many women went straight into threat mode, thinking she had designs on their boyfriends or husbands, which she didn't of course. In those days, she had no true female friends. Now, however, she was a member of a group of women she loved and showed her love in return. Granted, she'd hated Lily in high school because Lily and Trent were a couple back then too and Rock's crush on Trent rivaled the size of the universe. But she and Lily got along very well now, mostly because Rocky had grown up.

Sheila had volunteered to be her wedding planner. "Rocky, you and I need to get together to talk details."

The only details Rocky enjoyed were on vehicles, which was why she was letting Sheila handle the wedding and had been putting off them getting together. "Okay."

While the party continued, the recently married Genevieve sat glued to her tablet. Tamar cast a baleful eye her way and asked, "Gen? Are we going to have to confiscate your electronics like we do the kids?"

"I'm looking for a dress for Rocky." And then she glanced up excitedly. "Rock! Come look at this."

Holding her glass of wine, Rocky walked over and viewed the picture on the tablet. "Oh my!"

"You like?"

"I heart that!"

Everyone crowded around to view the statuesque model wearing a flowing cream-colored leather duster over a matching, tastefully designed leather bustier and pants. "I don't suppose they have it in black?"

"No!" her friends cried.

Rocky laughed and sipped.

Lily said, "That's hot, Rock. You may not make it out of the church if Jack sees you walking down the aisle in that."

Sheila said, "I never thought leather was appropriate for a wedding but this is you, Rocky."

Gen agreed. "I think so too and it only takes three weeks for it to be made and shipped."

Rocky took out her phone and typed in the site's URL. "I'll check it out, asap. Thanks Gen." And once again, she felt loved. "Can I open my presents now?"

Laughter greeted that, so she sat and waited for the unveiling.

And what an unveiling it was.

Anna, already on her way to Mexico, gifted her a beautiful wrought iron candelabra for the dining room table. Marie and Gen went halfsies on a gorgeous black leather jacket and an indigo-colored helmet. The silver flute from Lily and Trent made tears flow down her cheeks. Tamar's badass set of socket wrenches made her wipe away the tears and want to try them out immediately. Paula gave her a book of affirmations, which Rocky knew she'd love. Sheila passed her a gift-wrapped box filled with sexy lingerie, and said, "Tell Jack, no need to thank me."

Everyone howled.

Bernadine handed her an envelope that Rock viewed puzzledly.

"Just open it and read what it says."

When she did, her eyes widened.

"What's it say?" Gen asked eagerly.

"For Rocky and Jack. Use of my jet to any-where in the continental US for their honeymoon." Tears pooled in her eyes again. "Thank you," she whispered.

"Have you two picked out a place yet?"

"Yes. New York City."

"When you're ready to go, just let me know."

Rocky was so moved all she could do was nod in reply.

Tamar presented the last gift. "Your godfathers,

Mal, Clay, and Bing, asked me to give you this."

It was another envelope. Inside were two season tickets to the Chiefs games for the upcoming NFL season. She pumped her fist. "Yes!"

Surrounded by her booty, Rocky took in all the smiles and the damp eyes and decided she might be the luckiest motorcycle chick on earth. Since she was a little girl, she'd dreamt about having a life as perfect as this one with its great job, fantastic love, and an amazing group of friends. "Thank you, everybody."

"You're welcome."

Lily called out, "And now, cake!"

Cheers filled the air.

Walking on air after the shower, Rocky rode the short distance across the street to see if Jack was home. She wanted to tell him about the great gifts and see if he wanted to get together later. There was an unfamiliar car parked in his driveway. Not wanting to butt in on anything, she sent him a text saying she was going home, to not disturb him and his company. Her phone rang. Caller ID showed JACK. "Hey, babe."

"Hey," he replied. "You aren't interrupting anything. Come on in."

"You sure?"

"Positive. Eva's cousin is in town on business and I want her to meet you."

"Eva's cousin?"

"Yes. Please, Rock."

"Is she giving you drama?"

He didn't answer, which she took as a yes. "Be right there." She walked to the door. Steeling herself for what she'd find on the other side, she turned the knob and went in.

The woman, a petite brunette, looked so stunned when Rocky walked in, Rock almost smiled.

Jack did the introductions. "Helen, my fiancée, Rochelle Dancer. Rock, Eva's cousin Helen Simon."

"Pleased to meet you," Rocky said.

The woman appeared to shake herself out of her shock and said, "Same here. I wasn't expecting—"

Rocky spoke into the breach. "Someone who rides motorcycles? I know." She placed her helmet on a table. "Many folks are shocked that I do." She sat down on the arm of the couch where Jack was sitting.

He looked up at her and smiled. "How was the shower?"

"A lot of fun. Got some pretty nice stuff, too." She turned to the cousin, who continued her assessment. "Are you going to be in town for a while?" Rocky asked her.

"About two weeks. I'm doing some consulting work over in Franklin."

"Ah."

Jack said, "I thought she might like to have dinner with us later."

Rocky had nothing but respect for Jack's ties to his late wife, but the woman eyeing her with barely veiled, narrowed eyes didn't impress her as a friendly dinner companion. "I just stuffed myself at the shower but if you don't think I'll be intruding on you two catching up, I'll go."

"You won't be intruding," Jack insisted.

Rocky looked to the visitor and asked, Helen?" The woman seemed to be still sizing her up.

"Oh," she replied, as if startled. "Sure. Please come along. I'd like for us to get to know each other."

Rocky sensed the lie but if Jack wanted her to tag along, so be it.

They went to the Dog. Jukebox Gina was playing "If I Was Your Woman" by Gladys Knight. It was Sunday evening so the diner was crowded. Helen cast a critical eye around the place and voiced, "How quaint. Looks like a diner in Mayberry or *American Graffiti*."

"We like it," Jack said.

"Music is extremely loud, though."

Rocky disagreed, but then she was accustomed to the sound levels of the jukebox.

In his role as shift host, Eli approached them and Helen squealed, "Eli!" and threw her arms wide for a hug.

His responding hug appeared more polite than heartfelt. "Hi, Cousin Helen. Dad said you were in town." He then stepped back.

"Yes. How are you?"

"I'm good. You?"

"Good. You're all grown up, and you look so much like Eva."

Eli didn't reply, just sort of nodded in response. "Booth or table?" he asked his dad.

Jack turned to Rocky. "Do you have a preference?"

"No, we'll take whatever you have open, Eli."

"Okay. Right this way." He grabbed some menus and led them to a booth on the back wall. "I'll send your server right over."

As they settled in, Bing Shepard, sitting at a table with his housemate, Clay Dobbs, and a couple of local farmers, leaned over and said, "Rock. Spaghetti is excellent tonight. Just excellent."

"Why thanks, Bing. I'll let Siz and Randy know."

Helen appeared puzzled by the interaction so Jack explained, "Rocky's the co-owner here."

"Ah, I see. So, is this the only place to eat in town?"

Rocky heard the dig in her voice but didn't glance up from her menu.

Jack answered, "Yes. Best food in the county."

"How long have you been co-owner, Rochelle?"

"A few years." Had Helen's tone held genuine interest, Rocky would've added that she'd worked as the lone cook for years before being offered partial ownership, but it didn't, so she kept the expanded version to herself. A glance over the top of the menu showed Helen still assessing her coolly. Ignoring that, Rocky asked Jack, "What are you having, Professor?"

"The snapper and fingerling potatoes."

Their server, a short redhead named Lisa, appeared at the table. "Oh hi, Ms. Dancer. I didn't know you and Mr. James were here. So sorry for the delay. We're really busy as you can see. What can I get you to drink?"

Rock and Jack asked for waters and colas. Helen turned the menu over and looked at the back. "Can I see a wine list?"

"We don't serve alcohol."

"Why on earth not?"

Rock said, "Because the principal owner's continued sobriety is important to us."

"Oh," Helen replied sounding and looking displeased. "I'll have water and a cola too, then."

"Coming right up. Do you want to place your dinner orders now, or do you need a few more minutes?"

They were ready. Rock ordered the spaghetti. She'd eat a little of it and take the rest home.

Helen asked, "Is it really snapper or just a pretense for the menu?"

Rocky drew in a deep breath.

Lisa looked offended but kept her tone professional. "It's real snapper, ma'am."

Helen gave her a brittle smile. "I was just curious. I'll have the snapper then."

"I'll be right back with your drinks." Lisa sent Rocky an angry look before she moved on.

Helen asked, "So, Jack, how in the world did you and Eli end up here?"

"The school superintendent made me an offer I couldn't refuse. Plus, Eli and I needed a change."

"I understand. We were all devastated by Eva's death. It had to be doubly hard for you and Eli since you loved her so much." She then turned to Rocky. "I hope talking about my cousin Eva isn't making you uncomfortable."

"No. I'm fine." Rocky met Jack's eyes and lingered there for a moment before shifting her attention to the well-ordered chaos of the Dog.

Helen kept the conversation going about Eva, asking Jack if he remembered certain family vacations and how beautifully Eva played the harp. Jack kept his responses short and did his best to include Rocky in the conversation, but Helen plowed right over his attempts and brought the conversation back to Eva.

"I remember the time we went to the shore and she and I won the sandcastle-building contest. We must have been eight or nine. She and I were the same age and resembled each other so much people often mistook us for twins." Her voice turned wistful. "I miss her so. You and Eli probably do, too."

She threw Rocky a look which was met with no reaction.

Lisa returned with their food and set the plates down. Helen studied her order. "Not many people can prepare snapper correctly. I hope this tastes as good as it appears."

Rocky chuckled to herself and started in on her spaghetti. The old Rocky would've already snatched Helen bald by now, but this was the new and improved Rochelle Dancer, and the last thing she wanted was to embarrass herself or Jack. At least publicly. But, as sure as she loved Jack and her motorcycle, Rock knew that before cousin Helen left town she'd be forced into finding out how she tasted with mustard. And truthfully, she was sort of looking forward to it.

"So, Rochelle. How long have you lived here?"

"All my life."

"How interesting. You never wanted to leave?"

"I did. Went away to KU, got a job, then traveled around the world for a year before moving back."

Her surprise showed. "Where'd you go?"

"Cambodia. Senegal. Rio. Mumbai. Tibet."

"You didn't see Paris or London?"

"No."

"How on earth can you go abroad and pass them up?"

"Had no desire to see Europe."

Her mouth dropped. Rocky twirled more spaghetti onto her fork and glanced up into Jack's humor-filled dark eyes. "I'm pretty unconventional."

"Which is how she stole my heart," Jack added.

"But so soon after Eva's death?"

Now we're getting to the meat of the matter, Rocky thought.

"It's been five years," he said with a smile that didn't reach his eyes. "Eva wanted me to remarry. In fact, she made me promise I would."

"I see," came the doubtful response.

Rocky asked, "Are you married, Helen?"

"No." And her eyes moved to Jack. "Unlike Eva I never found my soul mate."

Rocky wondered how long Helen had been in love with Jack. Although the Professor was a boss in the classroom, he was not the most observant guy and there was a good chance he might not know how she felt. Then again, maybe he did. Had Eva known? In the end the questions didn't much matter. Jack was her guy now and poaching by lovesick cousins would not be encouraged or allowed.

"So, Helen, what type of consulting are you doing in Franklin?" Jack asked.

"I'm working with the city's governmental leaders on how to fine-tune their practices. The company I work for does this nationwide."

"They have been having issues."

Helen nodded. "Yes, the former mayor nearly bankrupted the place, so I'm here to help put them back on the right track."

Rocky said, "I hear Mr. Proctor is doing a very good job."

"He seems knowledgeable. More importantly, he listens. I often run into situations where the men in charge don't want to take directions from a woman. It's been refreshing."

Rocky was admittedly impressed by that. On more than a few occasions, she'd had to fight the good fight on behalf of her gender, and her bank account was still smiling from the seven-figure settlement she'd won as a result a few years back. She was liking Helen a bit more.

"My Ivy League master's degree in public administration has given me a good life," Helen said and asked, "Do you have a degree, Rochelle?"

"Sure do. Graduated from Henry Adams High." Helen was back in the mustard category. "And with over a million in the bank, my degree has served me well, too."

Helen coughed and coughed some more.

Jack silently toasted Rocky with his glass of cola.

Rocky asked, "Are you okay, Helen?"

After wiping her mouth with her napkin, she replied, in a much less superior tone, "Yes. I'm fine."

Smiling, Jack asked, "Who's ready for dessert?"

After leaving the Dog, they rode back to Jack's place and Helen walked to her car. "Thanks for dinner."

Jack replied, "You're welcome."

"Nice meeting you, Rochelle."

"Same here. Let us know if you want to have dinner again before you leave town, or if you need anything while you're here."

"I'll do that."

Rocky kept the plastic smile on her face and, like Jack, waved when Helen backed out of the driveway and drove off.

"Thanks for coming along," Jack said as they climbed the steps to the porch.

"How long has she had the hots for you?"

"Since the day we were introduced."

"Was wondering if you knew."

He opened the door for her. "Oh, I do. Eva knew as well and wore the same fake smile you're wearing now every time Helen came around."

Rocky laughed. "I think Eva and I would've gotten along well."

"I think so, too." He took her in his arms

and placed a kiss on her forehead. "Thanks for putting up with her, I know that couldn't've been much fun for you."

"It wasn't, but I knew she and her master's degree in public administration would be going back to her hotel, and I was coming home with you, so that kept me from snatching her across the table."

"You're so wonderful."

"Yes, I am."

That night as Rocky lay in bed, she thought back on the encounter with cousin Helen. It was very apparent the woman thought Rocky not a good choice for Jack. In some ways, Rocky agreed, but she was becoming more comfortable with the idea that maybe she was. She wondered how pissed off Helen would be if they sent her an invitation to the wedding. Smiling, she turned off the lamp and snuggled in to sleep.

CHAPTER
7

Monday morning, Bernadine and Trent toured the newly rebuilt Sutton Hotel on Main Street. Constructed originally in the 1880s, the once glorious establishment, ravaged by time, had tumbled into disrepair. Now, it was ready to be occupied again and she couldn't be happier. Lily found an Italian family of old-school stonemasons, who, using some of Tamar's old photos, had re-created the elaborate structural carvings on the building's face. As Bernadine walked the interior and surveyed the five ground-level businesses, her heels echoed on the newly installed tile floor. Kelly Douglas's beauty shop would be occupying one of the places and Doc Reg would be moving his practice out of the school to take over another. Bernadine stopped for a moment to view the overhead skylights set into the ceiling of the courtyard-like interior, and the large potted plants taste-fully set about, courtesy of Sheila Payne. "This looks wonderful, Trent."

"I agree. Have you decided on the other tenants besides Kelly and Reg?"

"I have a couple from Vegas interested in opening a combination coffee shop and bakery coming in to visit next week, but I'm still trying to decide on the last two spaces. It has to be something that serves the community best." She'd had plenty of offers from outsiders, everything from spas and boutiques to bank branches. Whatever she decided would have to not only serve the community but also be sustainable. It made no sense to take on an enterprise that would go belly up in six months.

"And upstairs?" he asked.

There were four one-bedroom apartments available for rent. The tenants would be able to access their spaces through a private entrance on the side of the building. "Crystal will have one. The other applicants are still being vetted. I want to be careful there, too."

"Have you talked to Mal yet about possibly bringing in a new restaurant?"

"Not yet."

Smiling, he asked, "Scared?"

"Yes. On one hand, he might not take it as a threat, but on the other hand . . ." Her voice trailed off. A new eating establishment was needed. With Siz working his magic in the kitchen, diners were coming from far and wide, and wait times for tables, especially on week-ends, were getting longer and longer.

"Maybe we can just expand the place," Trent said. "Have fine dining in one part and keep the old Dog for casual meals."

She thought that might work, but then came the question of whether Mal and Rocky wanted to manage a larger place. "I plan to run it by him this evening. I'll let you know what happens."

"Okay. Wishing you luck. Who knows, maybe he'll surprise you. I'm heading over to the firehouse. Luis says he's noticed some drainage issues."

"Should I be worried?"

"Hope not. I'll let you know."

Alone, she surveyed the place again, imagining the way it might look with the businesses open and customers coming in and out. Having the building restored and on the brink of occupation was a big step for her growing town, and with growth came worries. There were at least five new families slated to move in over the next year, bringing with them new personalities, ideas, and maybe different ways of viewing the Henry Adams she'd come to love. Would the old residents lose the close connections they'd forged? What might happen with traditions like August First, the monthly town meetings, and the newly established Mexican Christmas celebration of Posada? A change in the connections of the residents was probably inevitable, but could the growth be managed so as not to impact the town's heart? She wanted neighbors to know each other, to continue Friday Night Movies, and for those moving in to know how

Henry Adams was established and why. Only the future would tell if that was achievable, and having no crystal ball, she contented herself with being pleased that the old hotel was alive again. She hoped the original owner, Virginia Sutton, and the other Dusters were, too.

Back in her office, she sent Mal a text to make sure they were still on for dinner and checked her e-mail. As she'd promised Gemma, she'd placed a call to the Kansas Department of Families and Children to get some direction on how to proceed with Lucas and Jasmine Herman. Her contact at the office, Gwen Frazier, had been very helpful with the paperwork tied to the fostering of Amari and his crew, and she'd been eager to help this time around, too. In fact, Ms. Frazier said she had no problem putting Gemma Dahl on the fast track to becoming a foster parent. The state of Kansas, like many others, was beating the bushes to find good people willing to open their hearts and homes, and Ms. Frazier didn't want to discourage someone willing to step up by making them jump through a prolonged series of hoops. In the meantime, though, Ms. Frazier promised to reach out to her counterparts in Ohio to see if the kids' files could be shared so she, Bernadine, and Gemma could get a handle on why no family members had stepped up to take the children after the death of their parents.

Lily stuck her head in the door. "Gwen Frazier just faxed over the files for the Herman kids. It's still printing. I'll bring it in when it's done."

"Thanks, Lil. I have a question?"

Lily walked into the office.

"How do you think having another restaurant in town will go over?"

She shrugged. "Not sure, but we do need one. I'm tired of having to wait a day and a half to get a seat at the Dog. Might also be nice to have a fancy place with nice tablecloths and candles. Not that the Dog isn't nice, but you know what I mean."

She did. The Dog was a diner, not a restaurant.

Lily asked, "I take it you haven't brought this up with Mal?"

"No, not yet."

"Thinking he might fight you on it?"

"My heart says no, but my head? Not so sure."

"It is his baby, and running that place was one of the things that helped him kick the alcohol. He might give you grief over competition."

Bernadine sighed. She hadn't thought about the Dog being tied to his sobriety. "You know, when we did all the dreaming about making Henry Adams bigger and better we didn't think about the growing pains."

"No, we didn't, but, She Who Turns the World always comes up with a solution."

135

Bernadine found that amusing. "Thanks for the support."

"IJS."

"Oh lord. Don't start that again. Go check on the fax." They'd kidded each other before about the Internet acronym for I'm Just Saying.

"Yes, ma'am."

A few minutes later, Bernadine had the printed copy of the file in hand. The report bore out the facts that no one wanted the Herman children after their parents' deaths. Not the father's dad or any of the mom's three married siblings, even though the State of Ohio caseworker contacted them repeatedly. That saddened her. Per the file, the dad owned a successful construction firm and the mom had an eponymous pediatric practice. She looked through the file for information on the Herman estate and found nothing. Thinking that odd, she picked up the phone and called Ms. Frazier

It was lunch hour at the Dog and a frazzled Rocky was helping her scrambling staff by taking orders and delivering them to the tables. There were twenty people waiting in line to be seated when she'd gone to the floor a few minutes ago, but she had to not think about them because she was also keeping an eye on the baskets holding the fries in the two deep fryers, washing veggies, and grabbing new order tickets from the line.

She and Siz and the tattooed new assistant cook, Randy, were also cooking and calling for side dishes from the two newly hired prep cooks who were doing their best to keep up.

"Let's move it people!" she yelled over the chaos while the staff hurried in to add more tickets to the line, and pick up completed orders so they could rush back out again. "Folks are hungry. Let's not keep them waiting!" The air was filled with the sounds of burgers and steaks sizzling on the grill and the kitchen was hot from the heat of the flat tops and the steam wafting from the big cook pots filled with veggies and pasta. Behind her, Rocky heard glass break and prayed it was the sound of empty dishes and not from a just-filled order. She turned. The kitchen gods were kind. The server, a new girl named Chrissy, stared at the mess on the floor with wide eyes.

"It happens, Chris," Siz reassured her as he added a done burger to a plate. "No big deal, but grab the broom."

"Will I have to pay for the glass?"

"No, but grab a broom and sweep it up before someone trips coming in. It's over there."

Chrissy hurried to where the broom and dust pan were kept and began sweeping.

Siz glanced over at Randy and the Texan drawled, "Just another slow lunch hour here in Dog and Cow heaven."

Rock grinned, snatched another ticket from the line, and called, "I need a number seven!"

From eleven o'clock until one thirty it was full-out nonstop, and not even the addition of the two new prep cooks made a difference. The staff was behind on orders, bussing tables, and seating people. Although none of the regular customers complained, Rock could tell by the disgruntled faces when she finally arrived with some of the orders that the long waits were not going over well. Her offered apologies were met by taciturn nods, and even a few glares that she knew were deserved.

When the rush finally ended, she slumped tiredly onto a stool, drew in a deep breath and used a towel to mop the perspiration from her brow. "I'm getting too old for this," she told Siz, who was seated on another stool and sipping a large cola. Beside him sat Randy Emerson, whose two full sleeves sported beautiful tattooed images of fruits, veggies, and cuts of meat.

"You and me both."

"And you want to leave me and Randy here while you go gallivanting off to Miami? I don't think so."

"You'll do fine."

Randy said, "The new kid Alex did really good for his first day."

"He did but even with him and the other newbie Pam, we still couldn't keep up."

"We need to start serving bad food," Siz offered. Rock tossed back, "Don't even go there because this is all your fault."

"Me!"

"Yes, you. Folks wouldn't be coming from miles around if you weren't such a wizard." And he was. There were never crowds of this proportion when Rocky had been the Dog's only cook. Her food was good, but there were no words to describe how well he could *burn*, as the old folks called it.

Randy said, "I'm going to go take a walk and stretch my legs."

"Make sure you don't run away and join the circus," Rocky told him. "I need you."

"Depends on what kind of food they have." He laughed and exited out of the back.

"I like him, Rock. A little quiet, but knows his way around a kitchen."

"I like him, too. I've never seen full sleeves of food, though."

"Neither have I. Kind of dope, though."

"Dope?"

"What you old people call cool."

"Ah. How are you and Stephen?"

"He's still acting like somebody in middle school, so I dumped him. Tired of his drama."

"I'm sorry, Siz."

"So am I, but like my dad said, I obviously didn't mean that much to him."

"Do you think you'll reconcile?"

He shook his head. "Even if a five-star restaurant opened across the street and I stayed here, I still wouldn't be with him. I can't be with someone who's too scared to be who they are."

She thought about her own issues. "Some people aren't as strong as others, baby."

"I know and I tried to be patient, Rock, I really did, but no. Sometimes you have to step up, and I don't see him doing that for a long time."

"Maybe this will be the push he needs."

"Maybe, but I'm moving on. Life's too short."

"Says the old, decrepit Kitchen Wizard."

He grinned and went back to sipping his drink.

Once the kitchen was cleaned, Siz left to take a short break too and Rocky sought out Mal in his office. He looked up from the computer screen. "Spreadsheets say we're doing box office business, baby girl."

"If something doesn't change, you may need some of those bucks to bury me and my staff. The crowds are working us to death and I hate the way we're always behind."

He shrugged. "Hire more people."

"There's only so much room in the kitchen, Mal, no real room for more bodies. Maybe Bernadine will bring in another eating place and take some of the heat off us."

"Bite your tongue. Profit is at an all-time high."

"High profits—dead staff. Take your pick."

"We'll be fine," he said. "Grab a seat and take a breath. Dinner starts in three hours."

Rocky sighed her frustration and left King Mal Midas to his spreadsheets of gold. She planned to speak with Bernadine as soon as possible.

Although Wyatt was old enough to be home alone, Gemma made arrangements for Crystal to come and stay with the kids while she went to class. The county had opened a community college extension in Henry Adams's big beautiful school, so she'd signed up to take some business classes with the hope of obtaining a business degree. Her first class would be Intro to Accounting.

When she entered the school the beauty of it blew her away as always. From the huge fish tank built into the wall to the skylights and kiva, it was state of the art. She was told that a good portion of the building hadn't been opened yet because there weren't enough students enrolled, but Bernadine was betting on future growth and she was rarely wrong.

There were other classes being held that evening, and Gemma found hers down the hall from the art labs. She was twenty minutes early, and when she entered, less than a third of the seats were filled. Seeing how young the occupants were made her wonder what she'd been thinking when she decided to go back to school. All were wearing earbuds and glued to their phones. They were not only younger but also probably smarter. Unease roiling her insides, she took a seat near the back and hoped for invisibility.

"Are you the prof?" asked a young blue-haired kid seated next to her. His sleeveless shirt showed arms tatted up with full sleeves and there were small hoops in the lobes of both ears.

She gave him a quick shake of her head. "No."

"You're a student?" His voice and eyes were filled with wonder and surprise.

"Yes." There were snickers from two girls seated nearby, but Gemma ignored them.

"That's dope," he said. "My mom just got her degree in nursing."

His kindness made her smile. "Thanks. I'm scared to death," she admitted.

He waved her off. "You got this. My name's Josh."

"I'm Gemma."

"Nice to meet you, Ms. Gemma. If you need someone to get the haters out of your mentions, just let me know."

Gemma had no idea what that meant, but guessed it was an offer of support, so she said, "Okay." She made a mental note to ask Eli or Crystal for a translation the next time she saw one of them.

The room filled up slowly and although she hoped not to be the oldest person in the class, she was. No one looked over twenty, let alone over forty, but she drew in a deep breath, swallowed her fears, and repeated inwardly what Josh said earlier, *You got this.* She'd always dreamed of going back to school but dreams don't come true if you don't show up so she was determined to get through this with the best grade possible. And who knew, maybe her life experience would mean something when it was all said and done.

Most of the seats were taken by the time the man she assumed to be the professor hurried in. He looked harried and carried a laptop case bulging with disorderly papers. He set his things down on the desk at the front of the room, pushed his black framed glasses up his nose, and said, "I'm Dr. LeForge, and this is Intro to Accounting, so if that's not why you're here, you might need to be somewhere else." He gave the class a shy smile, and Gemma and some other students in the room responded with smiles of their own, but she noticed more than a few remained plugged in to their phones. She wondered if they knew they needed to be listening to him and not to whatever was coming through their earbuds.

Gemma thought him not bad-looking, in a rumpled, disorganized sort of way. He appeared to be about her age and had light brown hair that brushed the collar of a faded blue oxford button-down shirt that was sorely in need of ironing. The blue corduroy suit coat worn over it was shiny with age and the elbows reinforced with the stereotypical patches professors were prone to sport, at least in the movies.

"Now," he said, breaking into her assessment, "for those of you in a deep, symbiotic relationship with your phones, if you don't have the respect to remove your buds, you probably aren't worth my time to teach. Whether you pass this class or not, I still get paid."

"Ouch!" somebody called out.

"He ain't playing with y'all," another amused voice added.

Gemma liked him. Some of those called out sheepishly pulled their buds free. The remaining few disconnected, but showed bored, disinterested faces.

He passed out the syllabus and the class began with him talking about the book that was required and the workbook that complemented it. Apparently, the book could be rented online but the workbook had to be purchased. Gemma had no idea you could rent textbooks and wondered how much it would cost. He then mentioned something about a code the students needed to access accompanying online materials and she was as lost as a country girl on her first trip to the big city.

"Any questions?" he asked.

Gemma was too embarrassed to raise her hand, so sat silently and hoped to catch Josh after class and have him explain what it all meant. The conversation shifted to the subject matter they'd be covering and how much weight the quizzes, tests, and homework carried toward their grades.

"Even though this is an intro course, it isn't a walk in the park," he told them. "You'll work hard in this class and if you do, you'll reap the benefits. My office hours are on the syllabus. If you need help come see me. Pride won't help you pass the midterm or the final."

Gemma swore he was speaking directly to her. Color rose in her cheeks. Once again doubts rose about her ability to handle this, but she beat them down.

"Now that we have the housekeeping out of the way, I like to know who my students are. When I call your name, raise your hand and if you'd like, share your dreams."

A few students rolled their eyes but many of their classmates did offer up their goals. A young woman named Brie wanted to be able to handle the books in her father's feed store, while another named Stacy wanted to be an accountant and move to New York City. When her story drew some snickering, LeForge said forcefully, "Never laugh at someone's dream. Ever."

You could hear a pin drop. Josh, whose last name was Miller, wanted to open a tattoo shop and needed the class to help him be successful financially.

LeForge called Gemma's name next. She haltingly raised her hand in response and said, "I just want to make a good life for me and my grandson, and I'm hoping this class will help me get a better-paying job."

"A worthy goal, Ms. Dahl."

"Thanks," she whispered. A quick glance over at Josh showed his smile and the thumbs-up he sent her way.

Class was only an hour long and when time came for dismissal, everyone grabbed their belongings and began moving to the door. Josh gave her a wave and was gone before she could ask him what she needed to know. Professor LeForge was still at the front of the room stuffing papers back into his portfolio. Grabbing her courage, she approached. "Professor?"

"Yes?"

"Can you explain these online codes you mentioned? I'm kind of new at all this."

He gave her a warm smile. "Sure can. There's another class coming in behind this one, so we need to leave. If you have a few minutes we can talk in the hallway."

They took a seat on one of the benches outside the classroom and he gave her the information she needed. Filled with relief, she thanked him. "I haven't been in a class since high school, so I'm sort of swimming upstream."

"Understandable but you're to be commended for coming back."

"It's a bit scary."

"That's understandable too, but as I said earlier, you have my office hours and e-mail. Shoot me a message if you need anything."

"I will. Thanks again."

"No problem. Anything else?"

She shook her head but noted he didn't wear a wedding ring.

He stood. "I'll see you Thursday."

"Bye." And as he walked away, Van Halen's "Hot for Teacher" began playing in her head. Laughing to herself, she stood and headed for the parking lot.

"So, how'd your day go?" Mal asked Bernadine over dinner. They were seated at her dining room table and his question was one of the many things she loved about him. He was always interested in her day.

"I looked over the files of Lucas and Jasmine Herman and found the oddest thing. Their dad owned a construction company and the mom had her own pediatric practice, so I assume they had money, but there's nothing in the records concerning the estate."

"That is odd. No will?"

"Nothing in the record about that, either. I called Ms. Frazier, who helped with the paperwork for our kids. She said she'd reach out to the folks in Ohio and see if we can get some answers. I was a social worker for a long time and I've never known kids with money to go into foster care if they have relatives. Most people will take them in for the money alone."

"So how are the kids doing?"

"Okay, considering. Ms. Frazier is going to try and push Gemma's foster parent paperwork through as quickly as possible. They need some stability after all they've been through."

He seemed to agree. "What else did you do today?"

"Went with Trent to check out the Sutton Hotel. It looks fabulous."

"So I hear. I haven't been inside yet."

"I'm still trying to decide what other kinds of businesses I should let lease the space." And she told him about the choices she was considering.

"I like the bank branch idea. Having to drive to Franklin to make the daily deposits is a pain. Not that it's far but it's the idea. Also be nice to have more than that one ATM at the Dog."

"Yes, it would." She wondered if now might be the time to bring up the possibility of a new eatery. "I'm also interested in any ideas

148

you might have about the situation with the Dog."

He paused. "What situation?"

"It's become so popular and crowded, I'm wondering if maybe we need another restaurant."

"No."

"Then maybe we could expand the building."

"It's fine the way it is."

She sighed inwardly. "Mal, sometimes it takes twenty minutes to get a table. People are getting frustrated. We need to come up with a solution. Why are you so opposed?"

"If you want to open a new place, go ahead, but don't expect me to clap. This town has always had only one place to eat and one place is all we need."

She sat back. "Really? That's your answer?"

"Rock and I worked hard to build that place up."

"With my help," she reminded him gently. The place had been a hot mess of a dump when she purchased the town and she'd sunk good money into the rehab.

His jaw tightened. "With your help."

"Look, I'm not trying to close the place."

"Then let's talk about putting in more tables."

"Where? It's at maximum occupancy now. There's no room for more tables." She'd been hoping this conversation wouldn't blow up in her face but it seemed well on the way. This wasn't what she wanted so she tried a different tack. "Will you at least consider enlarging the place?"

"The Dog is fine the way it is."

She countered in a reasonable tone, "No, babe, it isn't. Can you tell me why you won't even talk about this with me?" She was doing her best to try and understand his resistance, but so far, he'd given her nothing tangible.

His silent, tight-faced response showed he wasn't budging, either. "Okay," she said, "I'll go ahead and make my decision without your input."

"What's that mean?"

"It means, I'm going to consider bringing in another restaurant, probably for fine dining."

"I thought we were a team?"

"We are."

"Not if you're going behind my back."

"I'm not going behind your back. Why do you think I asked for your opinion in the first place?"

"Why ask if you'd already made up your mind?"

She fought hard to rein in her rising temper. "Look, Mal."

He cut her off. "No, you look. Since this is obviously your way or the highway, do what you want."

"Mal?" She was stunned at how quickly this had gone sideways. Was he that afraid of change? "A new place won't close down the Dog. That's not what this is about."

He responded by pushing back from the table. "I just remembered there's something else I was supposed to do this evening."

Rather than say something that would pour more gasoline on the fire she remained silent.

He glared. She kept her reaction passive.

He left.

Outdone, she sat in the silence and wondered, *what the hell just happened?*

Crystal came into the house on the heels of his exit. "What's OG so mad about? Just saw him tearing out of the subdivision like—" She stopped and took in Bernadine's face. "Did you two have a fight?"

Bernadine drained the last of her wine. "I think so."

"Over what? Or am I being too nosy?"

"You're not. I asked him what he thought about bringing in a new restaurant because of how crowded the Dog is getting."

"And he wasn't feeling it, I take it?"

"No." And she wanted to rant about him being stubborn and hardheaded but instead asked, "You work there. What do you think?"

Crystal shrugged. "I like the money I'm bringing in from the extra hours we're working, but it's crowded twenty-four seven and it's running the staff raggedy. Have you talked to Rocky?"

"Not yet, she's next on my list."

"How about we just make it bigger?"

"Mal wasn't feeling that, either."

"He's got issues."

She agreed. As Trent mentioned earlier, the Dog was Mal's baby. She understood that. No way was she trying to undermine his interests, or how much the diner meant to him personally, but the crowding and wait times were a problem that needed to be addressed.

"Maybe he'll come around," Crystal said.

"I hope so." Although, knowing Mal, it wouldn't be soon. She sensed this was going to test their relationship in ways nothing had before and that made her sad. "So how was your day? Did Gemma say anything about her class?"

"Only that the prof seemed nice and she was the oldest person in the room."

"I think it's wonderful that she's going back to school."

"Me, too. The kids were good while I was over there. W.W. said Jaz wants a chess set and Lucas needs a skateboard."

"Okay. I'll take care of it. And the rest of your day?"

"Pretty good," she said, taking a seat. "Have my classes picked out for the fall term. Helped Eli register online for his. Can't wait to get the keys to my new place."

"You'll be able to move in this weekend."

"Yes!" she said throwing a fist pump, then caught herself. "Not that I'm in a hurry to leave you, Mom."

"Uh-huh." Although she was amused, the idea of Crystal moving on with her life was something else that made her sad. Even though she'd still be living in town, they'd no longer be under the same roof and that was going to be a big adjustment on her part. "We've come a long way, these past what, five years?"

"Yep. Back when I had a bad attitude and blonde weave to match. I look at the pictures of me back then and wonder why you didn't just shave my head. That thing was awful."

"True, but it was your pride and joy. You would've never forgiven me had I done that."

Crystal quieted for a few moments and Bernadine could tell she was thinking. When she finally spoke, her voice was soft. "No telling where I'd be if it weren't for you. Probably dead someplace."

"Maybe not."

"I certainly wouldn't be an artist or a fashionista, or have visited places like Paris and Madrid. Thank you for adopting me."

"You've been a blessing."

"Not all the time."

"No, but I can't imagine my life without you in it."

Concern filled Crystal's eyes. "Are you going to be okay with me moving out?"

"I'll get used to it. It'll be practice for when you really leave Henry Adams, and I only get to text or talk to you by phone." Bernadine paused. "Do you think you're ready for wheels?"

A smile beamed from her daughter's face like the sun in June. "Yeah."

"Then sometime this week, we'll go over to the dealership in Franklin and see about a used car. With Eli leaving for good you're going to need a way to get around. And since you already know how to drive, you shouldn't have a problem taking the driving test."

Crystal threw herself on Bernadine in joy. "Thank you!"

Bernadine held her and thought about how different this grown-up version of Crystal was compared to the child who once slept on her bedroom floor to keep from messing up the décor. "You're welcome."

"I love you, Mom."

"I love you more."

Later, upstairs in her bedroom, Bernadine's thoughts returned to Mal. To try and smooth things over, she'd sent him a text. He'd yet to respond. In their two years together they'd never run into a situation they hadn't been able to work out. It made her wonder if his refusal to consider her suggestion meant there was

154

something going on beneath the surface that he didn't want to share. She knew the place was tied to his sobriety but his responses sounded off to her, almost as if they were tied to something else entirely. Their relationship had put such joy in her personal life. Finding love with him had all but banished the anger and bitterness Leo's perfidy had left in her heart. Mal wasn't perfect and neither was she, but together they'd built something special. Now, she wasn't sure where they stood. Standing in front of her vanity's mirror, she removed the promise necklace he'd given her from around her neck and set it beside the bangles and earrings she'd picked out for the next day, and crawled into bed. Her worry over their future was still on her mind when she finally slid into sleep.

CHAPTER
8

Tamar walked into the kitchen for breakfast and found her son, Malachi, seated at the table sipping coffee. Knowing his devotion to the diner, she asked, "Did the Dog burn down overnight?"

He shook his head. "Took the morning off."

Deciding something must be very wrong for him to be with her and not at his post, she left the why of it for a moment to take a skillet down from the cupboard and set it on the stove. Opening the refrigerator, she took out some bacon and two eggs. Because he still hadn't offered a reason for his visit, she remarked, "I have many superpowers, Mal, but mind-reading isn't one, at least not this early in the day, so how about you tell me why you're here?"

"I've decided I hate change."

"Join the crowd." He was her only child, a product of her brief relationship with Joel Newton and, to be honest, she'd resented him at first. As a result, they didn't begin life together with the typical mother and son bond until her mother pointedly reminded her that he hadn't asked to be born. After getting over herself when he was about six months old, she came to love him fiercely but that love was tested when he came back from Nam and gave his life over to alcohol. She put a couple strips of bacon in the now hot skillet and poured herself a cup of coffee. Studying his face, she saw sadness and the stubbornness that lay beneath the surface. "You and Bernadine fighting?"

"Yeah."

Tamar thought Bernadine Brown to be the best thing to ever come into her son's life. Before her arrival, he'd chased women young enough to be his granddaughters and been proud of it. She on the other hand found it pitiful. That his initial interest in Bernadine didn't make Bernadine instantly swoon at his feet had puzzled him but Tamar cheered. He'd had to grow up to step to Bernadine. "So, what was the fight about?"

"The Dog. She wants to bring in another restaurant."

"Good. Folks can stop waiting for hell to freeze over to be seated."

He cut her a look that she ignored in favor of tending to the bacon frying.

"But we're making a record profit."

"At the expense of what?"

He didn't answer.

"I'm having issues with change, too," she admitted. "And waiting to eat at the Dog is one of them."

"You're no help."

"You knew the job was dangerous when you sat down at my table." She removed the cooked bacon from the skillet and placed the strips onto a paper-towel-covered plate. "Have you eaten?"

He nodded.

She cracked the two eggs into the skillet. Once they were over easy the way she liked them, she took a seat and joined him.

He asked, "Besides waiting to be seated, what else is on your list?"

For a moment, she debated whether to be truthful or not and finally settled on the former. "Wondering if I've outlived my usefulness."

"You haven't. This town would crack wide open without you steering the ship."

"That's Bernadine's job."

"And she doesn't care who knows it. I tried to tell her to bring in more tables, but that's not what she wants to do."

"Where are you going to put more tables, on the ceiling?"

"You're supposed to be taking my side."

"Not if your side's illogical."

"So now you're Mr. Spock?"

"Could be worse, I could be agreeing with you."

He sighed. "I want everything to stay the same."

"As much as I hate to say it, the town needs

change, so don't let your July stubbornness mess up what you have with Bernadine."

"*She's so in charge,* sometimes."

"Nothing wrong with that. Remember where we were before she got here?"

"Yeah," he muttered.

"Do you remember where you were before she got here?"

He didn't respond.

"You survived Nam, you beat alcohol, you'll survive another restaurant opening. You may not survive not having her in your life, though."

"I'll survive that, too."

She knew he was wrong, but he'd been charting his own path since he learned to say the word *no,* so she held her tongue. The love Mal and Bernadine shared kept them both balanced, but stubbornness was in the July DNA, which is why their ancestor Teresa July Nance wound up serving time in a territorial penitentiary. She mulishly stuck to the family's outlaw ways in defiance of Judge Parker's gavel and the changing times.

He stood. "I'll see you later."

She nodded.

When he left, she took out her phone and called Bernadine to see if she had time for Tamar to pay her a visit.

Later that morning, Tamar set out for town. She was still weighing Mal's visit and therefore not paying attention to the speedometer when she and Olivia hit the curve at eighty. She did pay attention to the siren and flashing bubble on top of the brown county sheriff car that pulled out onto the road behind her. *Dammit!*

"Morning, Ms. July."

Fuming, Tamar responded to Deputy Ransom's greeting by holding out her hand.

Ransom placed the speeding ticket on her palm. "Have a good day, ma'am." She touched her hat respectfully, walked back to her vehicle, and drove off.

With lightning sparking from her eyes, Tamar drove off in the opposite direction. At warp speed.

She was still simmering when she arrived at Bernadine's office.

"Are you okay?" Bernadine asked.

"No. Will's new deputy gave me *another* speeding ticket and if you say I drive too fast too, I will take off my belt."

Bernadine held up her hands defensively, "No, ma'am. My lips are sealed."

"Good. Now, talk to me about this new restaurant."

"Are you against it, too?"

"Of course not. I think it's a great idea. Mal doesn't but he's not the one having to stand in line."

"Did he tell you we argued?"

161

"Yes."

"I sent him a text last night hoping we could iron things out, but he still hasn't responded. I don't want to fight with him, Tamar."

"I understand. I love my son, but the Julys don't do well with change, never have. So, tell me what you have in mind."

"I'm not real sure at this point. Maybe a fine dining place with white tablecloths and candles, but Mal has me wanting to be the owner just so I can stick out my tongue and go, nah nah nah nah nah."

"Not the most mature response but an understandable one. If you do decide to build, I think it should be called The Three Spinsters."

Seeing the confusion on Bernadine's face, Tamar explained. "They were three unmarried ladies who helped found Henry Adams. Daisy Miller, secretary for the first AME church; Rachel Eddings, telegraph clerk and one of the town's surveyors; and town milliner Lucretia Potter. They were known as the Three Spinsters. Per the stories, they were highly educated and opinionated."

"That's fascinating and the Three Spinsters is a perfect name."

"Be a nice way to honor them and keep their memory alive."

"I agree. Do you have any pictures of them?"

"I doubt it but I will look."

"Let me know."

"Will do and don't worry about Mal, at least not enough to keep you from going forward. A fancy new place will be nice."

"Thanks for the support. Now, I just need to speak with Rocky. Mal's already mad at me, I'm hoping she won't be, too."

"Let's hope." Tamar stood. "I'm going to head to the rec. How are our new children?"

"They're okay. I'm dealing with a mystery surrounding their parents' estate, though." And she explained.

After hearing her out, Tamar said, "That is strange. Let me know if you find anything."

"Promise."

Feeling much better about her day, Tamar made her exit.

Once alone, Bernadine sat at her desk and mulled over the idea of the new restaurant and the more she thought about it, the more she liked it. Tamar's suggested name was perfect. Granted Bernadine knew nothing about the ins and outs of a restaurant, but more than a few of her sisters in the Bottom Women's group were owners of restaurant chains, and they'd give her all the help she'd need. Mal was going to throw a tantrum if she did decide to make herself a principal in the operation but that couldn't be helped. A knock on her door broke her from her musings and she looked up to see Rocky standing in the doorway.

"Hey, Bernadine. Do you have a minute?"

"I do, come on in. I was planning to call you."

"Is it about this restaurant that has Mal's drawers in a knot?"

"Yes."

"Do you think whoever builds it will want an investor?"

Bernadine was puzzled.

"No?"

She shook herself free. "You want to be an investor?"

"If I can. My tax lady says I need to invest some of the settlement I won from my sexual harassment suit at the truck place I was working. So, what do you think?"

"I'm thinking I want to be the owner and having you on board would be a dream come true."

Rocky grinned. "Then I'm in, and if Mal has a fit, so be it."

Bernadine didn't want to give her honey fits and knew the news would put a further strain on their relationship, but the train seemed to be leaving the station and she couldn't think of a better conductor than Rochelle Dancer.

"So, what do we do first?" Rocky asked.

"No idea, but let me make a few calls and I'll get back with you as soon as possible."

Rocky stood. "Okay, and thanks, Bernadine."

"Can I ask why you want to do this besides the tax implications?"

"I love the Dog, but I've worked there most of my adult life and I want a change. I'm also getting married and I want to kick back a bit. I'll never see Jack if I'm chopping onions twenty-four seven."

"Nothing wrong with that."

"Good. I'll wait for your call. Now, I need to go back to work. Time for lunch madness."

And she left.

As Rocky walked back to the Dog, she thought back on her response to Bernadine's question as to why she wanted to invest in the new restaurant. It had caught her off guard and she'd said the first thing she could think of, but was it true? Until that moment, she'd never acknowledged being tired of the Dog. Was she? She was still wrestling with the answer when she entered the kitchen, but set it aside to get to work.

An hour in, the place was so crowded, they were behind. Eli had been running orders in and out nonstop, so Rocky called, "Eli. Take a ten-minute break. I'll grab your next two orders."

Looking beat, he said, "Thanks, Rock. One of the orders is for cousin Helen and four of her co-workers."

Rocky wasn't looking forward to seeing Helen again. "Thanks for the warning."

He exited through the back door to the dock

for his break, and she loaded up the tray with the order for cousin Helen. Expertly balancing the groaning tray, she wove her way through the full diner and over to the booth. Gina the jukebox, always on point, was offering up "Smiling Faces" by Undisputed Truth. *"Smiling faces, sometimes—they don't tell the truth."*

"Hello, Helen," Rocky said cheerily as she arrived. "Good to see you again."

"Rochelle."

Rocky nodded a greeting at the four men with Helen and said, "I didn't take the order so you'll have to tell me who has what."

They complied and once everyone had their plate, Rocky asked, "Anything else I can get you?"

The men were staring her way with glazed-over smiles as men were prone to do upon meeting her for the first time. Rocky was used to it. Helen appeared highly perturbed at their responses and stated briskly, "We're fine. Thank you."

"Enjoy." Seeing Lily and Trent seated and waiting patiently to put in their orders, Rocky hurried over. "Sorry for the delay."

Trent looked around at the crowd and said, "It's getting insane in here."

"No kidding. What can I get you?"

She took their order and as she turned to leave, saw Helen waving impatiently her way. *Now what?*

Keeping her voice even she asked, "Do you need something?"

"Yes. This chicken breast is not cooked through. I'm sending it back. Bring me one that is."

Rocky had grilled the breasts personally, so she knew Helen was bent on causing trouble. "I'm sorry about that." Rocky picked up the plate.

"Ken's is half-raw as well," Helen added in a superior tone. The way Ken froze and then glanced quickly in Helen's direction told all. His breast was about a quarter eaten.

"So, yours is raw, too?" Rocky asked.

His face reddened.

"She your boss?"

He nodded tightly.

"Then let's take yours back. We don't want you getting in trouble for not agreeing with her."

Helen's eyes widened with outrage.

Rocky ignored her and quizzed the rest of the party. "Anybody else having issues?" None of the men appeared willing to meet her eyes. Everyone shook their heads, no. "Good. I'll be back shortly."

Taking their plates, she left with Helen's eyes burning a hole in her back.

After the lunch rush was over, Rocky went to speak with Mal. She owed him the truth. As always, he was inputting the receipts into the computer. "Want to let you know I'm going to invest in the new restaurant," she said.

He turned. "The one Bernadine's talking about bringing in?"

She nodded.

"Why?"

"Tax issues. And I think having a new place in town is a great idea."

"I don't."

"I heard."

"But you're going to take her side over me." It was more statement than question.

"This isn't about taking sides, Mal. What is going on with you?"

"Yes, it is. And if you were the girl I thought you were, you'd be on mine. I put my life's blood into this place."

"I know."

"Then why are you trying to help her shut it down?"

"No one's trying to do that. Not me. Not Bernadine."

"Then what do you call it?"

"Choices. Breathing room for the staff. Timely seating for our diners."

"*Our* diners?" he echoed derisively. "What do you mean, *our* diners? If you join her you can kiss your job goodbye."

That hurt. "Really?"

"Yeah."

"Then you can write me a check for the money I invested."

He appeared startled by that, then caught himself. "No."

"You kick me to the curb; you kick my money to the curb."

"No."

"Stop acting like a spoiled brat. If you want me out, I want my money, or I'll see your childish behind in court."

He glared.

She glared right back. "And I'll be here for the dinner shift because if I'm not, you will close down. See you later." She stormed out.

Angry, hurt, and torn by guilt, she needed to talk to someone. Jack was teaching class down in Hays, so she set out walking to the church.

Paula was in her office at her desk. When Rocky appeared in the doorway she must've seen something in her face. "Bad day, Rock?"

"Sort of, yeah. Do you have a few minutes?"

"Of course. Come on in and sit. Can I get you something?"

"No, but thanks."

Rock sat on the couch and rested her head against the back of it for a moment while she gathered her thoughts.

"So, what's up?" Paula asked.

"Well, let's see. I was a bit nasty to Jack's cousin by marriage, and Mal's going to fire me because I'm planning to invest in the new restaurant Bernadine wants to open."

"I hear she and Mal are at odds."

"He's pretty mad. Accused me of taking sides and helping her close down the Dog. Both of which are ridiculous."

"He feels threatened by the competition."

"Yes, and I do feel like I'm abandoning him, even though I'm not."

"No, you aren't, but back up a minute and tell me about this cousin of Jack's."

"Her name's Helen and she's had the hots for him for years." Rock went on to explain why the woman was in town and what occurred at lunch.

Paula said, "If she sent the chicken back just to yank your chain, I think you showed remarkable restraint."

"I wanted to pour a pitcher of iced tea on her head."

Paula chuckled. "I'm glad you didn't. As for Mal, how are you feeling about that?"

"Truthfully, I'm mad that he's being so bullheaded, but feeling a little bit guilty, too. I mean, he's always been there for me. Is it wrong for me to want to do something different with my life?"

"No, but change always brings upheaval, Rock. Would you rather stay with the status quo?"

"No. The idea of this new restaurant is exciting. I've never done anything like this before. In a way, it feels like this is part of the new life I'm having. I have Jack, a bunch of lady friends, I have you. I don't want to go back to Rocky the Hermit. At least I don't think I do. That make sense?"

"Yes. But the new restaurant will impact the Dog and Mal. Maybe not in the way he perceives but it will. Are you prepared for him to pout and be angry and point his finger and accuse you of being part of the cause?"

"No. He's been like a second father to me."

"And maybe once the new place opens and he sees he hasn't been left high and dry, the relationship you've always had will repair itself, but for now, it might be difficult and painful."

Rock sensed she was right, but it wasn't something she wanted to hear or deal with. "Maybe Glinda the Good Witch will show up and wave her magic wand and make things better."

"Maybe, but in case she's busy, you need to prepare yourself emotionally for some fallout from him."

"Lord." Rock dragged her hands down her face.

"And don't keep your feelings inside. Let Jack help you stay balanced. Ideally that's what partners are for."

Rocky nodded. She wasn't accustomed to sharing her insides but she was getting better at it, thanks to Paula. "Okay."

"And I'm always here for you too, Rock."

"I know and that's great, believe me. I'd be even more of a basket case without you."

"You're not a basket case. You're human just like one hundred percent of everyone else."

Paula always knew exactly what to say to keep Rocky's shadows at bay. "So, do you think this investment is a good idea?"

"Your opinion is the one that matters the most. What do you think?"

"I do think it's a good idea."

"Then as the elders say: Name it and claim it."

Rocky grinned. "Thanks, Paula."

"You're welcome. Keep me posted."

"I will. Promise."

And with that, Rocky left Paula's office and walked back outside into the afternoon sunshine.

Gemma checked the time on the store's wall clock. Two thirty p.m. In another hour, her shift would end and she could go pick up the kids from the rec where they'd spent the day swimming and having fun under the watchful eyes of Tamar and crew. Gemma had promised Lucas and Jaz a trip to the Franklin library. They told her they were big-time readers so she hoped to be able to get them library cards. Wyatt loved to read, too. She was ringing up a big order when Sgt. Ma'am walked up. "Mr. Clark wants to see you in his office. Someone will be here to relieve you shortly."

"What's it about?"

Alma responded by walking away. Gemma growled inwardly. When her replacement arrived, Gemma took her drawer and left the floor to see what Gary wanted.

She entered his office and found him on the phone. He shot her a smile, gestured for her to take a seat and continued his conversation. "No. I don't want pears. I want the apples I ordered. I understand you're overstocked, but that's not my problem, frankly." The back and forth went on for a minute more and when it ended, he put his phone down. "Supplier thinks I don't know the difference between apples and pears."

She offered a small smile. "You wanted to see me?"

"Yes. I just got a call from Bernadine. The state social worker is on her way to Henry Adams to talk about being a foster parent. She wants you to come by her office asap."

Gemma felt a flash of panic. She'd already missed a day of work because of the Herman kids and having to leave early now was probably not going to go over well. "I can work an additional couple of hours on Saturday to make up the time."

"Not necessary. It's not like you're taking off to go shopping. The store will cover your time and Bernadine will take care of your pay."

Gemma blinked.

"You shouldn't be punished for wanting to help out two kids in need."

"Thank you," she gushed with relief.

"How'd the first day of class go?"

"Okay, I guess. I'm the oldest person in the room besides the professor. Some of the information about the textbooks was confusing but he took the time to explain it to me."

"Good."

"I don't think class will interfere with my job. I don't want any special treatment or anything."

"You're a single parent, soon to be raising three kids, and you're in school. If anybody deserves special treatment, it's you."

"I just don't want people to think I'm taking advantage."

"I know you're not, so if you need help don't be afraid to ask. You're one of our best workers and your fellow employees like you a lot."

"Thank you. I appreciate you saying that."

"Go on over to the Power Plant and get with Bernadine. If there's anything my girls and I can do to help with the kids' transition, let me know."

She stood. "Thanks, Gary."

"No problem."

Alma was seated at her desk in the office next to Gary's and gave Gemma the evil eye when she passed by her open door. Gemma was tempted to tell her that Gary had praised her job performance, but kept it to herself.

She arrived at the Power Plant to find Bernadine and another Black woman in the office.

"Hey Gemma, come on in. I want you to meet Aretha Krebs from the Kansas Department of Children and Families."

Gemma held out her hand. "How are you?"

For a moment, the woman stared at Gemma as if she had snakes in her hair, then seemed to catch herself, and shook Gemma's hand. "Pleased to meet you. Ms. Brown didn't tell my boss you were Caucasian."

Bernadine said coolly, "I did but Ms. Frazier obviously doesn't have an issue with it because she helped facilitate the adoption process for another mixed family living here."

Seemingly embarrassed by the pointed response, Ms. Krebs stuttered, "I—It's just that we like to place African American children with like foster parents."

Gemma glanced at Bernadine's granite set face and asked, "Do you have any *like* foster parents willing to take them in?"

"Well, no. Not at the moment."

"Then let's move on, shall we?" Bernadine replied.

The young, stylishly dressed woman didn't appear pleased. Gemma was equal parts angry and disappointed that in this day and age, anyone would be prevented from opening their hearts to children in need of home and love due to race.

She was living in a historic, all-Black town for heaven's sake. Yes, culture mattered, so what better place for Lucas and Jasmine to be raised than in Henry Adams? She was through with the caseworker.

Ms. Krebs said, "Ms. Dahl, your home will need to be inspected and if all goes well, as a favor to Ms. Brown we'll be putting your certification on a fast track."

"Thank you," Gemma replied. "I'm sure the Herman kids will appreciate your willingness to get them settled in quickly."

"I'd like to interview them."

"Certainly."

"Today."

Gemma really disliked her attitude and tone. "Of course."

"And where are they now?"

"At our rec center, being watched over by our town matriarch."

Bernadine smiled. "Let me give her a call."

"That would be good," Krebs said.

Gemma doubted the woman knew she'd get her head chopped off if she gave Tamar attitude. Bernadine's smug smile made Gemma think she was thinking the same thing. So, while they waited for Tamar to arrive with the kids, Gemma began filling out the paperwork the caseworker brought along to begin the process.

A few minutes later, Tamar entered the office

with the three kids in tow. Bernadine made the introductions.

Gemma saw Ms. Krebs startle at Tamar's looming height before she took in the flowing red-and-black caftan and silver bangles. Gemma wondered what she thought of their matriarch.

Tamar acknowledged Ms. Krebs and added, "We in Henry Adams want to thank you for your help with this. We'd like to get the children settled in as quickly as legally possible."

Krebs looked up at the towering Tamar and hastily shook her hand. "Yes, ma'am."

As Tamar sat down, Gemma noted the anger and suspicion Lucas was directing at the caseworker. Jasmine came over and sat next to Gemma. Gemma put her arm around her and Jaz eased closer.

Ms. Krebs said, "I'd like to interview the children if I might."

Lucas said, "The adults here can stay, right?"

"Usually, we like to talk to you privately."

"I want them to stay."

For a moment, she studied him silently. "May I ask why?"

"I trust them. The other social worker back in Ohio said we'd be going to good foster homes and we didn't."

"Oh. I'm sorry to hear that."

Gemma was pleased that he trusted them

to advocate on his behalf but it hurt seeing the rigidness and pain he exuded.

He added, "My sister and I want to stay here. We don't want to go to another foster home with people we don't know."

"Understood, but we always try and place children of color with families of color because of cultural concerns, so I have to ask, does it bother you that Ms. Gemma is of a different race."

Gemma saw Tamar tense and her eyes narrow.

Lucas said, "Our godmother was White."

Ms. Krebs reacted with surprise. "Oh."

Jaz asked, "What difference does it make?"

Tamar stepped in. "Ms. Krebs, you do know that this is a historic all-Black town, correct?"

"Well, yes, but I—"

Tamar waved her quiet. "Do you know the Negro National Anthem?"

"Yes, but I don't see—"

"Sing it."

Her eyes widened.

"Wyatt, sing it with her."

Wyatt's eyes widened too, but he knew not to balk, so he closed his eyes and sang, *"Lift every voice and sing, til earth and heaven ring. Ring with the harmony of liberty."*

"Ms. Krebs, sing the rest of the first verse."

Apparently scared to death, the visibly shaken woman closed her eyes as if trying to recall the words and when it became obvious she couldn't, Tamar said to her, "Your cultural concerns may be well grounded elsewhere, but not here. Wyatt knows the Anthem because the children in our school sing it every morning. The people of Henry Adams, of all races, live and breathe the culture of the race and not just in February." She looked to Wyatt. "Thank you."

He nodded. "You're welcome."

Tamar redirected her attention to the social worker, and her tone was kinder. "Ms. Krebs, I understand you're just doing your job, and that your agency has the best interest of the children at heart, but I hope I've helped to satisfy your concerns about whether Lucas and Jasmine will be raised within the context of their race and culture."

She whispered, "Yes, ma'am. You have. Perfectly."

Tamar sat back. Lucas and Wyatt shared a quick smile. Gemma wanted to cheer until she met the venomous glare the woman shot her way. It lasted only a second but it was enough to convey that she'd made an enemy, which made no sense. Tamar was the one who'd set her on fire, but Gemma supposed she made an easier target of Krebs's ire than the town's six-foot matriarch.

Ms. Krebs began gathering her things. "Ms. Dahl, I'd like to do your home inspection now if that's okay."

"Sure."

CHAPTER
9

Lucas hadn't been inside a library in two years. Browsing the titles filled him with both eagerness and sadness. He loved books, as had his mom and dad, and trips to the library back home had always been special. However, the foster mother had refused to take him, saying she didn't have the gas or time, so he'd placed his love for reading in the spot in his heart where he'd buried all the other neat things he'd cared about in his old life. Being able to take out books again was awesome. Ms. Gemma had gotten him and Jaz library cards. Wyatt said she brought him here at least twice a month, which was twice more than Lucas ever hoped for while in the foster care system. He took down the first Harry Potter book. He'd already read the series and remembered how great it had been to lose himself in the story of Harry and his friends, so he took down the second book also and added them to the ones he already had in his arms. With no school to interfere, he could read as much as he wanted.

Wyatt came up beside him and asked quietly, "How many books do you have?"

"Five. You?"

"Five."

They shared grins and walked over to the checkout desk. Lucas liked Wyatt and guessed they could be good friends but because life would never allow him to be happy again he wouldn't allow himself to get close. Less heartache that way.

On the ride back to Ms. Gemma's he savored the weight of the books in his lap and couldn't wait to dive into them. "Thank you, Ms. Gemma."

She smiled at him in the mirror. "You're welcome. We'll go as often as we can."

He glanced over at Jaz and she grinned. She had a bunch of books, too. It was good seeing her happy, even though he was certain it wouldn't last. He thought back on the visit with the social worker. He hadn't liked her. When she did the house inspection she'd been real cold to Ms. Gemma; wouldn't make small talk, never smiled. She was all about the business. He guessed she hadn't liked being called out by Tamar. Actually witnessing how scary Tamar could be made him never want to get on her bad side, ever. Lucas knew about the Negro National Anthem, but he didn't know all the words the way Wyatt did, and it made him wonder about the Henry Adams school. He'd seen the outside and Wyatt said their teacher Mr. James was amazing, but that the school only had one teacher was as puzzling as learning they sang the Anthem every day. Henry Adams was a really different place and one he wouldn't mind being in permanently, but he had about as much of a chance of that happening as he had of receiving a welcome letter from Hogwarts.

Seated in the backseat beside him, Jaz asked, "Ms. Gemma, what else do you have to do to be our foster mother?"

"Take a couple of online classes and fill out more papers."

"How long do you think it'll take?" Lucas asked.

"A month maybe?"

"That's a long time."

"I suppose but if all goes well, we'll have everything in place by the time school starts in September."

Wyatt added, "We're supposed to be getting another teacher. I hope I get to still be with Mr. James."

"I think you will. The new teacher is supposed to be teaching the younger kids, or at least that's my understanding."

"Lucas, you'll like Mr. James," Wyatt said. "He does what he calls topical teaching. Instead of just using textbooks, he teaches us about stuff in the news. It's kinda awesome. He's real serious about us getting a good education, but he also makes it fun. Sometimes."

Although Lucas was intrigued by Wyatt's enthusiasm, he refused to hope that he'd be around when the time came to go to school.

When they got back to Ms. Gemma's he and Jaz and Wyatt sat out on the deck and read until the sun began going down. Jaz and Wyatt went inside but Lucas stayed. He had so many thoughts running through his brain and for the past few days being alone with the silence of the countryside seemed to calm his insides.

"The mosquitoes will be out soon," Ms. Gemma said, stepping outside to join him.

He gave her a small smile. She walked over and stood beside him and, like him, gazed out at the plains.

"This is a lot different than being in Chicago," she said.

"Dayton, too."

"I grew up in Franklin, but being a kid I never appreciated the silence the way I do now that I'm an adult."

"I didn't know you were from here."

She nodded. "Moved to Chicago when I was sixteen."

"It's real quiet."

"It is."

They stood silently for a few moments before she said, "I like having you and Jaz here."

"Thanks." He looked over at her and the kindness reflected in her eyes made him turn away because he didn't want to acknowledge how much he could become attached to her as well.

"Things will work out, Lucas."

"No, they won't. They haven't since my parents died and it isn't going to change."

That she didn't try and convince him otherwise made him think she maybe understood.

"My daughter was in the Army and died over in Afghanistan."

He tensed and met her eyes. "Was she Wyatt's mom?"

"Yes."

"He and I have a lot in common then."

"Yes. Neither of us thought we'd ever smile again."

Lucas knew what Wyatt must have gone through and admitted with a whisper, "This is hard."

"Very, and it will be awhile before it gets easier."

Silence settled around them again.

She rubbed his back gently. "Don't let the mosquitoes carry you away."

With that, she went inside and he was left alone with his thoughts.

In the dream, she was making her way up the mountain's narrow path. Wind whipped at her black-and-red caftan, causing her gray hair to wave behind her like a banner. The harpy eagle flew above, its calls urging her on. She still had no idea why she was climbing but the urge to keep going was strong. On the wind came sounds of music; the faint tinkle of bells and the rhythmic beat of drums bringing with it the echoes of gunfire and screams. Fog descended, turning the dream world a ghostly gray. Suddenly, the ground was littered with mangled dead bodies of men, women, and children all wearing the colorful dress of her ancestors. Off in the distance, panicked voices cried out in Spanish, English, and in tongues she didn't recognize. Filled with dread, she searched the fog but saw no one. A charred wooden sign appeared. Negro Fort. She startled. She knew this place. The eagle screamed and she woke up.

It was 5:00 a.m. and still dark. Shaking, she sat up in bed and dragged shuddering hands down her face. Her heart pounded. *Why am I having these dreams?* Negro Fort was a Black Seminole enclave in Spanish Florida, blown up in 1816 by soldiers sent by President Andrew Jackson. Hundreds of warriors, women, and children died from the American cannons; some bodies were even found in the tops of trees. Survivors unable to escape were either sold into slavery or executed. It was the first skirmish in the Seminole Wars.

Tamar hugged herself against the chilling memory. Was this a sign of some kind? Was she on the final journey to join her Black Seminole ancestors? She had no answers, but wanted the dreams to stop because this one scared her to death.

Knowing she wouldn't be able to go back to sleep she got up and started a pot of coffee. When it was ready, she poured herself a cup, fired up her laptop, and did a search on harpy eagles. She knew they weren't native to the United States but per the information she found, they had at one time called parts of Mexico home, a portion of which encompassed areas the Black Seminoles settled in after fleeing Indian Territory. Places like Nacimiento and Piedras Negras. Tamar had never believed in coincidence and she didn't plan to start now. The dreams and the eagle meant something. But what, remained a mystery.

Later that morning, she was sweeping her porch when a cab pulled up to the house. Since she wasn't expecting anyone, she paused to see who would step out. It was her cousin. Eula. Age-old resentment rose. Eula Nance. Snooty, self-absorbed, and the wealthiest member of the widespread July family, she was the great-granddaughter of Tamar's great-aunt Teresa July Nance. Tamar had no idea what she wanted. That the cabbie was unloading luggage from the trunk meant she planned to stay awhile. Tamar would have Mal or Trent drive Eula over to one of the hotels in Franklin because she wasn't staying with her.

"Morning, Tammy."

"Eula." As always, her attire reflected her financial status: a nice pair of gray slacks, white silk blouse, gold in her ears and around her neck. She had on a wide-brimmed straw hat and pricey designer shades. She was using a cane, which made Tamar wonder if she'd had a stroke. She hadn't seen or heard from Eula in a good five or six years, and once again wondered why she'd come.

Standing at the bottom of the steps, Eula said quietly, "Surprised to see me, I'll bet?"

"Give the woman a cigar."

"Are you going to invite me in?"

"Do I have to?"

"Unfortunately, for both of us, you do."

"Why?"

"Because I'm dying, Tam, and I need you to bury me when the time comes."

Tamar was stunned. She certainly hadn't been expecting that. "Come on in, then."

The cabbie brought the luggage to the porch.

Eula struggled up the steps and followed her inside.

"Place looks nice," Eula said once she was seated.

"Thanks."

When Eula removed her hat and shades, Tamar saw the gray pallor of her skin and the dullness in her eyes. There were short, sparse patches of gray hair on her nearly bald head.

"It's cancer," Eula explained unprompted.

"Why come to me?"

"Julia wouldn't take my calls. So, given the choice of you or that brother of yours and his family of hooligans, you won."

Tamar forced herself not to remind Eula that beggars, especially dying ones, couldn't be choosey. "Julia still mad about you taking her to court?"

Julia was a cousin descended from Harper and Vivian July. They'd lived in Wyoming back when Olivia, Neil, Teresa, and her banker husband, Madison Nance, resided in nineteenth-century Henry Adams. Julia and her clan now lived in Florida.

"Yes, and I realize it was not one of my finer moments."

Twenty years ago, Julia borrowed a large sum of money from Eula. When she couldn't repay it, Eula took her to court.

"You warned me I'd need my family one day,

but I didn't believe you. I know better now that it's too late."

"How long have the doctors given you."

"If I'm lucky, six months."

"I'm sorry, Eula." And she was.

"So am I. I have a ton of regrets. A ton." Her lips trembled and tears filled her eyes. "I was so afraid of dying alone."

And with that, Tamar let go of a lifetime of animosity and eased her cousin into her arms. "You won't be alone," she whispered. "I promise."

Eula wept bitterly. As Tamar held her close, tears filled her eyes, too.

Tamar settled Eula into one of the spare bedrooms and while she slept, Tamar pulled out her phone. The rest of the family needed to know about Eula. She'd be needing a proper homegoing to mark her passing, and therefore hatchets had to be buried. The Spirit knew Tamar wasn't looking forward to another visit from Thad and his havoc-causing Oklahoma clan, but it couldn't be avoided. Setting thoughts of them aside for the moment, she brought up her contacts and called Julia.

Rocky and Siz were cleaning up the kitchen after the breakfast rush when he asked, "What's up with Mal?"

"He's mad at me."

"Why?"

She explained.

"I think a new place is a great idea."

She was glad to have his support. "He doesn't."

"I was wondering why he was so grumpy this morning."

"He's threatening to fire me if I invest."

Siz stopped. "Whoa. Wait. That's crazy. Who's going to run this place if that happens?"

"You tell me."

"I can't work here without you, Rock."

"I appreciate that, babe, but I think he's just blowing smoke."

"Hopefully, because that would be a disaster and I'd be wearing a tee shirt that said: 'Miami here I come.'"

"Have you heard anything from the chef down there?"

"Yeah. Got an e-mail last night. He's in Tokyo right now and wants me to come down when he gets back."

"Did he say when that'll be?"

"Probably first week of September. Be nice to be in Florida for the winter doing sunshine instead of snow and below zero."

Rocky agreed, but still she didn't want him to leave.

"So how soon will Ms. Brown's place open?"

"Not sure but she'll let me know."

Mal came into the kitchen. "I need to talk to you, Rock. In my office." And he walked out just as abruptly.

Rocky wanted to run after him and smack him on the back of his head. Instead, she calmed herself and said to Siz, "Be right back."

In the office, he was seated behind the desk.

"What's up?" she asked.

He said, "I have a solution to our so-called problem. Come look at this."

He turned the laptop her way so she could view the diagram on the screen.

"What am I looking at?"

"The new layout for the dining room. I took out the booths on the back wall and added four more tables."

She studied it for a moment. "How wide is this aisle here?" she asked, pointing to the space between the new tables and the old ones in the center of the room.

"About fifteen inches."

"The servers can't maneuver in a space that narrow."

"Sure they can."

"No, they can't."

"They'll adjust."

"Before or after they drop a tray on someone's head or in their lap?"

He glared.

She ignored it. "Have you shown this to Luis?"

Luis Acosta was Henry Adam's fire chief and fire marshal.

"No."

"I can tell you now, he isn't going to approve it. We're already pushing the envelope on code."

"I say we try it."

"I say we don't. Unless you want him to close us down. He does have the authority."

He blew out a breath. "Then what do you suggest?"

"You already shot down my suggestions, remember?"

"You're determined to take Bernadine's side, aren't you?"

"I'm not going another round with you on that. Everybody and their mother knows what this place needs, except you. What's with the blinders? Is there something going on that you aren't telling me?"

"No."

She'd known him most of her life and at that moment, she swore he wasn't telling the truth. "Are you sure?"

"Yes, so just go on back to the kitchen. Be time for lunch in a minute."

Rocky stood there for a moment. He wouldn't meet her eyes.

"Okay, Mal. I'll see you later." She left the office filled with the sense that something was going on and that it wasn't good.

The feeling stayed with her for the rest of the afternoon and she found herself discreetly observing him to try and figure out what he might be keeping from her, but he gave her no clues. She was convinced he hadn't fallen off the wagon; he took too much pride in his sobriety and there was no hint of alcohol on his breath or clothing. Of course, it was quite possible that nothing was amiss and she was simply looking for an excuse to explain away his pigheadedness when in reality it was him just being pigheaded, but her Spidey sense was tingling and it wouldn't go away.

After the lunch rush, she walked down to the rec center hoping to talk to Tamar but found Marie there instead.

"She's at home today," Marie explained. "A cousin of hers showed up this morning, so she's spending the day with her. Anything I can help you with?"

Marie knew Mal probably better than anyone so Rocky explained her concerns.

Marie nodded understandingly. "He is pretty bent out of shape over this new restaurant idea. He says Bernadine refuses to listen to reason."

"He's the one being unreasonable." And Rocky explained what she meant by that.

Marie sat back. "He didn't tell me all that, but then this is Mal we're talking about. He has a blind spot about his own issues sometimes. So, you didn't threaten to quit?"

"He threatened to make me quit if I threw in with Bernadine."

Marie sighed. "Lord."

"Something's going on with him, Marie, and I'm worried."

"You could be right. He's coming by tonight to watch baseball. Maybe he'll talk to me."

"I hope so. He's supposed to be giving me away. I don't want whatever this is to come between us."

"I understand." Marie changed gears. "Have you ordered your wedding leathers?"

She hung her head. "No."

"Rocky?"

"I know. I'll do it tonight after work. Promise."

"I'm going to call you this evening to make sure."

"Okay." Glad that Marie hadn't dismissed her concerns, Rocky left the rec and walked back to the Dog.

Seated behind her desk in her office, Bernadine reviewed some of the bids for the three remaining open spots at the Sutton Hotel facility. She'd halfway settled on one being a bank branch but had to decide which corporate entity to choose.

"Ms. Brown, can I talk with you a minute?"

It was Kelly Douglas, the town's hairdresser and Crystal's best friend. Kelly and her husband, Bobby, had moved to Henry Adams last winter with their twin toddlers: Bobby Jr. and Kiara. "Sure. Come on in," Bernadine said, smiling.

Kelly took a seat and Bernadine asked, "How are things?"

"Things are good. No issues."

"And Riley?"

"Doing his job, which is all I ask. Keeps talking about running for mayor, but I tune that part out."

"The last time he ran he got one vote. Genevieve's. He might get a goose egg this time around."

"He won't get mine. That's for sure."

"Mine, either. So, what brings you by?"

"I've picked out a name for the salon and want to know what you think."

"Okay."

"We're all about town history here and from talking with Tamar I know that back in the day there used to be a saloon called the Liberian Lady, so I want to call my shop The Liberian Lady and Gents Salon."

Bernadine beamed. "I love that, and the play on the word saloon is just perfect. Brilliant, Kelly."

"Thanks. I'd like to have the name either on

the glass on the front door or one of the windows. Maybe use a fancy, scrolly kind of font. Would that work, or be too expensive?"

"I'm sure we can find a way to do it and keep it cost effective. I love the idea of the old-fashioned font."

"Good. When Amari, Brain, and Leah get back from vacation, they're going to help me put up a web page, so we can let people know we're here."

"You're on the ball, my dear."

"Learning how to turn my world by watching you."

"I appreciate that."

Kelly stood. "Let me get back before Riley turns the shop into his campaign headquarters. Can't wait to move in this weekend."

"I'll get started on ordering your signage."

"Thanks, Ms. B."

"You're welcome, Kelly."

She exited and left Bernadine smiling. Lily and Trent had taken the week off and were in Kansas City acting out their own version of *Home Alone,* so Bernadine had the Power Plant to herself. She hoped they were having fun. She, on the other hand, kept being distracted by thoughts of Mal and the ongoing mess between them. He still wasn't responding to her texts, so she stopped sending them. She hadn't seen him, either. Rather than get caught up in a public confrontation at the Dog, she'd avoided the place and had taken to eating lunch at her desk and dinner at home. She missed him. She missed them.

"Hello, Ms. Brown."

Bernadine looked up to see social worker Aretha Krebs on the threshold. The smug smile on her face instantly set off warning bells. "Ms. Krebs. Good to see you."

"I've come to collect the Herman children."

Bernadine froze.

The smug smile spread. "They have a great-aunt in Cincinnati who's agreed to take custody, and my counterpart in Ohio has solved the mystery of their parents' estate. The businesses were sold and the money's been in an escrow account, along with life insurance payouts. The family's financial advisor had a stroke a few days after the parents' accident and the original caseworker retired before all the financial background work was finalized."

"And it wasn't caught."

"No. Their office dropped the ball, probably due to large caseloads and being overworked as we all are. The advisor isn't physically able to return to his practice, so his daughter's been going through the files and just found the estate paperwork a few days ago."

"So, the great-aunt has stepped up now that the kids have money?"

"I talked with her last evening. She said she didn't know the kids were in the system."

"And you believe her?" Bernadine asked skeptically.

"I believe the children will be better off with a family member than with Ms. Dahl."

Bernadine knew Krebs's feeling on the matter so she let it go. "Have you vetted the great-aunt?"

"I have and there are no red flags."

Bernadine sighed inwardly. She didn't like this outcome but lacked the authority to step in.

Krebs gave her another fake smile. "So if you can have the children brought here, we can get them on a plane to Cincinnati this evening. A caseworker and the aunt will meet them at the airport."

Bernadine thought back on Lucas's desire to stay with Gemma. "And the children get no say?"

"No. Not when there's family willing to take them in. My counterpart in the Ohio office agrees the aunt's a better fit, too."

Bernadine understood the policy but wanted to know where the aunt had been for the past two years. She also wondered if it was wrong for her to disbelieve the woman's claim of not knowing the kids were in foster care. "How old is the aunt?"

"Seventy-three. She's the grandfather's sister."

Bernadine didn't like this at all. "Okay. Let me call Gemma and we'll have the kids packed and ready to leave shortly." This news was going to break the kids' hearts, Gemma's too, but maybe the great-aunt would give them the stability and love they needed. She set aside her misgivings and called the store.

Lucas, Jaz, and Wyatt were spending the day at the rec center with Ms. Marie. He and Lucas were playing checkers and Jaz was in a chair reading. When Ms. Dahl showed up unexpectedly Lucas saw her red-rimmed eyes and wondered if she'd been crying. Rather than be nosy and ask about it, he studied her silently. He didn't like seeing her looking so sad.

She spoke to Ms. Marie first. "Marie, I need to talk to Lucas and Jasmine. Can I use Tamar's office?"

Lucas froze.

"Sure, go right in."

Wyatt, seated on the other side of the checkerboard asked, "What's going on Gram? Have you been crying?"

Her lip trembled for a second before she gave him a watery smile. "Let me talk with Lucas and Jaz first, okay?"

"Gram, what's the matter?"

"In a minute, Wyatt."

Lucas shared a look with the now serious-faced Wyatt. Something had happened and he sensed it wasn't good.

He and Jaz followed her into the office and she quietly closed the door. "You're going back to Ohio."

Jaz screamed, "No!" and began crying. "No!"

"I'm sorry, sweetheart. Your grandfather's sister wants you and Lucas to come and live with her in Cincinnati."

Lucas felt like he'd been turned into ice. "What if we don't want to go?"

"Ms. Brown asked about that, but Ms. Krebs said when a family member wants custody, you and Jaz have no choice."

Jaz continued to sob. Her shoulders shook with emotion. Ms. Gemma's tears rolled down her cheeks as she pulled Jaz close and held her. "I want you to stay here, too. But I don't have any legal standing."

All his fears were realized. He'd been right not to dream or hope or attach himself to anyone there. Empty inside, he asked, "When do we leave?"

"Immediately. Ms. Krebs is waiting for you at Ms. Brown's office."

Jaz looked up and cried, "Please! We don't want to leave. Please help us, Ms. Gemma."

"Sweetie, I can't. This breaks my heart, too. I'm so sorry. Your aunt is probably really nice."

Lucas thought the only good thing about this whole heartbreaking situation was that he and his sister would still be together. He took her hand and said softly, "Come on, Jaz. We need to get our stuff."

He met Ms. Gemma's eyes and her tears reflected the ones he had hidden inside.

Up in his room, Lucas was stuffing his small cache of belongings into the new trash bag Ms. Gemma had given him when Wyatt appeared in the doorway. He looked both sad and angry.

"Hey," Lucas said.

"Hey."

"Thanks for everything. It's been nice."

"You'll be back."

Lucas offered a rueful smile. "If you want to think that, go ahead." His packing done, he stared over at the boy he wouldn't have minded calling brother. "Will you take my books back to the library when you go next time?"

He nodded solemnly. "Do you have our phone number, in case you want to call."

"I do, but I probably won't."

"Why not?"

Lucas wanted to say it would hurt too much. "I just won't, that's all."

"Okay," he said as if understanding. "Was nice knowing you, Lucas."

"Same here."

They shared one last long look and Wyatt left. Alone, Lucas wiped away a tear and carried the bag down the hall to hook up with Jaz. "Are you ready?"

"Yes," she said softly. "I want to stay here so bad."

"But we can't," he snapped. Then he felt bad. "I'm sorry."

"It's okay. I need to stop acting like a baby."

He saw their mom's features in her face and all the pain and fear rushed up inside him again. He wanted to hug her tight and tell her everything would be all right, but then they'd both start crying again, and the Krebs woman was waiting. No sense in delaying the inevitable. "Hand me your bag."

"No, I can carry it." She met his sad eyes and said, "I love you, Lucas. You're a good big brother."

"Thanks. I love you, too, Jaz."

And together they set out to face life's next challenge.

Lucas managed to remain stoic when the time came to say goodbye to Ms. Gemma and to Ms. Bernadine in her office. He knew if he began crying he'd never stop. Beside him, Jaz stood quietly while tears ran down her cheeks.

"Take care of each other," Ms. Gemma said, hugging them each in turn. "I'll miss you both."

Lucas nodded. Jaz grabbed her tightly around the waist and held on. A teary-eyed Ms. Gemma rocked her gently.

Ms. Krebs cleared her throat. "We need to get going so we don't miss the plane."

Jaz stepped away, wiped her face, and took her spot beside him.

Ms. Bernadine said, "We're always here if you need anything."

"Yes, ma'am."

Krebs said impatiently, "They'll be just fine. My office recommends you have no future contact so you don't interfere with them bonding with their family member."

Lucas didn't like her and blamed her for being prejudiced against Ms. Gemma, and for why they couldn't stay. She'd be flying with them on the plane to Ohio and he hoped that once they arrived, he and Jaz would never have to see her again.

Storing Ms. Gemma's kindness in his heart, he followed Ms. Krebs out to her car. She opened the back door for them and said, "I was pretty excited the first time I flew on a plane. Have you ever flown before?"

Lucas said, "Yeah. I flew to Australia with my mom for a doctor's conference when I was seven."

She stopped, stunned. Rolling his eyes, he climbed in and helped Jaz with her seat belt before buckling his own. When Ms. Krebs entered, he saw her eyeing him in the mirror with an odd expression on her face, but he turned away.

When they arrived at the Cincinnati airport it was dark. Lucas pulled the rolling suitcase Ms. Krebs had given them to stuff their trash bags into and waited while she looked around the nearly empty baggage claim area. A tall African American man wearing a suit walked up with a short, round, elderly African American woman wearing a black-and-white polka-dot dress and a big wide-brimmed church lady hat. She smiled the moment she saw them, so Lucas assumed this was their great-aunt. Ms. Krebs told them on the plane that her name was Wanda Borden.

"Ms. Krebs?" the tall man asked.

"Yes."

"I'm Ed Gladwin from Ohio Social Services. This is Mrs. Borden."

Krebs smiled. "Glad to meet you, Mrs. Borden. These are the kids. Lucas and Jasmine Herman."

She was still beaming. "How are you? Welcome to Cincinnati." She opened her arms. "Come give your auntie some sugar."

He and Jaz shared a quick look before Lucas walked over and let himself be folded in against her round body. She smelled like peppermint and her face was a bit sweaty. When she turned him loose, Jaz took his place. After the hug, she said, "What a pretty name for a pretty little girl. I had jasmine in my yard when I lived in California and it made the night smell so sweet. How was the flight?"

"Okay," Lucas voiced quietly.

"You must be exhausted. Are you hungry?"

"A little bit," Jasmine said.

"I'm a great cook, and I left some stuff on the stove. We'll eat soon as we get there."

So far, so good, Lucas thought but he knew better than to hope. Ms. Krebs watched his face, but he didn't acknowledge her. She'd gotten them here; now she could go.

Aunt Wanda said, "Ms. Krebs, I want to thank you for letting me know about them. I'm sure we'll be fine from here on out. Won't we, kids?"

Lucas nodded because he knew it was expected. Jaz did the same.

Mr. Gladwin said, "Ms. Krebs, I'll take you to your hotel. Kids, I'm your worker and I'll be by tomorrow to check on things. Nice meeting you both."

Ms. Krebs met Lucas's cold eyes and, if she'd been expecting a fond farewell, she didn't get one. "Take care, kids."

He and Jaz nodded but that was all. She left with Mr. Gladwin and they followed Aunt Wanda out to her car.

Once they were inside, she drove off. "I'm so glad to have you two with me. Nothing like youngsters to keep an old lady young."

She asked what grades they were in, in school. They told her and she replied, "The one near my house isn't fancy like the one you probably went to when you lived with your rich mama and daddy but you'll be okay there."

She said the word *rich* as if it were a bad word and Lucas became instantly wary.

"Going to be lots of changes living with me, but again, you'll be okay."

In the shadowy backseat, Jasmine slid her hand into his and he squeezed hers gently in response.

The car left the highway and merged into an area like the inner-city neighborhoods he'd lived in during his first stint in foster care. A few minutes later, she pulled into the driveway of a house on a quiet street.

"We're here," she announced.

They took their suitcase out of the trunk and followed her up the two cement steps to the porch. By the light from the bare bulb above them Lucas saw the burglar bars on the door and the windows across the front of the house. Aunt Wanda stuck a key into the full-length bars first, and once it was opened, she fumbled for another key to unlock the main door that led inside.

The interior was lit by a lone lamp in the small front room. Lucas spied a brown couch, an old cracked-leather recliner and a big flat-screen TV. The air smelled like stale perfume.

She put down her purse and removed her hat. "Put those bags down. Got some work for you to do before you eat."

Lucas stopped. He was hungry after the long day and so was Jaz. "We're really hungry. Can we eat first?"

"You sassing me, boy?" she asked ominously.

He froze and whispered, "No, ma'am."

"Good because you don't want to find out if you do. Now follow me."

They climbed the worn, slick carpeted stairs to the second floor. She clicked on a light and led them down the short hallway. "You'll be sleeping in this room."

Another light was thrown on to reveal a space filled with boxes, furniture, and clothing piled high, and he couldn't tell what else lay beneath all the layers of stuff. He looked around with wide eyes.

"Take everything in here down to the basement," she instructed them. "There's some sheets and blankets beneath those big boxes in the corner. When you find them, go put them in the washer. Once they dry and you get the beds made, you can eat."

She exited.

He glanced over at his sister, who said in a voice bordering on a wail, "She's mean, Lucas."

"I know." He'd been stupid to hope. "Let's get started so we can eat."

At 1:00 a.m., after eating a cold plate of collards, pork and beans, and chicken, they fell into bed. Lucas could hear Jasmine crying softly in the dark in the bed beside his. He didn't try and tell her things would work out because they both knew it was a lie. Fighting exhaustion, he wanted to at least console her but his tired eyes slid shut and he dropped like a stone into sleep.

CHAPTER
10

The following morning, Bernadine sat in her office going over her agenda for the day. She'd be meeting later with Samuel and Brenda Miller, the middle-aged couple interested in opening a coffee shop and bakery inside the Henry Adams hotel. They were presently living in Vegas where he worked as a pastry chef at one of the major hotels. She was an accountant who'd recently taken a buyout from a brokerage firm. Bernadine had been communicating with them for the past few months via e-mail, phone, and Skype. Today would be their first physical face-to-face and she was looking forward to the visit and showing them the space. She was about to get up and pour herself another cup of coffee when the phone rang. Caller ID showed TINA CRAIG, and she smiled as she picked up.

"Good morning, Lady T. How the are you?"

"Stressed but blessed, B. How are you?"

"Having issues with Mal, but I'm surviving."

"Oh, no. What's going on?"

For the next few minutes, Bernadine gave her a rundown, and when she was finished, Tina offered sympathetic words of support. "I hope you two can fix things."

"Me, too. Did you call for something specific or just to say hey?"

"The latter, yes, but two other things, too. One, Merilee said you were looking for help with a restaurant you want to open?"

Merilee Worth owned a nationwide chain of seafood places, and, like Bernadine and Tina, was a member of the Bottom Women's Society, a club made up of divorced first wives of wealthy executives.

"I am."

"If you're looking for investors, I want in."

"Really?"

"Yes, ma'am, because I'm going to move to your little piece of heaven and open a bed and breakfast."

Bernadine stilled. "Really?"

"Yes. Doctor said either I slow down or I die. Blood pressure is through the roof, as is my cholesterol, and I'm exhausted all the damn time. I need a lifestyle change, B."

"I'd love to have you as a neighbor, but what do you know about running a bed and break-fast?"

"Other than having stayed in a bunch all over the world, about as much as you knew about running a town when you bought Henry Adams off eBay."

She laughed. "I guess that makes you qualified."

"I think so, too. I'd like to fly in sometime next week to talk to you about the restaurant and look at sites for my place if that's possible."

"Sounds good."

"You don't have a strip for my jet to land, do you?"

"No, but if you come in by chopper something can be worked out."

"Okay, I'll do that then. Thanks, doll. I'll let you get back to turning your world. Can't wait to see you."

"The feeling's mutual."

After ending the call, Bernadine sat back, stunned. Tina Craig moving to Henry Adams? All she could say was "wow!"

"Ms. Brown?"

In the doorway stood a woman who looked vaguely familiar but Bernadine couldn't place her. "Yes? May I help you?"

"I'm sorry for not making an appointment, but I'm Sandy Langster. Do you remember me?"

The name rang a bell but the face, framed by angled-cut brown hair with blond highlights, remained a mystery.

"I'm the PI who worked on the Astrid Wiggins, Tommy Stewart madness last year."

"Oh my goodness, yes! How are you?"

"I'm well. I look different, don't I?"

"Yes, you do. Your hair's lighter." When they first met, Sandy had mousy brown hair and was pretty nondescript.

"I'm wearing blue contacts, too. I'm on a case in Hays and I needed to not look like me."

"Have a seat. What brings you by?"

"I hear you've rehabbed the old hotel and have some spaces you're renting out. I'm wondering if you're still looking for tenants?"

"I am."

"Would it be okay if I applied?"

"Of course."

She smiled. "Good. Thanks to the Stewart case, I'm getting a lot more work, so I've decided to open an office."

"Very nice."

"Do you have some info I can look at on pricing and all that?"

"Sure do."

Bernadine opened her drawer and handed her an application. "Fill it out and get it back to me as soon as you can."

"Thank you. I will." She stood. "I'll get out of your hair. I need to get back to Hays. Have a good day, Ms. Brown."

"You, too."

She exited and, once again, Bernadine was left pleasantly surprised. First Tina, and now PI Sandra Langster. Not a bad way to begin the day.

214

• • •

Gemma was not having such a good morning. Still saddened by the departure of Lucas and Jasmine, she and a glum Wyatt shared a somber breakfast.

"I wish they could've stayed," he said, toying with the scrambled eggs on his plate.

"I know. But hopefully the aunt is a nice lady and things will work out for them."

"Do you think Lucas will call us and let us know how they're doing?"

"Ms. Krebs said that wouldn't be a good idea. She doesn't want contact with us interfering with them getting resettled."

"Oh."

Gemma felt especially bad for Wyatt. Even though the Hermans had only been with them briefly, Wyatt had been more lively with them being around than he'd been since leaving Chicago. There'd been laughter and an almost instant camaraderie between the three and now, they were back in Ohio and her Wyatt was alone again. "Are you and Eli going to take your boards out today?"

He shook his head. "He's working today, and then he's helping Rocky start packing up her stuff so she can move in with his dad after the wedding."

"I see."

"I'll go hang at the rec and swim and read until you get off work."

"Okay. I have class tonight, too. So, I'll shoot home, do us a quick dinner and then go over to the school."

He nodded.

She wanted to pull him onto her lap and hold him close like she used to when he was little, but he was too old for that now. "If you grab your stuff I can drop you off at the rec on the way to the store."

"No. I think I'll do my chores and ride my bike over later, if that's okay."

"If you want. But text me when you leave and when you get there."

"I will."

Looking at his sad face almost made her ask if he wanted her to consider other foster kids needing a home, but she sensed now wasn't the right time to have that conversation. She'd let his feelings heal a bit first.

"We were just getting to know each other and they were happy here, Gram."

"I know, and I'm sure they'll be happy with their aunt. Life is funny sometimes, Wyatt. You and Lucas may cross paths again in the future. Wouldn't it be something if you ended up going to the same college?"

"I guess."

She gently caressed his hair. "I need to get to work. Remember to text me."

"I will."

• • •

Gemma enjoyed her job. It provided her with a steady income, a small health care package, and the workplace was clean and safe. Standing at a register for six to eight hours a shift was physically exhausting, however, and yet another reason why she'd chosen to return to school.

Handing her customer his receipt and change, she smiled. "Thank you."

He nodded and moved on.

When she looked into the face of her next customer, she froze.

Kind brown eyes twinkled back in response. "Hello, Ms. Dahl. How are you?"

She stuttered. "I—fine, Professor LeForge, how are you?" To cover her befuddlement, she scanned his package of steaks on the belt and weighed up a bag holding two tomatoes.

"I'm good," he replied. "Had no idea you worked here."

She scanned a head of lettuce and a small five-pound bag of red potatoes. "I've been here almost a year." Handling a half gallon of two percent milk, she moved on to dishwasher pods and green grapes.

"Any problem getting your books and workbook for class?"

"No, and thanks again for your help." Gemma swore the man was looking at her with more than a teacher's interest, but chalked it up to an overly active imagination. She rang up his last few items, told him the total and waited while he went through the process of paying with his debit card. She also tried not to stare at how nerdishly good-looking he was in his glasses, worn black Green Day tee shirt, and jeans. As if having read her thoughts, he smiled her way and went back to his transaction.

Once he was done, she handed over his receipt.

"I'll see you in class, Ms. Dahl."

Blushing, she nodded, horselike. He flashed another soft smile and pushed his buggy toward the exit. "Hot for Teacher" blasted through her brain again. Shaking herself, she greeted the next customer in line. "Hello, did you find everything you needed?"

The employee break room was fairly crowded when Gemma entered to eat lunch. Nodding a greeting to people from all the store's departments, but ignoring smiling Wilson Hughes, she found Edith sitting at a table alone.

"What happened with the foster kids?" Edith asked as Gemma took a seat.

"Social worker flew them back to Ohio, last night." She unwrapped the turkey sandwich she'd purchased at the deli. "A great-aunt stepped up to take them in." She added mustard to the sandwich and opened the small bag of chips she'd also snagged.

"Hope it works out for them."

She took a bite and replied as politely as she could manage with her mouth full, "I do, too. It left me and Wyatt kind of sad. We'd both wanted them to stay." She wondered what Lucas and Jasmine were doing and if the aunt was as kind as Gemma hoped.

Butcher Candy Stevens sat down. Opening her lunch tote, she asked, "Either of you going to apply for the new assistant manager position?"

Confused, Gemma paused. "What assistant manager position?"

"Supposedly Mr. Clark's moving Alma to a new position."

"Where'd you hear this?"

"From the night crew. Not sure where they got it from, though."

"I'll pass," Edith said. "I'm too old to be stressed out as Sgt. Ma'am's mini me. Being under her as a lowly cashier is bad enough."

Gemma agreed. She couldn't imagine having to be trained by Alma and shadowing her for however long it took. "It would be nice to have the extra pay, but Alma would have a stroke if I applied."

"Then please do," Edith said with a laugh.

Candy said, "You'd make a great assistant manager."

Sybil Martin, Alma's current mini me, entered the lounge. As she sat down at Wilson's table, Ed Daniels from the meat department called out,

"Hey, Sybil. You know anything about this new assistant manager Mr. Clark's going to hire?"

"Only that Alma's going to make sure I get the job, so the rest of you losers may as well not apply."

The room quieted. Gemma shook her head and saw others doing the same. A few people rolled their eyes disdainfully while a cashier seated behind her hissed, "Witch." Gemma had sympathized with Sybil at the pool. She didn't now.

Edith leaned over and whispered, "She's not going to get hired. Mr. Clark's no fool. Being assistant manager involves way more than just holding Alma's clipboard. I don't think she even finished high school."

Gemma knew nothing about Sybil's level of education but the many mistakes she made with scheduling and time sheets, Alma fixed, so Gemma couldn't see her in the position, either.

To their surprise, Gary Clark entered the room. His appearance wasn't uncommon but he usually took his breaks and lunch in his office. "Can I have your attention, please."

Everyone quieted. Gemma noticed Alma slip in and take up a position by the door. There was fire in her eyes. Gemma wondered what had set her off.

Gary's voice refocused her attention his way. "I'm assuming you've heard the rumors about

220

the new assistant manager position? Well, they're not rumors. I'm looking to hire someone and will begin accepting applications in a few days. I'd like to hire in-house, so if you want to apply, feel free. Qualifications, salary, and the job description will be posted in the morning."

A soft buzz of speculation went through the room. Ed Daniels called out, "Mr. Clark, we were told the job's already been promised to someone."

Gary's jaw tightened. "The position has not been promised to anyone."

On the heels of that firm statement, more than a few people turned Sybil's way. She tried to feign ignorance but her beet-red face told all. Gemma saw the angry Alma make her exit. *Hmm.*

Gary continued, "We all know I knew zip about running a store when we opened a year ago, and were it not for your help, patience, and the extensive training Ms. Brown suggested I take, I'd still be in the dark. But now, I think I'm up to speed enough to take over the reins a bit more. I'm grateful to Alma—" He glanced around as if looking for her. "She isn't here, but I'll be taking over her duties in the day-to-day operations, which will free her to concentrate on training new employees and offering her expertise in other ways."

Gemma met Edith's look of surprise. So, was

Alma being promoted or demoted? People were whispering all over the room, and she wondered if they were asking the same questions.

Gary continued, "I know all the employees aren't here, so if you'd help me spread the word about the posting, I'd appreciate it. That's it. Thanks, guys." And with a wave he was gone.

After his exit, Ed Davis called out, "Hey, Sybil. Looks like you won't be getting the job. Guess you're a loser now too, huh?"

She hastily gathered up her stuff and left the lounge under mocking laughter.

Rocky had the day off and when she glanced around at all the items in her bedroom needing to be packed: books, artwork, clothing, she drew in a deep breath to keep from being overwhelmed. "Hey babe," she called out to Jack packing in the living room. "Can we just cancel the wedding so I don't have to move any of this?" Out of respect for Eli, she wouldn't be sleeping at Jack's until after he left for school, so basic things like her bed would be staying.

He appeared in the doorway. "Sorry, too late. Invitations have already gone out and the food's been ordered. You're just going to have to suck it up."

"You're such a meanie."

"But I'm your meanie."

"Which is a good thing. Maybe I'll just have a bonfire. No?"

He shook his head.

"Okay, I'll bite the bullet."

"Maybe we need to take a break. We've been at this since way too early this morning."

It was nearly noon. "I agree. How about lunch?"

The kitchen was filled with boxes already packed and sealed, but she maneuvered around them to get to the fridge and the sandwiches she'd made earlier. Grabbing a large bag of chips, some grapes, and sodas, they took everything outside to her small attached porch. The sun was nearing its zenith and it was hot, but it was nice and shady beneath the porch's metal awning. As they began eating, the silence of the plains rose as it always did, letting them relish it and each other. "I think I have my head on now about this marriage thing."

He paused for a moment and eyed her before responding. "That's good to know."

The seriousness in his gaze and tone told her he'd been worried. "I don't want you worrying about whether I'll really show up. I know everyone in town is worried too, but they're secondary. My main concern is you."

"Thanks. And I must admit, I have been wondering."

"I know," she said softly. "I've never been real

223

comfortable in my own skin. Tough biker chick on the outside, a low-self-esteem mess on the inside."

He didn't respond, simply waited for her to say more or not. That calmness and his willingness to listen without the need to interject were some of the other things she loved about him. "You've been a big help with my trying to figure all that out. Thanks for your love and your patience."

"You're welcome, but you've done the real work—you and Reverend Paula. I've just been along for the ride."

"Thank God for her. Sometimes we women, particularly women of color, think we can ignore the cracks in our souls by just keeping it moving. Talking with Paula for the past few years has helped me see that doing that just makes them wider." She savored the love in his eyes and spoke from the heart. "Honestly, Jack, I don't know if the cracks will ever fully heal, but my spirit's no longer leaking through. If it starts up again, it helps knowing she and you are my caulk guns."

He sang softly, *"Then keep on using me, until you use me up."*

"Okay, Bill Withers."

After lunch, they went back to packing when Eli rushed in. "Is your phone off?" he asked Rocky.

She stared. "No, but it's on silent. Why?"

"Siz has been trying to call you. He sent me to tell you. Go get your phone!"

She dug it out of her purse and looked at the screen. Twelve messages! Most were from Siz. They'd started about ten minutes ago. First one read: *Rock. Call. ASAP.* Another one followed thirty seconds later. *Rock. PLEASE CALL!!!!* Alarmed, she slid down to the last message which read: *Need you here!!! Mr. Acosta hutting us down!!*

She let out a curse and ran out the door. "Meet me at the Dog!"

Not waiting to see if they followed, she jumped on the Shadow and roared off.

When she arrived, she spotted the yellow tape draped across the door right away. Next, she saw Siz and the staff talking with Luis Acosta. With them were Bernadine, Tamar, a few other residents, and standing a few feet away a man and woman she didn't recognize. She parked and hurried over to Luis.

Seeing her, Siz said, "Thank God you're here."

Luis's eyes were cold. "Hey, Rock."

"Hey. What's going on?" Whatever it was, they all appeared equally stressed.

"I had to shut you down. Code violations."

She froze and stared back at the diner. "Tell me Mal didn't implement that new table configuration."

"You knew about this?" Luis asked.

"Yes, and I told him it violated code."

Bernadine threw up her hands. Tamar sighed angrily.

Luis replied, "He implemented it anyway. I told him this morning at breakfast he was in violation, and that if he didn't make changes by lunch, I'd have no other choice."

"I told him!" Rocky snapped. Tamping down her anger as much as she could, she asked, "If we are compliant by dinner, can we reopen?"

"Sure."

"Okay, thanks." She didn't see Mal in the crowd. "Where is he?"

Tamar answered, "Inside."

Rock turned to Luis. "Can I go in?"

"As long as you don't open for business until you pass inspection, go ahead."

The front door was locked, so she fished out her key, stuck it in, and walked inside. He was in his office.

"Come to say I told you so?"

"No, Luis already did that."

"Yeah, well."

"There are young people depending on the money they make here to keep their lives above water. How dare you put them in jeopardy by being selfish and petty."

No response.

"Luis said he warned you at breakfast. Did

you think he wouldn't come through, or did you expect him to jeopardize his livelihood for you, too?"

Still nothing.

"Mal, you are my family. This isn't like you. Please tell me what's going on."

"I already told you. Nothing."

"Liar, liar, pants on fire."

He eyed her but she didn't blink. He finally turned away. "I'm going to Vegas. If you still want me to be in the wedding, text me."

"I don't need to text you. The answer's yes."

"Then I'll be back for it."

"When are you leaving?"

"Soon as I can book a flight."

"You're going to talk to Bernadine before taking off, right?"

"Probably not."

"Mal?"

"You take care of your business and I'll take care of mine."

She wanted to rail at him, shake him until his teeth rattled, but knew that wouldn't help so she gave up. "Keep yourself safe." And she turned to leave.

"Rock?"

She stopped. "What?"

"I'm not going to Vegas to drink."

Tears stung her eyes and she whispered, "Holding you to that."

"Understood. Give me a few minutes and I'll be out of your way here."

She walked out of the office and left him alone.

Back out front, Tamar asked, "And?"

"He's taking off for Vegas. Says he'll be back in time for the wedding."

"What's he going to do there?" she asked.

"Who knows."

Bernadine asked doubtfully, "Vegas?"

"Yeah."

"Hopefully he and I can talk before he takes off."

Rocky went still.

Bernadine searched her face. "He doesn't want to talk to me, does he?"

"I asked. He said no."

"Well, okay then," she said with a false cheeriness. The hurt in her eyes made Rocky want to march back inside and kick Mal's butt until sunrise.

Bernadine said, "Okay. I have things to do. Thanks, Rock." She walked over to the mystery couple Rock noticed when she rode up, and she and the couple headed back in the direction of the Power Plant.

Groups of people began driving up, expecting lunch.

"We're closed until dinner," Rock told them. "Dishwasher's dead. Sorry for the inconvenience."

It was as good an excuse as any, she supposed. Much better than letting the customers know her co-owner was an idiot.

She turned back to Luis. "I'll call you when we're ready for the inspection."

"No problem."

"And Luis, I'm not mad at you. You're doing your job."

"Thanks for that."

Tamar, Marie, and Gen, along with the twins and Wyatt, set out for the rec.

That left Rocky with her staff, and Jack, who was seated out of the way on one of the benches by the door. She assumed by then Mal would be upstairs in his apartment over the diner, preparing to leave. She said to Siz and Eli, "Take everybody inside and see if you can find the booths Mal removed so we can put them back. I'll be in in a minute."

Alone, she dropped down onto the bench with Jack and rested her head against his shoulder. "Good grief," she said.

"Quite the excitement."

"I wish I knew what was going on with him."

"It'll come out eventually whether he wants it to or not, so just hold on."

"I want to shake him like an orca with a seal."

"That's a bit extreme."

"I feel extreme. Extremely mad, frustrated, sad."

He eased her closer. "Why sad?"

"Because I know something's wrong and he won't tell me. He's also breaking Bernadine's heart. No one's ever going to love him the way she does, and he's acting like it doesn't matter. He did promise me he wasn't going to Vegas to drink."

"You know him better than I. Do you believe him?"

"I do." And she did. His sobriety meant more than anything to him. Still, her frustration continued. "I need to get inside and put the place back together."

"Do you need my help?"

"Not with this, but knowing you'll be waiting for me at the end of the day fills my heart."

To emphasize that, she kissed him with all the love she had inside, then left him to ready the diner for the fire marshal's inspection.

Eli and Siz found the missing booths outside behind the building. They removed the tarps placed over them to protect the wood from the elements, then slowly maneuvered them back inside. Rocky was certain Mal hadn't done the moving of the heavy booths alone. More than likely someone like Clay had been his partner in crime. It occurred to her that he might know what was going on with Mal and so made a mental note to ask him about it as soon as she got the chance.

Once she and the staff got the place reconfigured back the way it was supposed to be, she put in a call to Luis. He came over, looked around, and gave his approval. "You can reopen whenever you're ready, Rock."

"Thank you!"

After he departed, she and Siz fired up the kitchen. The Dog and Cow was back in business.

After escorting Sam and Brenda Miller back to her office, Bernadine set aside the sting of Mal's actions and concentrated on the business at hand.

"So, will that place be opening up again?" Sam asked.

"Yes, and in time for dinner probably. One of the owners was just trying to add more seating and violated code."

His wife Brenda said, "When you said you wanted to give us a walking tour of the town, I didn't expect to see drama."

Neither had Bernadine. Rocky's voice echoed in her head. *He said no.*

Her husband added, "But I'm glad to know you have a fire marshal who takes his job seriously."

"Luis is very dedicated."

The Millers had been ecstatic over the Sutton Hotel space she hoped would house their coffee shop and bakery, but worried the drama at the

Dog would dissuade them. Apparently, it hadn't.

"If we decide to go ahead and sign the lease, how soon can we move in?"

"As soon as you like. We'll be having the grand re-opening on Saturday."

Sam, the big roly-poly husband, asked, "So what time does that diner open up in the mornings?"

"Six thirty."

"So, they'll be our competition?"

"Not really. The Dog serves full meals. People wanting just a cup of coffee and maybe something to go with it on their way to work or the highway, will bow down and kiss your feet. There was a coffee shop in Franklin but it closed recently."

He added, "I know we talked about the diner's presence before, but seeing it in person and how modern it appears initially caused me some concern."

Bernadine hoped the Dog wouldn't be a deal breaker after all.

Brenda, short and tiny as her husband was tall and round, said, "But I liked the apartments upstairs, and knowing that we could lease one for now and have a house built later if we can make this business a go."

Sam said, "This town is really small, though."

Bernadine agreed. "It is and it took me some time getting used to. But I've come to love the slow pace and the peace and quiet. We're hoping the new growth doesn't jeopardize that."

"I like that the place is small," Brenda admitted. "I grew up in LA, and then he and I met in Boston."

"Both big cities," he added.

"We may be small but we're not backward. We have some of the fastest Wi-Fi in the region. Our community centers like the rec, the church, and school are all state of the art and wired, too."

Brenda told her, "We really enjoyed the tour of the rec center. And thanks for sending that beautiful brochure on the history here. Sammy's quite a Black History buff and being in Henry Adams is exciting for him."

"Here's another plus you may not have thought about. The stars at night are breathtaking. You're not going to believe how beautiful they are."

Sam said, "Me? I'm sold."

His wife laughed. "Hold up. Now that we've finally seen the place, how about we talk first?"

"Always the voice of reason. That's why I keep her around."

Their shared smile was filled with so much love, Bernadine wondered if she and Mal would ever be that way again. "I think a talk and a good night's sleep is wise."

Sam hung his head. "Okay."

The mock pout made his wife smile. "He's quite the character as you'll find out if we do decide to sign on the dotted line."

"Which we will be doing, Ms. Brown. Trust me. She's as excited as I am, but she's logical and methodical as opposed to my let-it-all-hang-out spontaneity."

"That's a good balance," Bernadine said.

"It's worked for us for over thirty years," Brenda said, adoration still shining in her eyes.

They stood and Sam said, "We'll head back to our hotel over in Franklin and give you a call either this evening or in the morning. Will that work?"

"Perfectly. It's so nice to finally meet you face-to-face."

"Same here."

"Enjoy the rest of your day. If you have any questions you have my number. Feel free to call."

"Thanks."

After they left, Bernadine decided she felt good about them as potential business owners and residents. Neither impressed her as being outlandish or having personalities that would rub the locals the wrong way. However, she knew absolutely nothing about them and hoped she wouldn't be proven wrong. Alone now, she let her mind move to Mal. What was going on in Vegas that he needed to simply pick up and go. Was he running away from something, or to something or someone? She was honest enough with herself to consider that maybe he had found another woman. After all, he'd been quite the player when she first came to town. Back then, Tamar described him as being made of snake oil and she'd been right. But he'd won her over. Their first date had been a picnic in his pickup truck, of all places. He'd taught her to fly kites, shared his love for raptors, and given her a promise necklace that made her cry happy tears. She reached up and slowly fingered the chain. Last Christmas, he'd shown up in a Santa hat and with a horse and sleigh, and took her on a sleigh ride through the snow. And now?

She glanced up and found Mal standing in her doorway. Her heart pounded.

"Hey," he said.

"Hey," she whispered.

"Just stopped in to say goodbye."

"Okay." She had a thousand questions she wanted to ask but kept silent.

"I have some things I need to work out."

"If I can help—"

"Alone," he gritted out. "Let a man work out his stuff alone."

She drew back. "Sure." Why was he being so gruff?

He had trouble meeting her eyes after that, but finally said, "I'll be back for the wedding."

She wanted to ask if he'd call her while he was away, but held off on asking that, too. "Okay. Take care of yourself."

"You, too." He held her gaze for so long she thought he might have more to say. Instead, he turned and walked away.

She sat in the echoing silence unable to decide how she felt. Sad. Angry. Resigned. Finally, after an hour she did something she'd never done before. Bernadine Brown left work in the middle of the day and drove home.

CHAPTER
11

That evening, Gemma entered the classroom and was again among the first to arrive. Unlike last time, however, Professor LeForge was already there, seated at the small table at the front of the room, typing on his laptop. He glanced up at her entrance, sent her a smile, and went back to whatever he was working on. She sat, settled in, and waited for class to begin. As she did, she thought back on Gary Clark's announcement at the store. Although she wouldn't be able to see the job posting until the next day, she wondered if she met the minimum qualifications. She hoped so because more than likely the salary would be higher than what she made presently and the benefits package better, too. It would be nice to get a bump in her paycheck. Although the issue of having to be trained by Alma was daunting, she'd cross that bridge if and when the time came. In the meantime, she had to pass this class.

The rest of the students arrived shortly thereafter. She nodded a greeting to the tattooed Josh Miller and when the class began, focused her attention on LeForge.

"I've randomly divided you up into groups of

four. You and your partners will create a company and as we go through the course you'll be asked to apply the principles you're learning to get your company up and running and hopefully profitable." He added that each business would be given a fictitious amount of seed money from which to buy or lease a building, and to furnish it with whatever they needed.

There were twenty students. They all looked around the room as if wondering who they'd be paired with. He began reciting names. When Gemma's was called in conjunction with Josh, she felt relieved; at least he was someone she knew to be nice. The other two members of their team were Carrie Farway and Brad Young. Carrie moved to an open chair beside Josh. She had dark brown hair and an eager smile. Brad, however, was one of those LeForge had shamed into removing his earbuds on the first day. He joined them and looked just as disinterested as he had then. The group's first task was to decide what type of company to create. Gemma had no idea, but Josh did.

"How about we start a tat parlor?"

Gemma shrugged. "That's okay with me."

Carrie looked skeptical.

Brad rolled his eyes. "That's so gay."

Carrie spun on him. "Don't ever use that phrase around me again."

He drew back.

"It's a slur, you moron. Grow the hell up."

Josh raised an eyebrow.

As if the confrontation with Brad had cemented her decision, Carrie said, "Go ahead Josh, I think that's an awesome idea."

The now sullen-looking Brad put in his earbuds and ignored them while they planned.

LeForge quietly walked the room, listening to the group discussions and answering questions. When he reached Gemma's group, she did her best to ignore his standing presence directly behind her and failed badly.

He gave the disconnected Brad a brief glance but didn't address him. Instead he said, "This group has an advantage over the others."

"How?" Josh asked.

"You have Ms. Dahl, who can probably offer life and work experience no one else here has yet."

Gemma was embarrassed down to her toes. "I hope so."

He asked about their company. After hearing their initial plans, he voiced his approval and moved on.

As class ended, he gave out the homework assignment, which was tied to their accounting textbook. They were also told to continue building their companies.

Josh asked her and Carrie, "Do we want to get together online or IRL?"

Gemma was confused.

Carrie saw that and translated. "Means: in real life."

"I vote for IRL." Her response drew smiles from her young teammates. "I live nearby. We could meet there and use my dining room table."

Josh and Carrie agreed and they settled on a time that best fit their schedules.

Josh reached over and pulled the bud out of Brad's left ear. "We're meeting at Ms. Gem's house on Saturday."

"Yippee," he replied sarcastically.

Gemma's disapproving side-eye was mirrored by the others.

"Why are you even here?" Josh asked him.

"Because my witch of a mom said either go to school or get out of her basement."

Carrie asked, "Don't you think you should at least try and pass the class, then?"

"She said go to school. She didn't say anything about me having to pass."

"You really are a moron."

"Better than fat and ugly."

Her right cross knocked him out of his chair and onto the floor.

Everything and everyone in the class stopped.

While the stunned Brad stared at the blood staining his fingers from his bloody lip, Josh said to Carrie in a wondrous tone, "I think I'm in love."

Blushing, she smiled.

LeForge came over. "What's going on here?"

Brad picked himself up off the floor and whined, "She sucker punched me."

"You don't get to fat shame me, ever!"

"Mr. Young, do you need medical assistance?"

"No."

"Then head to the restroom and get yourself cleaned up." He then turned to Carrie. "Ms. Farway. No more punching."

Her chin rose. "Yes, sir."

He gave Gemma a speaking look that parents of squabbling children often shared, then returned to the front of the room.

Everyone gathered up their belongings and before Gemma could head out the door, LeForge said, "Ms. Dahl, can I speak to you for a moment?"

She gave Josh and Carrie a wave goodbye and made her way to him. "Yes."

"I hope I didn't embarrass you by talking about your life experience."

"No, you didn't."

"Good. Just wanted to check."

They stared at each other for a moment and Gemma, feeling her attraction to him rising, fought to clear her head. "You handled that craziness between Carrie and Brad very well."

"I've been teaching for a long time. You learn."

"I see." She added, "I don't want to tattle, but

241

Brad didn't participate at all in our discussion."

"Go on without him. You seem to have two smart teammates. He'll either engage or he won't."

"So, we operate shorthanded?"

"If need be. Sort of like life, right?"

She thought about the years she'd spent raising her daughter, and now Wyatt, alone. "I suppose."

"Your group will be fine. Are you heading to the parking lot?"

"I am."

"Okay if I walk with you?" he asked, gathering up his stuff.

Nervous, but determined not to let it show, she replied, "Sure."

The hallway was crowded with students going to and from other classes. She spotted Josh and Carrie talking. Josh, seeing her with LeForge, gave her a thumbs-up and she hoped her cheeks weren't red in response.

When they reached the door, LeForge pushed it aside so she could exit first. It was summertime so even at that late hour it wasn't dark yet. They walked across the lot, and he asked, "Have you lived here all your life?"

"Born in Franklin. Moved to Chicago. Came back to Kansas a year ago. Where's home for you?"

"Milwaukee. Living in Hays about five years now."

She wondered why Hays? Not wanting to

appear nosy, she didn't ask. "Ah. My car's over there."

"And mine is on the other side of the building." He stopped. "I'll see you at the next class."

Once again, they stood staring for a long moment, until he said softly, "Have a good weekend, Ms. Dahl."

"Thanks. You do the same."

Walking away, she felt his eyes follow her retreat. *Don't look back,* she told herself. Inside the car, she started the engine. Feeling like a crushing teenager, she drove out of the lot and wondered where, if anywhere, this might be heading.

The next morning, Tamar and Eula shared a silent breakfast. Accustomed to having her home to herself, Tamar was a bit irritated with Eula's presence, but knowing her cousin had nowhere else to go, she swallowed her pique along with her coffee.

"I know my being here isn't easy for you, Tam."

Tamar wondered when Eula had acquired mind-reading abilities. "It's okay."

"No, it isn't, so thank you for your graciousness."

"You're welcome."

"You probably don't know this, but growing up, I always envied you."

That was surprising. "Why?"

"Because you were so confident. You knew all the latest dances and you were so tall and gorgeous."

Tamar looked up from her plate at the unexpected praise.

Eula smiled. "I know. I always acted like you and the others were beneath me, but it was to overcompensate for how intimidating your branch of the family was to me."

"Meaning?"

"Here I was, an only child. A Nance. Even though Teresa was my great-gran, I was raised in Philly, far away from all the true Julys here. You and the other cousins knew each other intimately. You joked about things, talked trash about each other. And when I would come for the summers, I didn't feel like I belonged."

"I never knew that."

"I sure as hell wasn't going to admit it, so I threw my nose in the air and pretended I didn't care, but I did. And as we grew older and my visits became less frequent, I convinced myself that I was indeed better and didn't need you country Julys."

Tamar sat back and let that soak in. The truth in Eula's eyes showed just how honest she was attempting to be. Tamar's respect rose as did her empathy. "You never acted like you wanted to belong."

"I was scared."

"Of?"

"For one thing, how many there were of you."

Tamar smiled. She got that part. She and Thad were direct descendants of Neil and Olivia's second child, Neil Griffin July, and his wife, Lacy Trenton. Add in the four descendants of Neil and Olivia's only daughter, Teresa, the five children from the marriage of Neil's brother Harper and his wife, Vivian, along with the first Diego children, and you had enough Julys to start their own town. Tamar never thought the numbers were intimidating but to an only child like Eula, they undoubtedly were. "We never knew you were scared. We just thought you were stuck up. Being as poor as we all were, you intimidated us with your nice clothes and proper speech. I remember Julia saying to me, 'Damn, Tam. How many shoes does she have?'" And Tamar smiled at the memory. "We'd never been around anyone who had more than one pair of shoes, and you seemed to wear a different pair daily."

"The Nances always had money."

"We knew that but to actually see it left us intimidated as well."

"Is Julia going to come to see me before I die?"

Tamar paused. She wanted to reassure her but couldn't. "I don't know, Eula. You hurt her pretty badly taking her to court like you did."

"Hubris, pure and simple."

"Maybe I can convince her to talk to you on Skype."

"What's Skype? I retired from teaching thirty-five years ago. I haven't kept up with the technology."

She explained Skype.

"My goodness. And you know how to use it?"

Tamar enjoyed the wonder in her voice. "I do. Amari, Trent, and the rest of the people here make sure I stay current."

"You're very blessed to have caring people around you."

That Eula didn't pulled at Tamar's heart in ways she couldn't have imagined before Eula showed up at her door.

"So, do you think Julia will speak to me so I can apologize?"

"All I can do is ask her. Do you want to do it now?"

"In a little while. I want to finish breakfast and get my thoughts together first."

Tamar noticed she hadn't eaten much of her eggs and grits and had taken only a few bites of her toast. "You need to eat more to keep your strength up."

"Not much of an appetite these days. Probably because I'm at death's doorway. No hunger in heaven. There might be in hell, though."

"You might stick around longer than you think."

"Nice of you to say, but I probably won't."

"The doctors could be wrong."

"True, but First Tamar usually isn't."

Tamar stilled. "She visited you?"

Eula nodded. "In a dream, a few weeks back. Told me to go home. And since this is where Madison Nance and Teresa July began their married life together, I came here. To you."

Tamar thought back on the odd dreams she'd been having lately. The woman she'd been named for had yet to show herself in them but Tamar sensed her presence. Because the family viewed the matriarch's visits as a harbinger of death, Tamar didn't really want to see her. In truth, she did though, as long as she didn't die with the day's following sunrise.

They finished breakfast and Tamar was loading their dishes in the dishwasher when a knock sounded on the door.

"It's open," she called.

In walked Mal.

They eyed each other silently.

Eula, having been told about yesterday's incident at the diner, stood and said, "I'll let you two have some privacy."

Once she was gone, Tamar didn't bother beating around the bush. "Why Vegas?"

He shrugged. "I have something I need to take care of."

"Meaning what?"

"My business."

It wasn't what she wanted to hear but it had been expected. He'd always played his cards close to the vest, even when he'd been drinking—especially when he'd been drinking. She really wanted to know what was going on with him, but he was far too old to be sent to his room until he told her the truth and she got the sense that learning the truth was only going to make things worse.

"I'll be back for the wedding."

"Permanently?"

"We'll see."

She sighed with frustration. "Okay. Have you talked to Bernadine?"

"For a minute."

"Did you at least explain to her what this is about?"

"No."

"Mal?"

"Look, I didn't come here for lectures, I came to let you know I'm leaving as a show of respect."

"Thank you for that."

"You're welcome. I'll see you at the wedding."

"Okay."

And he turned and strode out.

Holding in her anger, she put her hardheaded

son out of her mind as best she could, and went back to filling the dishwasher.

Later that morning, she and Eula were watching *The View* when they heard what sounded like car engines revving outside. Sharing a look of confused curiosity, they walked to the front door and what they saw through the screen rendered Tamar speechless. Roaring onto her land were pickup trucks, dune buggies, Jeeps, and motorcycles. Followed by more pickups, motorcycles, and cars of all make and in all conditions. Each vehicle was packed with men, young and old, all bearing the signature dark skin of the Julys. Knees weak, she stepped out onto the porch.

Eula followed and asked, "Are they who I think they are?"

"Yes."

The Oklahoma Julys were doing wheelies in front of the porch, racing each other across the field, kicking up dust and clods of dirt and grass, and generally behaving like the coyote cubs that they were. The last time they'd visited, for Lily and Trent's wedding, they'd entered the Dog like a raucous, chanting war party. There'd been drummers and dancing and singers. They'd caused such a commotion that Tamar had to fire her shotgun into the ceiling to bring the situation under control. She knew they'd be coming for Eula's eventual funeral, but what were they doing in her front yard now—beside acting like the rodeo come to town. The last vehicle to pull up was a big silver and black RV that she assumed belonged to her brother. By then the other vehicles had cut their engines and the occupants were making their way to her side.

"Hey, Aunt Tammy," they said, wearing her brother's grin. Each gave her a peck on the cheek, and all she could do was smile and receive the tributes in the spirit in which they were given. Although the visit was bound to cause so much mischief Will Dalton and his deputies would be pulling out their hair, they were her family and she loved them even when she didn't want to.

A panel on the side of the RV slowly opened and a whirring ramp descended. Seconds later, her brother, wearing a snow-white Stetson, powered his motorized wheelchair down the ramp. Behind him walked his half-Sioux grandson Griffin, who was also the father of Tamar's great-grandson, Amari. Griffin was one of the few members of Thad's clan with any sense.

"Hey Tammy," Thad said as he rolled up and stopped at the foot of the porch steps.

"Hey, Thad."

"Hey there, Eula."

"Thaddeus."

"Sorry to hear about what you're facing."

"Thanks, Thaddeus."

Tamar said, "You didn't tell me you were coming."

"Because you would've just said don't. Correct?"

"More than likely."

"Exactly."

"And you're here, why?"

"To celebrate Eula's life with a cookout, and some dancing and home brew, and who knows what else."

"A cookout?"

"Brought our own meat, fixings, and grills. We'll set up everything in the yard and have us an old-fashioned, August First wang-dang doodle, July style."

"Lord," she whispered.

"We'll sleep in tents and in the vehicles." He looked out at the open prairie. "Might take us a while to dance down all that grass so we can raise the tents, but it'll be a full moon tonight. Should give us plenty of light."

She turned her attention to Griffin. "I thought Amari was with you."

"No, he's still with my mother. I'll ride up and get him when the family gets settled in here. This will be a fun gathering, Aunt Tam."

"Uh-huh, okay. Get yourselves situated and I'll call Trent and let him know you're here. Calling Sheriff Will Dalton, too."

Thad grabbed his chest. "You wound me, sister."

"I'll do more than that if you put your mitts on Olivia, again."

He smiled like the coyote he was. His progeny from his three ex-wives did as well. Tamar shook her head. She and the stunned Eula went back inside.

While Tamar was texting Oklahoma July warning alerts, Eula asked, "Where are their wives?"

"Probably at home, happy the men are away. Most of Thad's sons and grandsons are either divorced or single. Keeping wives is not a male July strong suit."

Tamar looked down at Will's responding text: *Oh lord. Alerting my crews. Thx.*

Trent: *Your house stil! standing? Lily and I back later tonight.*

Seated at her desk, Bernadine read the message from Tamar about the arrival of Thaddeus July and his Wild Bunch and smiled. There'd been no town-wide plans for a big August First celebration because they were focused on Rocky and Jack's Labor Day wedding, but it wouldn't hurt to liven things up, and she was sure Thad and his family would do just that. As for Mal, her pity party was over, or at least she'd convinced herself it was. No more moping, wondering, or angst. If he had something to do that needed doing, have at it. She had a town to run and a world to turn. With that in mind, she printed out the lease papers for the Millers. They'd sent her a text late last night to let her know they wanted the space in the hotel for their shop and she couldn't be happier. As they'd discussed previously, it would be a few weeks before they'd be open for business, but she thought their coffee shop would be a plus for Henry Adams. They'd also be renting one of the upper apartments, and per their text, were hoping to move in as soon as possible. It was her hope that they'd be good neighbors to Crystal, now home getting the last of her packing done. Tomorrow was the big move-in day for her and for Kelly's Liberian Ladies and Gents Salon. The name continued to amuse her because it was so perfect. She couldn't wait to see the online website the kids were going to put up on the salon's behalf.

"Bernadine."

She looked up. It was Rocky. Bernadine paused because of what she saw on Rocky's face. "What's wrong?"

"I can't log into the Dog's payroll account."

"Why not?"

"Password's been changed."

Bernadine stared back, confused.

"I can access the menus, the website, the

vendor files, but not payroll, which means I can't print out checks for the employees. Mal usually does it and I've had my hands full with him being gone so I forgot about today being a pay week until an hour or two ago."

"Why would he change the password?"

"I don't know. I had the kids write down the hours they worked and add them up. I can try and compute taxes and all that and pay them with checks out of my personal account, but I'll need access to that payroll file eventually because the IRS will want their money."

"Have you tried contacting him?"

"No reply to my texts or calls."

Bernadine's mind whirred with possible solutions. "Okay. You go ahead and pay your people and I'll reimburse you. I'll also call Lily and Trent, to let them know what's going on. Maybe one of them knows of a firm that can hack their way in so we can figure out what the heck is going on."

"I have a really bad feeling in the pit of my stomach."

"Don't go there. I'll keep you posted."

She exited, and Bernadine sat back against her chair. *Lord, Mal. What does this mean?* She returned to her laptop. Because she'd invested in the diner's rehab, she had admin access to its financial records accounts. She keyed in her password but instead of being allowed in, a message in bold letters appeared on the screen: "Access denied. See admin for further assistance." Eyes wide, she entered her password again, only to have the denial message reappear. *Oh, my god!* She tried a third time. Same result. The hair on the back of her neck stood up. She grabbed her phone and called Brain down in Florida.

He answered right away. "Hey, Ms. Bernadine. How are you? Is something wrong? My parents okay?"

"Everyone's fine, but I have a quick question."

"Okay."

"Did you help OG change one of the passwords on the Dog's computers?"

"Yep. He said he thought somebody had been trying to hack in and he wanted me and Leah to add another level of security."

Bernadine almost fainted.

Brain, sounding worried, asked, "Did we do something wrong?"

"No, babe. Do you know what he changed the password to?"

"No."

"Would you be able to go back in and undo the added level?"

He got real quiet. "No. We did do something wrong, didn't we?"

"No, but he's gone to Vegas and we can't get

into payroll. No biggie. We'll just wait until he calls us back."

"Oh, okay. You scared me, not going to lie."

She spent a few more minutes asking how he was doing and if he was having a good time with his bio mom. He assured her that he was and she ended the call.

She ran shaking hands down her face. After drawing in a deep calming breath, she called Rocky and had her try and access the financial files as the account's third administrator of record.

"It won't let me in," she said.

Bernadine related the conversation with Brain.

Rocky was quiet for a long moment before saying, "Tell me he hasn't been embezzling? Oh, god, Bernadine."

"I know. We'll keep a good thought until we can get into the account and look around."

"Jesus."

After the call, Bernadine hated to think that the man she loved was guilty of embezzlement. There had to be a rational explanation. There just had to be.

CHAPTER
12

Lucas Herman was so exhausted he could barely keep his eyes open, but he had to get the dishes washed and then mop the kitchen floor before he'd be allowed to eat breakfast. He'd decided that Great-aunt Wanda was really Professor Dolores Umbridge from the Harry Potter series in disguise. Nice on the outside but hateful and mean on the inside. Since their arrival two days ago, she'd been working them nonstop—washing windows, sweeping floors, moving furniture, doing laundry—and if they didn't do it fast enough or made a mistake, they were punished. Last night, he'd been washing their dinner dishes and while drying a plate it slipped out of his hands and broke on the floor. She screamed at him about the plate having originally belonged to her mother and slapped him so hard he wound up on the floor in the broken glass. His face still ached.

"Are you done in there?" she yelled from her spot in front of the TV. She watched TV a lot.

"Almost."

"Hurry up. I need that floor mopped, too."

"Yes, ma'am," he whispered.

She entered the kitchen. She was wearing a

gray sweatshirt and pants. "What did you say?"

He pitched his voice louder. "I said, yes, ma'am."

She walked over and pinched his upper arm so hard he whimpered. "Don't be sassing me now."

"No, ma'am. I'm not."

"Good. Spare the rod, spoil the child. Jasmine!"

Lucas heard his sister running down the stairs from the second floor.

She entered, looking wary and afraid. "Yes, ma'am?"

"Those bathrooms clean?"

"Yes, ma'am."

It broke his heart seeing Jaz's scared face. They were both scared.

The doorbell rang.

Aunt Wanda snapped, "Upstairs, both of you! Get in your room, close the door, and do not make a sound!"

They ran up the steps. Jaz flew into the bedroom but Lucas stood out of sight at the top of the stairs to listen in.

It was the social worker, Mr. Gladwin. He asked to see them.

"Oh, you just missed them," she lied. "They've gone to the library with the kids next door."

Lucas hadn't seen any kids and wondered if any existed.

Aunt Wanda added, "When you didn't show

up yesterday like you said, I wasn't sure what was up, so I told them to go on ahead. They'll be back in an hour or so. Library is having some kind of summer program."

"So, they're settling in?" Gladwin asked.

"Yes. No problems, so far. They're the sweetest things."

"Okay, good. Glad to hear that."

"But they both need clothes, pajamas, things like that. Ms. Krebs said their parents left an estate? I almost fainted when she said it was worth about three million dollars. Never seen that much money in my whole life. How do I get access to it, so I can get them what they need? I promise not to spend all three million, at least not today," she said, apparently making a joke.

Lucas stilled. *Three million dollars!*

Mr. Gladwin replied, "Most of the estate is being held in escrow for them until they turn eighteen, but as their guardian you'll be able to tap into a small monthly amount."

"Oh," she said as if that wasn't the answer she'd been expecting. Lucas wondered if Mr. Gladwin was suspicious.

Her voice turned cheery again. "Do I need to fill out paperwork, or what?"

"I have everything with me, but I'm really supposed to see the kids before we start the process, so how about I come back later? I don't want you to have to wait any longer than necessary."

"That's fine. Can I call you when they get back?"

"Sure. I've got a full plate today and may not be able to come as soon as you call, but I will stop back by."

"That's good enough."

Not only was Aunt Wanda vicious and mean, she was greedy, too. Hearing Mr. Gladwin leave, Lucas tiptoed down the hall to their room and shared with Jaz what he'd heard.

"Three million dollars!" Jaz whispered excitedly.

He nodded.

"She's going to try and spend it all. We won't be eighteen for a thousand years."

"I know."

She took in his face. "Does your face hurt?" she asked with concern.

"Yes. Be nice if Mr. Gladwin does come back and gets us out of here." But the way their lives had been going, Lucas didn't hold much hope.

That afternoon, Aunt Wanda sent him outside to cut the grass in her backyard. The yard was small so he didn't think it would take very long. He worried that the ancient-looking mower wouldn't work, but when he pulled the starter, it started right up. When he lived with his parents, he'd been ecstatic when he grew old enough to take on the job. He'd listened intently to his dad explain how the mower worked and the safety measures that needed to be adhered to, like wearing safety glasses. Thinking about his dad brought back the sadness, but knowing Aunt Wanda was waiting for him to get done, he put it aside and got to work. He was cutting a path from the house to the shed at the back of the yard when he saw a woman exit the house next door. She was wearing a blue uniform that made him think she might be the police and she was carrying a trash bag. He kept mowing while she put the bag into a brown Dumpster, and then she stopped and looked at him as if surprised. She waved. Not wanting to draw Aunt Wanda's wrath, he put his head down and pushed the mower. When he peeked over she was at the fence that separated the two homes waving again as if wanting him to stop. Because she was an adult, he did.

"Hey there," she said, "I'm C. C. Crane, and you are?"

"Lucas Herman."

"You visiting?"

"I live here now. Me and my sister."

She paused and concern filled her face. "Since when?"

"Wednesday."

"Really?" She looked over at Aunt Wanda's

house for a moment, then back to him. "Foster kids?"

"No. She's our great-aunt. Our parents died two years ago. We went to foster care but now we're here."

"She treating you okay?"

Lucas hesitated. He didn't know what might happen if he told the truth and Aunt Wanda found out, so he nodded. "Yeah."

C.C.'s lips tightened as if she knew he was lying. "Tell you what," she said, voice kind. "I'm a police officer. If you or your sister need anything, come knock on my door. Even if it's in the middle of the night, you come. You hear me?"

He whispered, "Yes, ma'am."

"Lucas!" Aunt Wanda was standing on the back porch. "Get back to work."

C.C. stared at her coldly. "Morning, Ms. Borden. How are you?"

"Fine. Go bust some crackheads and let him finish his chores."

She ignored that but told Lucas, "Remember what I said."

He nodded and restarted the mower. He took a quick glance over at the fence and saw C.C. going into her house.

Aunt Wanda said, "Don't let that uniform of hers fool you. She's as corrupt as they come."

"Yes, ma'am."

Once he was done, he put the mower back into the small shed and went inside the house. He was hungry but there was no guarantee she'd let him eat, so he tried not to think about his stomach.

"What was she saying to you?" Aunt Wanda asked as soon as he stepped in.

"She just introduced herself and wanted to know who I was."

"And you told her what?"

"That we'd just come to live with you and you were raising us."

"She ask you about your face?"

"No, ma'am." He hadn't looked in the mirror since getting up so he guessed the bruise was starting to become visible.

"Anybody ask you what happened, you say you tripped over something in the dark on your way to the toilet."

"Yes, ma'am."

"Wash your hands and go make some sandwiches for you and your sister."

"Yes, ma'am."

A few hours later, Mr. Gladwin returned. "You kids doing okay?"

For the second time that day, Lucas hesitated over his reply, but Aunt Wanda was sitting on the couch watching him intently. She had a smile on her face and a glare in her eyes. "Yes, we're fine."

Gladwin turned and viewed Aunt Wanda for a long moment before bringing his attention back to Lucas. "Do you like to read?"

"Yes." No hesitation.

"What books did you bring back from the library?"

He heard Jaz give a tiny gasp of surprise.

Aunt Wanda answered in her fake cheery voice, "They weren't allowed to check out any books. They said I had to be with them to get a library card. Right kids?"

"Uh, yes. That's what they told us."

Gladwin studied him in a way reminiscent of the way police officer C. C. had earlier. *Does he know I'm lying? Please, God, let him know.*

Gladwin got to his feet. "Ms. Borden, I need to see the kids' bedroom to make sure it meets the specifications."

She stood. "I can take—"

"No. You stay here. They can show me. We'll be right back."

Up in the room, he let them enter first. "Have a seat." They sat down on their beds and waited. He closed the door.

"I want to ask you a few questions and I want you to tell me the truth, okay?"

They nodded. Lucas began shaking.

"Did you really go to the library this morning?"

Lucas and Jaz shared a look. Jaz said, "We can't say. She'll hurt us."

Gladwin's jaw tightened. "Not on my watch, so tell me everything that's happened since she brought you here."

In a halting voice, Lucas began with having to clean the room before they could eat.

Gladwin appeared angry. "I saw this room when I did the inspection the day before you arrived. She told me she'd have it cleaned up for you."

"We cleaned it up for us," Jaz said.

Lucas added, "And we had to take all the stuff out and wash and dry the sheets before we could eat."

"And the food was cold," Jaz said tightly.

"It was one in the morning when we went to bed."

"And she slapped Lucas in the face last night because he accidentally broke a plate."

Mr. Gladwin bent down and gently turned Lucas's face so he could see it better. "I saw it when I came in. I wanted to wait until we were alone to ask you about it. You have a good-sized bruise blooming there. I'm sorry about all this. My office placed you here on the recommenda-tion of the worker in Kansas, Ms. Krebs. She said she checked Ms. Borden out thoroughly."

"I think she just wants our parents' money," Lucas said.

"I got that impression as well when she and I

265

spoke this morning. Gather up your things. I'm getting you two out of here."

Tears sprang into Lucas's eyes but he quickly wiped them away. "Thank you, sir."

"Is there someplace you want to go?"

"Yes, back to Ms. Dahl and Henry Adams."

And after they explained why and answered a few questions he had about Ms. Gemma and the town, Gladwin said, "Let's see if I can't make that happen. No. I will make it happen. Again, I apologize on behalf of the state of Ohio for placing you here."

They stuffed their belongings back into the trash bags. When they reached the bottom of the stairs, Aunt Wanda stood up. She looked confused. "What's going on here? Where are you taking them?"

"Away. I'm rescinding your guardianship."

Her eyes went wide. "Why?"

"Abuse."

"What abuse? If he said I hit him, he's lying."

He met her hostile glare. "There are two kids standing here. How did you know Lucas was the accuser?"

She froze.

"You'll be hearing from the state, Ms. Borden. Have a nice day."

As he escorted them out the door, she began cursing and screaming and calling them all kinds of nasty names but Mr. Gladwin didn't respond.

Outside, a police car sat at the curb. C.C. stepped out. "Hey, Ed."

"C.C. Thanks for the call."

Lucas looked between the two adults with surprise.

Mr. Gladwin explained. "C.C. and I grew up together and now attend the same church. After she met you earlier she called me and told me about the bruise she saw on your face, and how hesitant you were when she questioned you."

She gave Lucas a kind smile.

Ed Gladwin continued, "Even if she hadn't called I knew something was up when I stopped by this morning. You learn to listen to your gut in this business, so I went back to the office and ran the background check on her that Krebs out in Kansas should've run."

"What did you find out?" Jaz asked.

"That thirty years ago, Wanda Borden had three of her kids taken from her home by the state of California because of neglect and abuse. She should've never been allowed anywhere near you and your brother."

Lucas glanced over at Jaz and something in his own gut told him the bad times were over. He didn't know why he felt that way, but he did. "Thank you, C.C."

"Anytime. Have a good life, Lucas." She turned to Jaz. "What's your name?"

When Jaz replied, C.C. said, "Nice meeting you, Jasmine. You have a good life, too."

She walked back to her cruiser and Gladwin called, "See you in church."

"You, too."

She drove away and Lucas and Jazz climbed into the backseat of his car. Once they were buckled in, he said, "Next stop, my office, and then, Henry Adams, Kansas."

Jaz cheered.

Three hours later, after stuffing themselves at McDonald's and sitting in Mr. Gladwin's office while he made calls and faxed papers, Lucas and Jasmine went with him to the airport There was a white jet sitting at one of the hangars. As they approached it, the door opened and stairs appeared. Lucas looked as confused as Jaz did, but when they saw Ms. Gemma, Wyatt, and Ms. Brown descending, their eyes widened and they ran.

Ms. Gemma scooped them up. "I'm so glad to see you!"

Lucas couldn't put into words how glad he was to see her, too.

Wyatt stuck out a hand and he and Lucas embraced. "Told you you'd be back," Wyatt laughed.

Ms. Brown had tears in her eyes. "Thank you, Mr. Gladwin."

"You're welcome. I like that fancy chariot you have there."

"Comes in handy for things like this. You kids ready to go home?"

Lucas spoke for them both. "Yes." But first he turned to Mr. Gladwin and said sincerely, "Thank you, sir, so much." He was thankful for him and for his friend Officer C.C.

"You're welcome. I'm glad things worked out. Take care."

He walked back the way they'd come and the Henry Adams crew climbed into the white jet and buckled up.

The jet gathered speed and, once in the air, Lucas viewed the city of Cincinnati getting smaller and smaller. He was not leaving with good memories, but he was thankful to have met C.C. and Mr. Gladwin. Across the aisle, he saw Jaz watching Cincinnati disappear, too. They'd survived Aunt Wanda, were still together, and, for the first time since their parents' death, the future looked bright.

Beside him, Wyatt said, "Brought you something." He handed Lucas the Harry Potter book he'd had to leave behind. Although it had only been a few days ago, it felt like an eternity. Emotion bubbled up. "Thanks,, Wyatt."

"You're welcome."

The bookmark he'd placed inside was still

there, so he removed it and picked up the story where he'd left off.

When they arrived at the Hays airport, Leah and Tiffany's uncle T.C. was standing next to a big black car waiting to drive them home. His welcoming smile and the memory of Pizza Saturday added to the happiness Lucas felt inside. Henry Adams was going to be their home now and these people, his and Jaz's extended family, and that made him happy, too.

To pitch their tents the Julys needed to flatten the grass, so, mimicking the Plains Indians of old, they danced under the light of the full moon. The night air pulsed with the steady beat of the drums while the wind carried the voices of the singers chanting songs passed down through time; songs of the Lakota Sioux, the Cheyenne, and the Cherokee alternated with songs rooted in the Black Seminoles of Florida, the border town of Brackettville, Texas, and Nacimiento, Mexico.

Tamar sat on her porch in the darkness, letting the familiar songs fill her soul and transport her back to Wewoka, the small town founded in the 1840s by legendary leader John Horse back when Oklahoma was known as Indian Territory. Slave catchers allied with the hated Creeks followed her people west, bent upon returning them to masters who viewed them only as property and not the fierce warriors who'd bested Andrew Jackson's soldiers again and again in the swamps and high grasses of Florida. Wearing the traditional headdress and a long calico dress she imagined herself among the women and other tribal members who followed John Horse and the Seminole Chief Wildcat south as they fled Indian Territory on a cold November night in 1849 to seek freedom and peace in Mexico. They walked to Texas and, with the women, she crossed the Trinity River and helped plant corn with the hope of staying long enough to harvest it, only to abandon it because it was too risky to stay with slave catchers dogging their trail like rabid bloodhounds. As they journeyed on, the young and the old died of starvation, drownings, and attacks from other tribes like the Comanche. By March they were crossing the river the Spanish named Los Brazos, the Arms of God, and called on the African deities of their ancestors to protect them as they walked on. Eight months later, in July of 1850, having evaded slave catchers, bands of Creeks, outlaws, bounty hunters, and the US government, John Horse and the Black Seminoles crossed the Rio Grande and found sanctuary in Mexico.

Tamar came back to the present. As the drumming, singing, and dancing continued she looked up at the stars. Her heart was filled

271

knowing that in towns along the borders of Texas and Mexico there were other women just like her, riding the songs and rhythms of the past with the blood of the Black Seminole diaspora flowing in their veins.

"Tamar?"

It was Eula, seated in a chair nearby. "Are you okay?"

"I am. Was lost in the past for a moment, but I'm fine."

"You were so quiet, I thought you'd fallen asleep."

In the darkness, Tamar smiled. "Not sleep." She gazed out at the full moon and saw the dark outline of a large winged bird crossing the glow. She froze. The now familiar caw of the harpy eagle from her dreams sounded on the wind. "Did you hear that?" she asked Eula.

"What?"

When Tamar looked again, the eagle was gone. The night sky held only the moon and the stars. "Never mind. I thought I heard something."

"I can't hear anything but the drums and the singing."

The logical parts of Tamar chalked up the odd sight to her imagination, but the traditional self knew better. She checked her phone for the time. One a.m. The July men had been dancing since sunset. By the light of the moon, she saw them starting to pitch tents, hammering in stakes to the beat of the drums. In another hour or so, it would be quiet enough to sleep. "I think I'm going to bed."

Eula stood. "I'm right behind you."

Lying in bed, Tamar thought back on the day. She'd bypassed the Friday Night Movies to make sure she'd have a home to come back to because vigilance was necessary with her brother and his cubs around. Trent and Lily stopped by right after sunset. She shared what little she knew about the situation surrounding Mal, and their concern mirrored her own. Rocky's call earlier about the locked-down computer added alarm to her ongoing worries, but that troublesome news was balanced by the rescue and return of the Herman children. She'd yet to hear the full details but knowing they were safe and sound and back with Gemma was a good thing. She turned on her side and burrowed deeper into the fresh sheets. In spite of her issues with her brother, she was glad they were there. Of course, come tomorrow they might do something to make her grab her shotgun and want to shoot the lot of them, but for the moment, as the drums outside continued to beat, she let the rhythms usher her into sleep.

CHAPTER
13

Bernadine surveyed Crystal's new digs and hoped her smile covered her sense of sadness. It was official. Her daughter had moved out and they were no longer living under the same roof.

"Do you like it?" Crystal asked, excitedly indicating her newly decorated and furnished space.

"It's you," Bernadine replied. Crystal's paintings graced the walls and there were small sculpted pieces from Eli accenting the end tables. Although her bedroom at home had been done mostly in shades of orange the apartment was a sophisticated mixture of grays and pale blue. "I like the color palette."

"Thought about using orange again, but it was a little too girlish."

"And you are no longer that."

"You look sad, Mom."

"It's a happy sad, though. You're grown up."

"Thank goodness. Growing up takes so long you think you're going to be a kid forever."

"Well get ready. You're going to be an adult for a very long time and it can get real old real quick."

"Right now I'm enjoying it, though. And thank you for my car. Again."

"You're welcome." It was used, but would serve her well for the next few years. Once she was ready to leave town and go out and make her mark on the world, Bernadine planned to purchase her a brand-new one, but Crystal didn't need to know that for now. "Is there anything you forgot to get, but need?"

"Nope. Going to go over to Gary's in a little bit and buy some groceries to fill up my fridge." She rubbed her hands together. "So excited. Getting my own food for my own fridge in my own place."

Bernadine chuckled.

"I've been saving a little money out of each check all summer so I can splurge and buy everything I want."

"Good for you." She was growing up and Bernadine couldn't be more proud.

Crystal threw her arms around her. "Thanks for being the bestest mom ever."

Bernadine held her tight, fought back her tears, and kissed her cheek. "Enjoy your first day." When they parted, she said, "Now, let's go downstairs and see how Kelly and Riley are doing with their move."

Crystal grabbed her purse and bounced to the door. Bernadine exited first and Crystal closed the door behind them.

"You have your door key, right?" Bernadine asked.

Crystal paused as if thinking and then her eyes widened. "Dammit! It's inside on the counter."

Bernadine shook her head. "Call Trent. He has a master set."

She looked so put out, Bernadine patted her on the back. "Welcome to the world of grown folks, Crys."

Downstairs, Kelly, her husband, Bobby, and Riley were moving into their new salon. Bobby was doing most of the heavy lifting, while Kelly and Riley opened boxes and pointed where they wanted things placed.

Seeing Bernadine and Crystal, Kelly walked over and gave Bernadine a big hug. "Thank you!"

"You're welcome. You've earned this new space."

"And I plan to bring in lots of dollars."

"Do you need anything?"

She shook her head. "We have everything under control."

"Call me if you do. Riley, how's my mansion?"

"Doing good. No issues."

"Okay." The mansion once owned by his ex-wife Eustacia Pennymaker had been abandoned and trashed. Bernadine purchased it for a dollar, rehabbed it, and let the then home-less Riley move in. He tended to be crazy as a bedbug, but so far, their agreement that he pay rent and not move in any hogs was holding.

Doc Reg would be taking one of the new spaces but he was waiting on a few pieces of equipment to arrive and would be moving in after they were shipped and delivered.

Since everything else was under control, she left Crystal to help Kelly and headed up the street to check on the Dog. The lunchtime rush was just about over so she hoped to be able to sit and talk to Rocky about how things were going.

She found her in Mal's office along with a young African American woman dressed in jeans and a KU tee shirt. The woman was pecking away at the computer keyboard.

"Hey, Bernadine."

"Rocky."

"This is Barbie Weaver. Barb, this is the town's owner, Bernadine Brown."

The girl stood and shook Bernadine's hand. "Great meeting you, Ms. Brown. Never knew anyone who owned a whole town before."

Rocky explained the young woman's presence. "Barbie runs a tech firm. She's trying to get into the files we need."

Barbie returned to the keyboard. "But as gifted as I am, I've been at this for over two hours and I'm having no success breaking this password. Who did the coding, IBM?"

278

Bernadine said, "No. A couple of our teens did it."

Barbie stopped and looked up. "Teens?"

Bernadine nodded. Had the situation not been so serious she would've laughed at the stunned look on Ms. Weaver's face.

"How old?"

"Sixteen, I believe."

"Goodness. Are they looking for jobs?"

Rocky answered, "Not with computers. They're physics geeks."

Barbie shook her head as though amazed and went back to work.

Leaving her in the office, Rocky led Bernadine to a booth in the back. There were only a few diners inside, and the staff was clearing tables to get ready for the dinner rush.

"Do you want something to eat?" Rocky asked. "Kitchen is still open."

"No, but maybe some water. It's hot out there and I walked from the hotel."

When Rocky returned with the ice-filled glass, Bernadine took a sip and asked, "You haven't heard from Mal, I take it?"

"No. I spoke with Tamar this morning and she hasn't, either."

Bernadine spoke with Trent last evening. His texts and phone calls to his father had gone into a black hole, too. She was at a loss as to how to proceed. "Should we bring in another tech company?"

Rocky shrugged. "Your call."

"Let's give Ms. Barbie until the end of the day."

"She's costing us about two-fifty an hour."

"If she succeeds it'll be worth it. Either way, we get to write it off."

"And if she doesn't?"

She had no idea. A thought occurred to her, though. "Maybe Sandy Langster has time to run down to Vegas and snoop around."

"The lady private detective that worked on the Astrid Wiggins mess?"

"Yes, because at this point, we don't know if he's really in Vegas or not."

"True."

"This is so frustrating."

"It really is."

"How are things here?"

"Okay. Some of the administrative stuff is going unattended, like bank runs, and some of the vendors have been late in getting paid, but they say they're willing to work with me if the invoices aren't left open too long."

"Good. Let me see if Lily has time to help out, and I can make the bank runs."

"That would be great."

"You aren't letting this impact your wedding planning, are you?"

"Trying not to. Between Mal, the wedding, and Siz relocating to Miami I should be a basket case, but I'm surprisingly mellow. I have Jack to thank for that. Who knew love could keep you from jumping off a roof."

"Your guy's a good man."

"You have a good man, too."

"I know." Stubborn and maddening, but good. Rocky turned toward the entrance to the dining room and said, "Lord, what is she doing here?"

"Who is she?"

"Jack's cousin Helen."

"A problem?"

"Ms. Snooty Booty of the Month. Let me get her seated. Be right back."

But when Rocky escorted the woman to the booth where they'd been sitting, Bernadine was surprised.

Rocky began, "Bernadine—"

Helen waved her off. "That's okay, Rochelle. No need to introduce me, I can take it from here." And without a word, she sat down.

A Rude Ms. Snooty Booty, Bernadine thought to herself.

"Can you get me a menu, Rochelle. Thank you," she added dismissively.

Bernadine and Rocky shared a look. Bernadine hoped Rock would let the ill-mannered chick live long enough for her to find out what this unexpected visit was about.

"Kitchen's closed," Rocky told her. "We open again at four for dinner."

"Surely you can make an exception for someone in Jack's family."

Rocky ignored her. "Bernadine, we'll talk later."

Bernadine nodded.

Helen glared at Rocky's retreat. "Not sure what Jack sees in her but if he wants to marry her it's none of my business."

"No, it isn't. And she's a very good friend of mine, just so you know."

Helen blinked.

"So, what can I do for you?"

"You're a hard person to track down. I went to your office, no one was there. Just happened to see some people moving into that hotel office building, and they told me you might be here."

Bernadine sipped her water and waited.

Apparently realizing she needed to get on with it, she said, "I'm Helen Simon, and I'm working with Lyman Proctor and his people over in Franklin. I'd like to discuss something with you."

"And that is?"

"Have you ever considered combining Henry Adams with Franklin?"

Bernadine sat back. She knew where this was leading. "No."

"It might be something to think about."

"There's no advantage in a merger for Henry Adams. Franklin is barely solvent."

"But in a few years, they will be. Their town is larger and they'll have a larger tax base."

"And who would oversee this larger town?"

"Franklin, of course, since they'd be bringing more to the table."

"Then why do they need us, or, specifically, me?"

"Because they could use your investment power. Think how much you'd stand to gain financially."

Bernadine wondered sarcastically if Jack's cousin knew Riley Curry? During his tenure as mayor he'd tried to float a similar nonsensical scheme that would have given him a substantial monetary kickback. "Who do you work for?"

"Bantam Enterprise. We specialize in turning around communities."

"I've heard of Bantam."

"Really? Then you know our reputation."

"I do. Your CEO Pete Denton is being investigated for tax evasion, manipulating the company's stock prices, and is scheduled to testify before a New Jersey grand jury next month."

Helen froze.

Bernadine gave her a crocodile smile. "I know his first wife, Terry. Talked to her on the phone just last week, which is how I know Pete's probably going to jail." Bernadine loved the astonishment on her face. "So, no, I won't be doing any business with you."

Waiting a moment to let that sink in, Bernadine further admonished her in a calm tone. "You should've done more homework on me and my town, Helen. If you had, you would've known better than to waltz in here treating Rocky like the help, or think I'd be so financially ignorant I'd entertain such an ill-thought-out, one-sided proposal."

Helen's mouth opened and closed like a fish.

"A brief background search may have also shown that Franklin's matriarch and ours have been best friends since grade school. Guess who I'll be calling to suggest Bantam be replaced by a more honest firm?"

"You can't do that!"

"Sure I can." She enjoyed watching her try and search for a comeback, and when she couldn't, Bernadine ended the gutting with, "It's been nice chatting with you."

After Helen stormed out, Bernadine got up from the booth and walked into the Dog's office. Rocky was there watching Barbie still pecking away at the keyboard.

"What did Helen want?"

"Nothing really."

"Is she gone?"

"Probably permanently."

"You don't say."

"Yes. Pretty sure she's on her way back to her hotel to pack. I hope she isn't on your guest list."

"So, what happened?" Rocky asked, laughing.

"Can I steal you away for a minute?"

"For this, I have all the time in the world." But before they exited, Rocky turned to Barbie. "Do you need anything?"

"No, but I have a question. Are you sure teens created this?"

Rocky and Bernadine hid their smiles and left her working.

Gemma's shift started midmorning, but she went in a bit early to check out the posting for the assistant manager's job. Just as Gary promised, it was pinned to the notice board inside the employee lounge next to notes from people wanting subs for their shifts, and offers of items for sale like used cars, pit bull puppies, and a cracked flat-screen TV. She read the job's requirements: at least one year of grocery store experience, the ability to use a computer, and some college. Realizing she met the minimum, she smiled.

"You won't get the job," Alma said behind her.

Gemma turned. "And why not?"

"Because there are a lot of people better qualified."

"Like who, Sybil?" she tossed back. "Gary already said no one has the inside track, so I'm applying."

Alma looked her up and down disapprovingly.

"You really think you're hot stuff, don't you?" Her eyes were hard with hate.

Gemma was so tired of her. "I'm just me, Alma. A single woman trying to make a life for me and my kids."

"And before that, a fast piece of tail who didn't care who she slept with."

Gemma froze. When she could speak again, she replied softly, "You don't know anything about me."

"I know you got yourself pregnant by a man you had no business messing with. A man who was happily married until you showed him your tits and spread your legs."

Gemma's jaw dropped.

"His wife was my baby sister, you whore!"

Gemma wanted to shout back that she'd been sixteen, Owen Welke had come on to her first and had promised to marry her, but she knew whatever she said in defense of herself wouldn't matter. Instead, she angrily snatched down one of the blank applications for the job and fled.

In the restroom, after a good cry, she put cold water on her face and studied herself in the mirror. *How long will my past dog me?* At least now she knew why Alma was so hateful. The sister of Owen's wife. Gemma couldn't recall the wife's name or even remember if she'd ever even known it. *Goodness.*

"Honey, what's the matter? Why are you crying?"

She turned to see a concerned Edith standing behind her. "No reason. I'm okay."

"Those red eyes say you're lying, so if you want to talk about it, I have a couple of minutes."

Gemma mulled over the request for a moment then asked sincerely, "How long do the mistakes you make in life follow you?"

Edith paused and searched her face. "I don't know. It depends, I guess. Why?"

Gemma gathered her courage and told her the story of her past and about the confrontation with Alma a few moments ago.

"That's why she's so nasty to you."

"Yes."

Edith let out a sigh. "That's hard on everyone involved. Except the man who caused it all of course."

"Of course, lay the blame at my naïve sixteen-year-old feet," Gemma said bitterly.

"So sorry you're having to deal with this."

"Me too, but now that I know what I'm up against, I can deal with it. I'm not going to be shamed into quitting my job. I've worked too hard to make something out of my life, and Alma or no Alma, I'm applying to be assistant manager."

"You go, girl. Alma better ask somebody, as the kids say."

"Amen!"

Buoyed by Edith's support and her own inner determination, Gemma grabbed her cash drawer from the office where they were kept. On her way down the hallway, as she passed the store's security offices, Barrett Payne stepped out. Taking a deep breath and hoping her eyes weren't still red, she faked a cheery voice, "Hey, Barrett."

"Hey, Gem. How are you?"

"I'm fine." The retired Marine's face was set so seriously, she wondered if she was about to be called on the carpet for something.

He said quietly to her, "Every inch of this store is wired for camera and sound, and I saw what happened with you and Alma."

Embarrassment burned her cheeks. "Oh."

"The past is the past. Don't allow that harpy to run you off, and you'd better apply for the job."

That caught her so off guard, she began laughing before she realized she was. Tears filled her eyes again.

"You got that?"

"Yes, sir."

"Good. Now, carry on." And he went back into his office and closed the door.

Floating on air, Gemma logged into her register. Sgt. Ma'am could kick rocks.

Gemma was good for the rest of her shift, and

things got even brighter when Professor LeForge came through her line. With so few items, he could have easily gone to one of the express lanes, but she was pleased that he hadn't.

"How are you, Ms. Dahl?" he asked as she ran his steak, a small bag of red potatoes, and a plastic container of salad greens over the scanner.

"Doing okay. How are you?"

"I'm good."

She relayed what he owed for the three items. Today, he wore a black tee with a graphic touting the Red Hot Chili Peppers across the front, and some nice-fitting jeans. Still no ring on his finger, though. He used his debit card for payment and she handed him his paper receipt.

"See you Tuesday," he said, then departed with a quick smile that melted her from the knees down. When she turned her attention to the next customer in line, she noticed Alma standing in the crowded store like Waldo hidden in a picture, watching her with that familiar ugliness in her eyes, and it spooked her a little. Gemma knew without a doubt that Alma had seen the harmless interaction between herself and LeForge and would probably try and make something out of it. Knowing the colonel was watching too helped her shake off the unease, so she greeted her next customer and focused on the job at hand.

At the end of her shift, Gemma drove home. She was looking forward to seeing the kids. Later, her classmates would be coming over to work on their company project. She wondered if Brad would show. If his mother had truly offered the ultimatum he said she had, the woman was probably at her wits' end. Gemma wondered what he enjoyed doing besides listening to whatever he had coming through his earbuds. She couldn't imagine Wyatt or the Herman kids being so disinterested in life that she had to threaten to put them out of her house to force them to make something of their lives. She remembered the joy on the faces of Lucas and Jaz the day she'd taken them to the library and how Lucas had practically hugged the books in the backseat of the car. Then came the sobering thought of how their lives might have turned out had they stayed in Cincinnati. Would there have been books? Would Jaz's love for chess have been fed? Neither Lucas nor Jaz had talked much about their experience with the great-aunt, and Gemma hadn't forced them to, but the bruise on Lucas's face said enough for her to know the stay hadn't been pleasant. According to Bernadine, Ms. Krebs had been fired for lying about having done the background check, and although Gemma didn't want anyone to be without a job, Krebs's single-minded agenda had placed the children in real danger. While

Gemma finished up her last few online foster care classes, the kids would be officially under Bernadine's supervision, but Ms. Frazier said she had no problem with them residing with Gemma until her licensing came through. They'd been moved around enough.

She pulled into the driveway of her home and there was Jaz sitting on the porch sofa reading. Gemma loved Wyatt very much but as Jaz waved and gave her a smile, Gemma had to admit there was something about raising a girl again that filled her heart. She'd never get over losing Gabby, but having Jaz in her life seemed to help balance the pain. Turning off the ignition, she got out and walked up the steps. "Hey there, Miss Jaz."

"Hey there," she replied happily. Closing the book, she came over and hugged her around the waist. "I missed you."

"Missed you, too. Were the boys good?"

"Yeah. Can I ask you something?"

"Sure, go ahead."

"Can I call you Gram, like Wyatt does?"

Gemma looked down into her little face and knew she'd never be able to deny this child anything. "Yes, I think that's an awesome idea."

"You do?"

Gemma nodded and, after receiving another strong hug, she and Jaz went inside.

Two houses away, Jack was listening to Rocky's

tale of How Cousin Helen Met Bernadine and laughing when his phone signaled an incoming text from Trent. After reading it, Jack's confusion showed on his face.

"What's the matter?" Rocky asked.

"Trent wants to know if I'm busy this evening because Dads Inc. is having my bachelor party and I might want to come."

"Guess you should go then."

"I've never had a bachelor party before."

"I never had a bridal shower before the Ladies Auxiliary threw mine, so that makes us even. Did he say where this is all happening?"

"Yes. His basement."

"Forget about strippers then. Not in Lily's house."

He laughed. "Then I think I'll stay home."

"Yeah right." She picked up her helmet. "I need to get back to the Dog for the dinner shift. Go and have a good time. I'll send you a text after we close."

"Okay." Once alone, he texted back his RSVP and a few hours later, made the short walk over to Trent's place.

"So, whose idea was this?" Jack asked as Trent pulled some six-packs from the fridge and loaded them into Jack's arms.

"Mine. It's basically just an excuse for us to get together and drink some cold ones. That okay with you?"

"Perfectly."

"Then follow me. Everyone else is already here."

And downstairs, Trent proved to be right. All the members of Dads Inc. were there and greeted him with waves and smiles while helping themselves to sandwiches, meatballs, chips, brownies, cake, soft drinks for the underage Bobby Douglas, and beer for the rest. Jack had grown to adulthood without many friends, so these men were special. They'd taken him in as one of them, no questions asked, and he'd become comfortable being with them and discussing whatever was on his mind. The others seemed to feel that way, too. As a group, they'd helped Barrett get over himself and learn to give his wife Sheila the love and respect she deserved; raked Reg over the coals for being such a butthead about his wife Roni's resurgent career; and listened to Luis's heartbreaking story of losing his wife in the fire that burned down the Acosta home. Jack didn't know of any other male support groups, but he was glad to be a part of this one.

"So, Jack," Barrett asked, grabbing two ping-pong paddles and tossing one to Bobby, "you sure you're ready to take the plunge back into matrimony?"

"Sure am."

Luis, across the room watching the baseball

game on the big flat-screen, called out, "Bob, let the old Marine live this time, okay?"

Until the arrival of Bobby Douglas, Barrett had ruled Trent's ping-pong table like an Eastern European dictator. Grinning, Bobby took up his position on the other side of the table and replied, "Not a chance. Being humbled is good for the soul. You ready for this whipping, sir?"

"Shut up and play."

Bobby's first volley streaked past Barrett with such speed the former drill sergeant was caught flat-footed.

"That your version of the Mannequin Challenge?" Jack asked.

Trent snorted beer through his nose.

Barrett flashed his best glare but Jack smiled. Yes, he loved Dads Inc. "Think I'll get myself a beer."

For the next little while, they watched Bobby beat Barrett like he stole something, ate more food, and drank more beer. They finally gravitated to the sofa and loveseat near the flat-screen and took seats.

Reg said to Trent, "I hear your Uncle Thad and his Oklahoma clan's here."

"Yes. They got in yesterday and are bunking out at Tamar's. So far, she hasn't had to shoot anybody and Will hasn't arrested any of them, but the visit's still young."

"Any word from Mal?" Luis asked.

He shook his head. Because Henry Adams was such a small town, rumors about the locked-up computer, why Mal might have disappeared, and whether he was in Vegas or not were flying right and left. From the tense set of Trent's jaw it was obviously not a subject he wanted to discuss, so no one pressed him for more.

Gary dipped a chip into the salsa on his plate and directed a question Jack's way. "How many people are invited to the wedding?"

"Too many, as far as Rock and I are concerned, but my mother seems to think half the planet should be in the church." He hadn't told Rocky that she'd called him earlier wanting to add another five people to the guest list. His answer: No.

"Honeymoon?" Barrett asked.

"Yes. New York City. I haven't been there in years, so I'm looking forward to it."

Bobby asked, "Are you getting yourself a bike?"

Jack laughed. "No. We'll remain a one-bike family." Although he had toyed with the idea until he talked himself out of it. Rocky was the adventurous one and he was okay with that.

Luis said, "I think you should get one. The family that rides together stays together."

"Hear! Hear!" they cried out in unison, raising their cans and glasses.

Jack chuckled.

Trent stood. "Since Lily refused to let me get you a stripper, and you don't want a bike, we thought you might like this." He turned to Bobby. "Mr. Douglas, if you would please."

Bobby stood and opened the door to what Jack knew to be a large storage room. He entered and returned pushing a large hand dolly with a huge box strapped to it. Jack stared.

Bobby let the handcart rest on its two wheels but held on to the handles so the weight of the box didn't tip it over.

Gary asked, "You going to go over and see what it is, Teach?"

Taking in their secretive smiles, he got to his feet. The lettering and the large picture on the front brought him up short. Heart pounding, he moved closer. "Oh wow!" He looked back at his friends. "If you're punking me with an empty box I will murder every last one of you."

"Not an empty box," Trent assured him.

It was a telescope but not just any scope. It was a top-of-the-line one every amateur and some professional astronomers dreamed of having. "You guys actually bought this? Do you know how much one of these babies costs?"

"With tax and shipping, about ten grand," Barrett replied. "Sucker weighs almost eighty pounds, too."

Jack was stunned by the thoughtfulness of the gift. They knew how much he loved stargazing.

The telescope, a Meade LX850-ACF, was enough to make a man swoon, but knowing they'd never let him live it down if he did, he pulled himself together. "I don't know what to say."

"Thank you usually works," Reg pointed out, using his fork to spear a meatball on his plate.

Jack dropped his head. Unsure what he'd ever done to deserve such an awesome group of buddies, he eyed the men with wonder and affection, and in a voice thickened with emotion whispered, "Thank you. This is so much better than a stripper."

A chuckling Luis raised his beer can in toast. "Spoken like a true nerd."

"Hear! Hear!"

Later, with Bobby manning the dolly, and all the dads following, the Meade was wheeled out the basement door, around to the driveway, and across the street to Jack's house. It took four of them to lift the dolly safely up the steps to the porch so it could be rolled inside. Jack decided to build it in the living room so the pieces could be spread out and he could work at his leisure, but wasn't sure when that would be due to all the boxes and totes holding Rocky's belongings stacked up everywhere. "Once it's built we'll have a Dads Inc. viewing party," he promised. "I can't thank you all enough. Best gift I've ever received in my life."

"Guess the bachelor party is over," Gary said with a mock pout.

Jack laughed. "Yes, it is. If anyone needs me, I'll be right here."

After sharing manly hugs and offering their congrats on his upcoming marriage, the men filed out. Alone, Jack noted that even if the living room had been clear, he'd had a bit too much beer to try and tackle the build then, but that didn't stop him from grinning at the box and feeling like the luckiest man alive. First Rocky agreed to marry him, and now he had one of the most kick-ass telescopes on the planet. He loved Henry Adams!

Wanting to show Rocky his gift, he took a picture of the box with his phone and was about to hit send when he heard a knock on the screen door. Sending the picture while walking to see who was there, he was surprised by the sight of Helen.

"Hi, Jack," she said through the screen. "Can a girl come in?"

He thought back on the story Rocky had related about Helen being flayed by Bernadine and wondered what she wanted. "Sure." He pushed the door open and she entered.

"Are you moving?" she asked, taking in all the boxes.

"No. Rock's moving in."

Her lips tightened. "I see."

"Have a seat."

She did and she didn't look happy.

"What can I do for you, Helen?"

"I'm flying out in the morning."

He found that good news, but kept his tone even. "I hope your work with Franklin went well."

"Things were fine until Bernadine Brown trashed my company's name. The town board canceled my contract just now."

"Sorry to hear that."

"Their loss, is all I can say."

"I'm sure there will be other opportunities."

"There will be, but maybe not for you."

"Excuse me?"

"After Eva passed away, I waited for you to contact me but you never did. Why?"

He wondered if this was a trick question. "Why would I have contacted you?"

"To take Eva's place in your life. Surely you knew how I felt about you?"

He was suddenly stone-cold sober. Reverend Paula's advice of kindness over rightness came to mind so he tried to be diplomatic. "I did, but I wasn't looking for you to take her place."

"Why not? Eva and I look alike. We were raised the same. Of course, my IQ was much higher."

That sealed it for him. She wasn't owed kindness. "You should drive back to your hotel, Helen. It's been nice seeing you."

"But I don't get it. You knew how I felt, yet you're marrying a woman who calls herself Rocky?"

Jack stood. "Time to go, Helen."

"Fine," she said getting to her feet. "But explain to me why her?"

"I don't owe you an explanation, but I love her. I've never loved you and I never will. Maybe because my IQ isn't high enough."

Anger flashed in her eyes but he ignored it and walked to the front door. He held it open.

"You're making a big mistake," she said. "If you come to your senses, call me."

"Goodbye."

Chin high, she breezed past. He didn't watch her drive away.

CHAPTER
14

O n Monday morning, Bernadine was on the phone with a Los Angeles data recovery firm recommended by Barbie Weaver after her unsuccessful attempts to bypass Mal's new password. After talking with one of the reps and getting all the info she needed, she ended the call and walked down to Lily's office.

"Can they help us?" Lily asked as Bernadine took a seat.

"They say they can. We'll need to ship them the computer, though."

"That shouldn't be a problem. Did they give you a timeline on how long the recovery might take?"

"No. We send it and pray they're as good as the rep I spoke with claims they are."

"Crossing my fingers."

Bernadine had hers crossed as well. Rather than descend into the funk of further worry, she asked, "So, is Tamar ready for August First?" It was a week away.

"I spoke with her last night. She says she is. Gary has the meat, chips, and the rest of the food and paper products on order. Clay and Bing are adding their grills to the ones Uncle Thad's

301

crew brought along. Trent said he and the dads will dig the horseshoe pits later this week. Not sure what other kind of activities we're having, though. I should know in a day or two. I figure the kids will want to be at the pool most of the time, regardless of what's planned."

Bernadine agreed. Most of the kids were back. Roni and Zoey were presently in Paris and would be heading home after concerts there. Griffin was on his way to Pine Ridge to pick up Amari. They were scheduled to return later in the day.

Lily searched her face. "How are you holding up?"

"I'm okay if I don't think about it." It was difficult not to, though. "Hoping once we get some answers from the Dog's desktop I'll be better."

"I think we'll all be."

"On a happier note, the Millers signed the contract for their coffee shop."

"That's great."

Bernadine gave her the details, adding, "They'll be taking one of the apartments upstairs, too." She also let her in on Tina Craig's interesting phone call.

Lily voiced her surprise. "Tina wants to move here?"

"She says she does, and I've never known her to propose something she isn't serious about."

"A bed and breakfast might do well here."

"I think so, too."

"A lot happened while Trent and I were away."

"Yes, indeed. Mal. The Herman kids. Luis shutting down the Dog. Me sending Jack's cousin Helen packing—which Rocky greatly appreciated. And Will's wife, Vicky, has gone into hospice." Bernadine took in Lily's stricken face and nodded sadly. "I talked to him last night. He said she's tired of fighting." Vicky Dalton had been battling ovarian cancer for the past few years.

"That's so terrible. Poor Vicky. Does Will need anything? Food? We can bring over some dishes he can freeze and microwave."

"I asked, he said no. Just our prayers. He told me he and Vicky have been together since elementary school."

"And now he's going to lose her."

"Yes." The Daltons weren't churchgoers but Reverend Paula was offering the family what support she could.

"I'm so sorry to hear this. I thought she had it licked after the last round of chemo. Her hair was growing back and everything."

"I know." Everyone had been glad to see her out and about this past spring, but now it appeared as if she'd be gone before autumn.

"I hope Will knows we're here for him and his kids."

"He does." Bernadine stood. "I'm supposed to be meeting with PI Sandy Langster in a few minutes. Hoping she'll be able to find out where Mal is. If the tech firm can't unlock that computer, we'll need him back here whether he wants to be or not."

Her meeting with Sandy didn't take long. The lady detective took the case and let Bernadine know she wanted to lease the office space at the refurbed hotel. Bernadine handed her a lease, and a check to retain her services in the Mal matter.

"I'll keep you posted," Sandy promised and exited the office.

Sitting there alone, Bernadine thought about all that was going on. The past seven days had been an emotional roller coaster. Her thoughts moved to Mal, but she set them aside because it only added to her heartache.

Over the next few days, Henry Adams prepared for August First. The horseshoe pits were dug, the foodstuffs began arriving, and Lily took suggestions for the games and other activities people wanted to participate in. To make room for the gathering on Tamar's land, the tents of the visiting Julys were relocated and set up down near the creek. Tamar was seated on the porch with her brother and Eula watching the move. So far, none of the Julys had been arrested for anything, and she hoped the good behavior held.

"I think I want to add Little Brother of War to our August First wang-dang doodle," Thad said.

"Why?" Tamar asked.

"To pay tribute to Eula. Back in the day, the chiefs would sometimes ask for a game on their deathbeds."

Eula, who appeared frailer than she had upon arriving last week, smiled. "That might be fun."

Tamar mulled over the idea of adding the ball game Americans knew as lacrosse to the day. "Are you going to play against each other or against a Henry Adams team?"

"Against a Henry Adams team, but we'll put Griffin and some of the other Julys with your people. Last time we played here you all took a pretty good licking."

It had been a football game held a few days before Trent and Lily's wedding.

"Have you run this by Trent?" she asked.

"Not yet, wanted to talk to you about it first, seeing as you're the matriarch."

"I appreciate the respect." And she did.

He gave her a slight nod.

Tamar made her decision. "Since Eula likes the idea, I do, too. I'm assuming you have enough sticks?"

"We do. We always travel with extras in case a game breaks out and somebody has left theirs at home."

"Might be nice for the kids to learn the history behind the game, too," Tamar said, thinking out loud. "Do you want to do the honors?"

"I'd love to. Be a nice way for me to get to know the ones that weren't here the last time I visited."

"Then we're agreed."

Eula said, "Thanks, Thad. Never had anything done in my memory before."

"You need to be honored, Eula. It's what family's supposed to do. That old saying about giving you your roses while you're living is true. You can't appreciate them if you've passed on." Neither he nor Tamar mentioned that it might be their last chance to make her feel special.

Eula asked, "Tam, have you talked with Julia about the two of us speaking?"

"I have. She said she has to think about it, and will let me know."

Sadness dimmed Eula's face and Tamar felt bad for her. A reconciliation between the cousins was warranted, but Julia carried a large helping of the July stubbornness gene.

Thad reached out and patted Eula's thin hand. "Don't worry, Eula. You'll get your talk. Julia will do what's right."

"I hope so," she whispered. "I don't want to die with this guilt on my soul."

Tamar shared that hope.

Eula struggled to her feet. "I think I'm going to lie down for a while. Will you wake me in a few hours, Tam?"

"Will do. Do you need any help?"

She shook her head. "I can manage."

Watching her slowly make her way inside, Tamar wished they'd had their own reconciliation earlier in life so they could have enjoyed the passing years. In the days since her arrival, Tamar learned not only why Eula had been so standoffish growing up, but that her cousin played a mean game of dominos, loved Prince, and, like their nineteenth-century ancestors, still voted Republican.

"How long are the docs giving her?" Thad asked once she'd gone inside.

"Not very."

"Sad."

"I know. She said First Tamar sent her here."

He didn't seem surprised by that. "You two getting along?"

"We are. I was put out at first, but admitting this wasn't about me fixed things."

"Good. So, have you heard anything from my nephew?"

A different type of sadness tugged at her heart. "No and I don't think we will, at least not until he's ready."

"I know he's not a child anymore, but I worry about him."

"I do, too. Bernadine shipped the computer to Los Angeles, so hopefully we'll know something about that at least, soon."

"We may have outlaws in our family, but I refuse to believe he's been embezzling."

"I do too but . . ." She looked out to see the last tent being moved. The land was now a wide-open field again. She turned back to her brother and noted how much he resembled their father, Trenton. "I don't know what I'll do if it turns out that he has."

"You'll deal with it like you've dealt with every other storm in your life. Fearlessly."

"After someone puts smelling salts under my nose to wake me up."

He smiled.

She thought back on Mal playing in that same field as a child and the awful years when alcohol ruled his life. "Mal may be many things, but he isn't a thief."

"Then hold on to that, Tam, and let it give you strength. The answers will come."

"Since when did you become so wise?"

"Always have been. You've just been too mad at me to appreciate it."

And once again, the past and her disastrous relationship with Joel Newton rose between them. "Why didn't you tell me the truth about him?"

"As I told you before, I didn't know how. I

really didn't. You were so in love and he swore to me he'd gotten divorced, but that's no excuse for remaining silent. Every time I look out at that field, I remember that day: the bower with all those flowers, the tables filled with people. You may never forgive me, but the hurt on your face when his wife stood up is something I'll take to the grave."

"Sixty-five years later, it still hurts."

"I know, Tammy. I know. That I played a part in it still hurts me, too."

And for the first time, she believed him. They'd had a similar conversation during his last visit but this time his words and feelings resonated with a clarity that hadn't touched her before. Maybe he was right. Maybe she'd still been too angry.

His voice sincere, he continued, "Aunt Teresa was the last of the original Julys, and you and I are the only ones left who knew her. That means something, or at least it should."

"It does." It made them the last living links to the family's past and purpose.

"Then can I please spend what time we have left as your brother again?"

Growing up he'd been her friend, protector, and confidante, but for the past sixty years, even though he'd remained in her heart, he'd been her bane. It needed to stop. She nodded with a sincerity of her own. "Yes."

He closed his eyes in relief and held out his hand. "Pax?"

She took it and squeezed gently. "Pax."

"Thank you," he whispered. "Now, how about you get us a couple of glasses and we drink some home brew to celebrate a new beginning."

She stood and went inside.

Sheila Payne had graciously volunteered to be Jack and Rocky's wedding planner, and for the past few days, had been hounding Rocky about the need to meet. After the third pleading text today, Rock called Siz and Crystal into the Dog's office.

"If I don't go talk with Sheila Payne about this wedding," said Rock, "she's going to hurt me."

Crystal and Siz exchanged smiles. Rocky knew the idea of Sheila harming anyone was amusing; she was one of the most even-tempered persons in town. However, her threatening to throw up her hands and quit got Rock's attention. "Siz, you're in charge of the kitchen. Crys, keep an eye on the floor and handle the cash register." Both had taken on the duties before, so she knew the place would still be standing when she returned.

Crystal said, "We close in another two hours. How about you just go home when you're done with Mrs. Payne. You've been working nonstop since Mal left."

Crystal was right about the hours she'd been putting in, but Rocky wasn't sure about taking the advice. She was confident about their ability to steer the ship for a short time but she was co-owner; the place was her responsibility and she took that seriously.

Sensing her hesitation, Siz said, "Go. Handle your business and we'll see you tomorrow. We can take care of things here and close up."

"But, I need—"

Crystal cut her off. "Bye, Rock." She made shooing gestures with her hands.

Rock dropped her head and surrendered. "Okay."

Swallowing her guilt over not being on-site when the Dog closed later, she shouldered her purse and left to meet with Sheila at the church. It was a short walk, and on the way, she had to admit it felt good to be away from the chaotic hustle and bustle of the diner. Her breathing slowed, heart rate too, she guessed, and even though it was hot as Hades, the heat was a perfect antidote to being stuck in air-conditioning since dawn.

Reaching the church, she pulled open the door and was met by the coolness of the air. She found Sheila in Reverend Paula's office.

"No Paula?" Rocky asked, taking a seat.

"No. She got a call from Will's daughter over at the hospice place. I think Vicky's time is close."

Rocky was sorry to hear that and hoped her transition was an easy one.

"Thanks for coming," Sheila said.

"Can't have you quitting on me. Sorry getting with you took so long."

"No problem. I know this whole Mal thing has you going. Anything new?"

She shook her head. She'd contacted everyone she knew with a connection to him, from the members of his AA group to some of his old lady loves. No one had heard a word. "So, what do you need from me?"

They spent the better part of an hour talking about guest lists, RSVPs, seating arrangements for the ceremony and for the reception at the Dog, before moving on to what kind of flowers Rocky preferred on the altar, and had she asked Roni to sing. "I talked with her about it before she went on tour."

"Do you know what you'd like for her to sing?"

"No."

"Get with her then and let me know."

Rocky had no idea what constituted wedding music. She wanted to ask Sheila to take care of it, but seeing as how Sheila was handling everything else, asking her to add that to her already long list of duties didn't seem fair. So, she kept her mouth shut and would rely on Roni's help to select something appropriate.

Their phones went off simultaneously with

alerts for incoming texts, and they laughed at the coincidence. Sheila glanced at her phone's face. "Is yours a summons from Tamar?"

"Yes. Looks like the whole town has been tagged. Prep for August First."

Setting the phones aside, they returned to the wedding plans.

Once they were done, Rocky said, "Thanks so much, Sheila. You're a lifesaver."

"I love doing this kind of stuff."

"I'm glad you do, believe me."

They stood in preparation for leaving. "I'll see you at Tamar's."

Rocky said, "See you there."

Leaving the church, Rocky was tempted to go back to the diner but, having been told to take the rest of the day off, she bit the bullet, walked back to the parking lot for her truck, and drove home. She still had a few more boxes to take to Jack's place so the free time gave her the opportunity to take care of that. Once that was done, and Jack came home from class, they could go to Tamar's.

After bringing in the last box, she set it down in the living room and took in the wealth of the rest of the stacked boxes, plastic totes, and suitcases holding her possessions. It was official. She was embarking on a new life. Admittedly, it was still somewhat scary but the small fear was dwarfed by the comforting knowledge of who she'd be sharing her new life with.

Hearing footsteps she looked up to see Eli coming down the stairs. "Hey, Rock."

"Hey you."

"That the last of your stuff?" he asked, indicating the box at her feet.

"Yes. The trailer is now almost as bare as Old Mother Hubbard's cupboard."

"Who?"

She laughed and waved him off. "Never mind. Are you packed?"

"I am." His classes started next week, so he'd be flying out to California in the morning.

"I'll miss you."

"Miss you, too."

"Thanks for being such a rock at the Dog this year."

"Thanks for helping me grow up."

"Really?"

He nodded. "Didn't like you at all when we first met, though."

"You weren't very charming back then."

"I know. That first day when you started calling me Oscar the Grouch, I didn't know what I hated more, you or the nickname." He added, "No offense."

"None taken. I was hard on you."

"You and everybody else here."

"That's how we roll."

"Lucky for me."

Rocky loved this new matured version of the angry, heartbroken teen brat he'd been back then.

"Do you know when I changed how I felt about you?"

"No, when?"

"The night Dad wrecked his car and you went to pick him up from the ER in Hays."

Rocky remembered that night as the beginning of her relationship with his father. Thinking back, she realized she was already half in love with him but was too scared to acknowledge her feelings.

Eli continued, "I figured he must have been special to you if you were willing to drive all that way in the middle of the night. It kind of made me rethink who you were."

"I'm glad, and he is special. Not many men would be willing to take on a woman like myself, but he didn't seem to be bothered by it."

"I'm glad you two are getting married."

"Why?"

"Because I can stop worrying about him."

"What do you mean?"

"Now that I've grown up a little, I realize just how sad he was after my mom died. He probably didn't get the chance to grieve like maybe he was supposed to because he had to deal with me and all the stupid crap I was doing. He wasn't happy. You made him smile again, Rock, and you'll always have my thanks for that."

Rocky's heart swelled with emotion. She'd been so focused on the many ways Jack had saved her, she hadn't given much thought to the idea of her having saved him. "Come here."

He gave her the side-eye for a moment but complied.

"Now, bend down," she said softly. When he did, she placed a kiss on his forehead. "Thank you."

"For what?"

"For wanting your dad to be happy."

"He deserves it."

"I think so, too."

Flashing her a grin that was a younger version of his dad's, he said, "Now that we've had our mushy moment, how about you tell me which boxes you want upstairs."

Working together they managed to clear out most of the living room. When they were done, Eli left to go and wait for Crystal to get off work so they could hang out.

A short while later, Rocky was in the kitchen making space in the cabinets for all her pots and pans when she heard Jack come in and say, "Whoa! I have my living room back."

She called out, "Do you like?"

"I like very much."

He entered the kitchen. "Hello, lovely lady, are you my new French maid?"

She chuckled.

He came up behind her, linked his arms loosely around her waist, and placed a soft kiss on her neck. "I think I'll buy you one of those skimpy little maid outfits so we can act out a novel I'm going to write."

Laughing, she asked, "What's the title?"

"The Professor and the French Maid, of course."

"Right. Now that the living room's clear you're going to be so focused on building that monster telescope, I could walk around in my birthday suit and you'd never even look up."

"I dare you."

She turned in the circle of his arms and faced him. "You need a keeper."

"That's why I have you."

She studied him and hoped they'd have this much fun until death did them part. "Would it be okay if I bought Eli a truck?"

His brow furrowed. "Why?"

"Because he's as special and as dear to me as his dad."

"My Eli? Oscar the Grouch? The kid who's eating me out of house and home?"

She playfully hit him on the arm. "Stop that, but yes, your Eli. Our Eli."

Jack shrugged. "I guess, but he's going to want

317

to take it to California and I'm not comfortable with him driving across country."

"How about I find him one online? Trent's mom Rita Lynn and her husband Paul can go with him to pick it up." Eli would be staying with them while attending school in California.

"That would work. So, what do I get for agreeing to Eli's boon?"

"Boon? Who talks like that?"

"Quit hating on my vocabulary and tell me, woman."

She answered coyly, "I could find a French maid outfit online. That a nice enough *boon?*"

His responding grin ignited one of her own.

Down the street, Lucas and Wyatt were on kitchen cleanup. Wyatt washed the dinner dishes while Lucas dried. As they worked, they talked about the invitation everyone had received from Tamar.

"Why does she want everyone to come to her house?" Lucas asked, drying a plate. He thought about the plate he'd dropped back in Cincinnati and the punishment he'd received from Evil Aunt Wanda, but put it out of his mind.

"Not sure. Gram just said we were going. Could be something fun. Could be work." He placed the casserole dish he'd washed and rinsed into the dish drain. "I'm hoping Zoey is there, though."

"She the girl with the singer mom who was in South Africa? The one with the gold coins?"

"Yeah. I'm crushing on her."

Lucas paused mid-dry. "Really?"

"Big time. She doesn't know it yet, but we're getting married when we get older."

Lucas's mouth dropped. He'd liked a few girls back when he lived with his parents but he'd never thought about marrying any of them. He wondered if it was because Wyatt was twelve and he was only ten.

Wyatt rinsed a glass and placed it in the drain. "She and her mom flew home last night and she sent me a text when they got here."

"Does she like you?"

Wyatt shrugged. "I think so."

"You think so," Lucas echoed dubiously.

"Yeah, I'm pretty sure she does."

Lucas thought you had to be real sure whether a girl liked you back if you were going to marry her someday. He wanted to ask Wyatt more about that, but didn't think they knew each other well enough yet. Rather than risk making him mad, Lucas kept his misgivings to himself and picked up some forks to dry.

When they arrived at Tamar's house, Lucas hadn't expected to find that she lived in the country. Open land surrounded the place as far as he could see. Getting out of the car, he eyed all the cars, motorcycles, Jeeps, and the big silver RV parked out front. He was surprised to see a bunch of tents off in the distance and to hear drums. This being his first time visiting he asked Ms. Gemma, "Are the tents here all the time?"

"No. They belong to Tamar's relatives. They're visiting."

"Are they playing the drums, too?"

"I think so."

He and Jaz followed Ms. Gemma and Wyatt to the house. There were picnic tables spread over the yard with laughing and talking adults seated t them. He saw Ms. Brown, Uncle T.C., Doc Reg, and many others he'd met at the Dog but whose names he didn't remember. Because some of them were playing cards and others dominos, he thought maybe they'd been invited to have fun.

"Our crew's over there," Wyatt said. "See you Gram."

"See you."

She headed for the adults and Wyatt led Lucas and Jaz over to a white picnic table where the kids were. The kids greeted them with smiles and made room for them to claim seats. The only unfamiliar face belonged to a short dark-haired girl sitting next to Amari. Judging by the smile she gave Wyatt, Lucas guessed her to be Zoey. The quick introduction that followed proved him correct.

"How was South Africa?" Wyatt asked from his seat across from her.

"Awesome. Awesome. Awesome. The next time Mama Roni and I go, I'll ask if you can go with us."

"Nice," Wyatt said.

Lucas noted her southern accent and wondered where she was from, and if she'd been in foster care too at some point in her life.

Brain asked, "Anyone want something to drink?"

Everyone said yes, so he and Leah got up and walked over to a table holding munchies and drinks. While the Acosta kids talked about their trip to Mexico, Lucas found himself taking in the gathering and listening to the faint beat of the drumming. The entire scene brought to mind again how different Henry Adams was from every other place he'd been. It wasn't anything like the subdivision he'd lived in growing up, or the cities he'd traveled to with his parents, or the ones he lived in as a foster kid. But he liked how relaxed everything seemed to be and was glad he and Jaz were back.

Brain and Leah returned with cups of grape Kool-Aid, paper plates, and two large mixing bowls filled with chips and pretzels. Everybody helped themselves. Amari was telling everybody about riding back from South Dakota on the back of his bio dad's motorcycle when Tamar walked over. Lucas doubted he'd ever forget the way she'd verbally smacked around Ms. Krebs that day in Ms. Brown's office. He also reminded himself to avoid getting on her bad side at all costs. Accompanying Tamar was an older man in a motorized wheelchair. He had two long gray braids hanging from beneath an awesome-looking white cowboy hat.

"Hey, youngins," he said.

The kids laughed. "Hey, Uncle Thad."

Tamar turned to Lucas and Jasmine. "Lucas and Jasmine Herman, I want you to meet my brother, Thaddeus July."

They greeted him respectfully.

He replied, "I hear you're my sister's newest pups. Welcome to the family."

"Thank you, sir," Lucas and Jaz said in unison.

A grinning Devon asked, "Uncle Thad, are you going to mess with Tamar's truck before you leave?"

Amari's mouth dropped and he stared at his little brother as if he'd lost his mind. Preston, warily eyeing Tamar, moved to the far side of the table, which left Devon sitting by himself. Lucas had no idea what was happening but the look in Tamar's eyes pinned Devon to his seat. In response, Devon appeared to shrink, giving the impression that he probably shouldn't have asked that question. Lucas made a mental note to find out later from Wyatt what this all meant.

But Uncle Thad was grinning and said, "I'll let you know, Dev."

Tamar smacked her brother on the back of his head and sent his white hat flying before she whirled and marched off. Leah caught the hat before it reached the ground and handed it back.

"Good hands, Leah," Thad said.

"Thanks."

Uncle Thad put his hat back on over the two long gray braids and said, "Sisters are a pain."

Jaz, hand on hip, said, "Hey!"

Everyone laughed at that.

Uncle Thad turned his twinkling dark eyes on her. "Do you know the significance of August First, Ms. Jasmine?"

"Does it have anything to do with knocking your brother's hat off?"

He laughed. "No, but you're quick. I like that. You could grow up and take Tamar's place around here." He turned to Amari. "Would you give the Lady Jasmine a quick rundown."

So, Lucas and Jaz listened and learned that England freed their slaves in the West Indies on August 1, 1834. In commemoration, abolitionists in the United States began celebrating the date with picnics, parades, and speeches.

"They hoped the US would get the message and free its slaves, too," Amari explained. "And after Emancipation here in the States, some places like Henry Adams kept the celebrations going."

Brain added, "You should've seen the August First parade Amari and I put together a few years ago. It was pretty awesome."

Jasmine looked confused. "But August first isn't until Monday. Why's everybody here today?"

Uncle Thad said, "To iron out the last few details of the picnic we're planning, and to pick teams for what the Native people call Little Brother of War."

Tiff asked, "Which is what?"

"The game known to Americans and the Europeans as lacrosse."

Everyone looked surprised.

Leah asked, "Why'd the Natives give it that name?"

"Because sometimes the tribes back east used the game instead of wars to settle disputes with other tribes over territorial boundaries, personal disagreements, things like that. Some chiefs called for games on their deathbeds as a means of tribute, which is why we're going to play. Our cousin Eula may be passing on soon, so we'll play to honor her."

Even though he looked sad about that, Uncle Thad turned out to be a lot of fun. He went on to tell them the Cherokee myth behind how the game of lacrosse began. "According to legend it comes from an incident known as How the Bat Got Its Wings. Picture this: land animals against the birds of the air. On the land team are bears, deer, and turtles. The winged team members are birds led by the hawk and the eagle. After the teams were set and ready to get started two little furry guys show up wanting to play, but the land animals said, 'You're too small. Beat it.'"

"That's rude," Zoey declared, looking outraged.

Uncle Thad chuckled. "Real rude. But the winged team took pity on the newcomers and said they could be on their team."

"Nice," Brain said. "When I was little, kids would tell me I was too fat to play, so mad love for the wings."

Amari grinned and Preston did, too.

Lucas was enjoying himself.

"But there was a problem," Uncle Thad said, continuing. "For the little furries to play on the bird team they had to be able to fly. They were land animals, remember, and didn't have wings."

"Oh, that's right," Alfonso Acosta said.

Alfonso's sister, Maria, asked, "So, what did they do?"

"The birds found some groundhog leather left over from the making of a drum head and they attached it to one of the little guys and changed his name to Tlameha."

Leah asked, "Which means?"

"Bat."

Everyone smiled.

"But there wasn't enough leather left to fix the second little furry, so you know what they did?" He glanced around at their rapt faces and when no one answered, said, "The eagle got on one side of the little furry and the hawk got on the other and they pulled his skin until he stretched."

"What?" Devon voiced skeptically. "You can't stretch somebody like that."

Amari snapped, "Dev. It's a myth. Just go with it. Okay? Jeez."

Uncle Thad chuckled softly, "Thanks, Amari. So anyway, they stretched him and changed his name to Tewa—the flying squirrel."

"Yes!" Brain cried.

Wyatt and Alfonso shared a high five.

Tiff said, "I love this story."

Jaz asked, "So who won the game?"

"Picture this," he said again. "The ball is tossed up. The flying squirrel, on the ground repping the wings, grabs it and runs it up the tree to his crew. The birds start flying the ball to the goal, but they drop it. Before it hits the ground, here come Tlameha, the bat. He dives out of the sky at warp speed, grabs the ball by his teeth and takes off toward the goal. He's dipping and dodging so wildly not even the fastest deer can catch him. He finally makes it to the goal, throws the ball in and scores!"

The kids' cheers drew smiling glances from the adults seated nearby.

Uncle Thad ended the story by saying, "And for many years it was traditional for players of the game to weave a piece of bat wing into the webbing of their lacrosse sticks for good luck."

Lucas knew he'd remember the story for a long time. Yes, he liked living in Henry Adams very much.

Amari asked, "So, who's going to be playing Little Brother of War for August First."

"It'll be my guys against Henry Adams," Uncle Thad said.

Leah groaned, "So you can kick our butts like the last time we played?"

"As I remember, you scored two touchdowns."

"Our only two touchdowns."

Amari said, "Yeah. We got slaughtered. 56–14."

"This time we're going to put both your dads on your town's team, Amari, and some of my boys will play for you, too."

"That might help," Tiff said. She turned to Jaz, Maria, and Zoey. "You want to be cheerleaders with me?"

Jaz replied with an excited "Yes!"

Maria did, too.

Zoey shook her head. "I want to play on the

team." She looked at the boys. "And don't tell me I can't."

Amari said, "No one's going to argue with ou, Zo. We'll need all the help we can get."

She folded her arms. "Good."

They were momentarily distracted by the sound of a motorcycle. A guy with dark skin and a long braid down his back got off, and there was a girl in a halter top and short shorts seated on the back.

Amari asked, "Is that cousin Diego?"

Preston replied, "Looks like it. Crystal's going to flip."

Once again, Lucas had no idea what that meant and wondered how long it would take to learn all the different personalities tied to the town. He hoped it would be quickly. Wyatt was right. Henry Adams did feel like a big family and Lucas wanted to be a full-fledged member.

He set his curiosity aside, and, with the others, followed Uncle Thad over to where the adults were gathered. The picking of the teams began. Griffin and Trent stepped forward as co-captains of the Henry Adams team. The Oklahoma Julys began arguing over who'd be their captain until Thad picked the newly arrived Diego, which set off more arguing. When Tamar stood up and threatened to end the fuss with a blast from her shotgun, they quickly deferred to their patriarch's choice.

A standard lacrosse game called for ten players. The Henry Adams team, after fielding all the boys, Zoey, Leah, the members of Dads Inc., Griffin July, and three of his cousins, topped out with sixteen members. The Julys went with eight.

Diego said, "We could probably whip you with five, but we'll go with eight."

The townspeople booed him and good-naturedly threw empty paper cups. Ducking, he grinned.

It was dark when Ms. Gemma pulled into the driveway. Lucas, Wyatt, and Jaz went to their respective rooms, took their showers and got into their sleepwear. Lucas had finished the two Harry Potter books he'd borrowed from the library. Wanting to know when they could make another trip so he could get more he went downstairs and found Ms. Gemma alone in the kitchen making her lunch for the next day.

"Hey, Lucas. Did you have a good time at Tamar's?"

"I did. I really like the people here."

"I do, too. It's a pretty special place."

"Can we go back to the library?"

"Sure. I have class tomorrow night but we can go Saturday morning if you want. Need more books?"

"I do."

She placed her now finished sandwich in a ziplock bag. As she stuck it in the fridge, she said, "When you get older, we'll see about setting you up an online account with one of the book sites so you can order what you want—with my approval of course."

He grinned. "Of course."

For a few moments, she didn't say anything else, just looked at him. He could tell she had something she wanted to say, but he wasn't sure what.

"Lucas, I know I told you this when we were at the airport in Cincinnati, but I'm really glad to have you and your sister back."

"We're glad to be back." His mind revisited the few short days he'd been with Aunt Wanda. The memories were still raw. "It felt like we were gone a million years."

"I'm sorry she was mean to you."

He was, too. "Mr. Gladwin said our parents left us a lot of money."

"They did."

"Can we buy you and Wyatt something?"

"That isn't necessary."

"But suppose I want to? To say thank you."

"You can thank me by doing good in school, always looking out for Jaz, and growing up to be the awesome young man your mom and dad wanted you to be. I don't need anything more than that, Lucas."

He nodded. "Has Wyatt ever been to Disney World?"

"No."

"Jaz and I used to go once a year. Can we take him so he can catch up?"

She didn't respond at first, but seeing the tears shining in her eyes made him feel terrible. "I'm sorry. You just told me no. I won't ask about stuff like that again. Please don't cry."

"No, honey. You didn't do anything wrong. I got teary because you have such a big heart." She tore a piece of paper towel from the roll and wiped her eyes.

Lucas said, "Wyatt and I are going to be like brothers, I think, so I just want him to get to do some of the stuff Jaz and I got to do. Do you think we can go to Australia too, maybe next year?"

She stared and laughed. "Australia? How about we see about Disney first, okay?"

He laughed, too. "Okay." When he left the kitchen, she was still wiping her eyes and he felt good.

CHAPTER
15

The next day, Gemma was scheduled to work the ten-to-four midday shift, so after breakfast, she left the kids watching a *Dexter's Laboratory* cartoon marathon and headed out the door. She'd gone to bed thinking about Lucas asking about Australia, and the over-the-top request made her smile again. Thinking about that helped take her mind off her impending interview for the assistant manager's job, scheduled for after work. She was determined to give it her best shot and told herself there was nothing to be apprehensive about but she was.

As she approached her car in the driveway, she stopped. For some reason the gray Taurus looked off balance. Not sure what was going on with it, she walked closer and her knees turned to jelly. All four tires were flat. *How could that be?* She took a slow tour around the vehicle.

"Hey, Gemma? Everything okay?"

She looked up. Across the street, Trent was coming down his steps, probably on his way to work, too. "Could you come look at my tires, please?" she called, still puzzled.

He came over. After hunkering down by the tire on the front passenger side, he looked up with concern. "Hate to tell you this, but this one's been slashed."

"What!"

He inspected the other three and found them all vandalized.

"Who'd want to slash your tires, Gem?"

"I have no idea." And truthfully, she didn't.

Colonel Payne lived next door and he came over to see what was going on just as her kids stepped out onto the porch.

Wyatt asked, "Something wrong with the car, Gram?"

"Just some flat tires," she explained, not wanting to make a big deal of this and have them worry. "I must've run over something. You guys go on back in the house."

They obeyed, albeit reluctantly.

Trent said to her, "I have some tires at the shop that might fit. If not, I'll run over to Franklin and pick up some new ones for you."

"Thanks, Trent." He left, and a few minutes later, she saw him driving away in his truck.

The colonel was on his phone. When he ended the call, he said to her, "Just talked to Gary. He said come in when you can. I also spoke with dispatch over at the sheriff's office. They'll send someone out as soon as they can. I'll stay with you until then if you want."

"I'd appreciate it." She'd been too shocked to think about calling the sheriff, but of course she needed to file a police report. Tires didn't slash themselves.

Barrett asked, "Do you think Alma may have done this?"

"I don't know. I hope not."

"Any other enemies?"

"None that I know of." She supposed Alma could be classified as an enemy, but Gemma had no idea who else might be upset with her enough to warrant this level of retaliation.

Concern on his face, Barrett cast a critical eye around at the houses on their street. "The only place in town not wired for security is our neighborhood. We'll get started on changing that today."

Gemma was outdone. Who hated her enough to slash her tires? Was she in personal danger? Were her kids? There were no answers, but she hoped there would be soon. If the person or persons responsible intended to scare her, they'd done their job.

A few minutes later, a brown county sheriff's car arrived. By then, she and the colonel had been joined by his wife, Sheila, and Roni and Doc Reg Garland. Across the street, Brain, Zoey, and Amari were watching from Trent's front steps. When Will Dalton stepped out of the cruiser accompanied by Deputy Davida Ransom, Gemma was surprised to see him. A town-wide text had gone out last night alerting everyone to Vicky Dalton's passing. When he walked up, there was weariness in his face and an abject sadness in his red-rimmed eyes.

"Morning, everybody."

They replied and offered their condolences.

"Thanks. I had to come to work to keep from losing my mind. The kids and I will let you know when the arrangements are finalized."

Gemma noticed her kids were back on the porch. So much for keeping this from them.

"Okay, Ms. Dahl, tell me what's going on here."

Deputy Ransom took pictures of the car and tires while Will asked her questions that echoed those put to her by the colonel: Did she know who might have done this? Did she have any enemies? She gave him the same answers she'd given Barrett.

"Have you ever been threatened by a customer?"

"No."

"Is there anyone you don't get along with or who doesn't get along with you at your job?" Dalton asked as he made notes in a small spiral-bound notebook.

She met Barrett's eyes and he gave her an encouraging nod. Seeing the kids still looking on, she asked Will quietly, "Can we move down the driveway a bit? I'd rather my kids not hear this."

They moved a few feet away and once there, not knowing how her neighbors would react, she drew in a deep breath and told Dalton about Alma and why the woman was so hostile. When she finished, Sheila rubbed her back gently. "This Owen Welke was obviously a louse to prey on a teenager."

"Amen," Roni chimed in softly. "None of us think less of you."

Their support was buoying.

Will said, "I'm going to question Ms. House and talk to Gary, too. We'll do our best to get to the bottom of this. Promise."

"Thanks, Sheriff."

"I'll be in touch."

Everyone offered their condolences again. He and Davida drove away.

Moments later, Trent returned with four new tires. Once he and Barrett put them on, Gemma asked, "How much do I owe you?"

"We'll talk about it later."

"Trent?"

"Later, Gem. No need to worry about that now."

She looked back at her kids. They weren't babies. She owed them an explanation.

Sheila interrupted her thoughts. "The kids can hang with me and the ladies at the rec today. I know you don't want them home alone."

And she didn't. Under normal circumstances, they'd be okay at home alone. Wyatt was twelve and very responsible. If anything happened, she and every other adult in town were only a text away. This wasn't a normal circumstance, however, and she'd feel better knowing they were being looked after at the rec. "Thanks, Sheila. I really appreciate the offer."

Sheila said, "Tell them to come knock on my door when they're ready and have them bring their suits so they can hang out at the pool."

Roni asked, "Anything you need from me or Reg before we take off?"

She couldn't think of anything.

Reg said, "If you do, send a text, I'll be in my office at the school."

Roni said, "And I'll be at the studio."

Grateful again for the cocoon of love and safety Henry Adams offered, Gemma thanked them and Barrett and walked back to the porch. The kids followed her inside.

"But why would somebody do that?" Wyatt asked angrily, once Gemma explained about the tires.

"I don't know, but Sheriff Dalton will find out."

Jaz said, "That's so mean."

"I agree."

"We have to go to the rec?" Lucas asked.

He'd learned to hide his emotions so well, Gemma couldn't tell if it was a complaint or not. "Yes, so go get dressed. Mrs. Payne is waiting on you."

But they stayed and Wyatt acted as their spokesman. "We want to go to the store with you."

She assessed the three determined young faces. "You can't."

"Why not?" Jaz asked.

"Because there's no place there for you to hang out."

Lucas explained, "We don't want to hang out. We want to be with you in case something happens."

She paused and studied them. They were determined but she sensed their fear as well. They'd each suffered a life-changing loss. She assumed they were afraid of losing her too, which made her want to pull all three into her arms and offer what reassurance she could. "Thank you for wanting to protect me, but I'll be safe. Brain's dad's there and he's not going to let anything happen to me. He can see the entire store from his computers."

"What if he doesn't see the person, though?" Wyatt asked.

"He will. Besides, whoever slashed my tires is probably satisfied they scared me and are done with me now."

Lucas wasn't buying it. "What if they're not? What if they come back and try and kill you or something?"

"I don't know Lucas, but that's why we have Sheriff Dalton on our side. I can't let this paralyze me and make me so scared I can't leave the house, otherwise whoever did this will have won, and I refuse to let them think that. So, go get dressed. We got this."

They looked at each other and then back at her.

"Go on," she encouraged softly. Once she was alone she cursed the person responsible, not for scaring her, but for scaring her kids.

The sheriff's cruiser was sitting outside the store when she turned into the parking lot. Will hadn't wasted time starting his investigation and she was pleased by that. Alma would undoubtedly throw a fit about being questioned but Gemma didn't care. Scaring her kids meant all bets were off and she hoped Alma had sense enough not to get in her face about it or try and write her up for being late to work.

There weren't many customers inside. She gave a quick wave to the co-workers she passed on her way to clock in and wondered if they knew why the sheriff was on-site. If not, they would soon and she braced herself for all the questions sure to come her way.

She'd been on her register about thirty minutes, when the phone rang at her station. She picked up. It was Alma. "A sub is coming to relieve you. When she arrives come to my office, immediately!" The last word was spoken with a snarl.

"What's this about?"

The line was dead.

Wishing she could ignore the summons, but knowing she couldn't, Gemma turned her lane over to the sub, a college student named Emily, and headed for Alma's office.

Inside, she found Alma seated at her desk. A thin, brown-haired woman Gemma didn't recognize was seated in one of the chairs.

Alma snapped, "How dare you sic the sheriff on me!"

"And how dare someone slash my tires and have my kids scared to death that someone's going to kill me! Dalton asked for names of people who had a problem with me and you're at the top of the list, or am I wrong?"

Alma looked surprised by the fiery comeback but Gemma wasn't in the mood to be nice. "So, what do you want?"

Alma gave her a cold smile. "I thought you'd like to meet my baby sister, Lisa. The one whose marriage you wrecked."

Gemma froze.

"Lisa, this is Gemma Dahl. Owen's little whore."

The woman paled visibly. Her wide eyes took in Alma and then Gemma before returning to Alma's smug, satisfied face. She stood and her eyes flashed with fury. Appalled, Gemma braced herself for an altercation.

"How dare you!" Lisa screamed. "How dare you!"

But to Gemma's shock, the words were flung Alma's way.

"Why would you do this!" she asked, now standing at the desk.

Alma stuttered, "I thought—"

Lisa slapped Alma so hard, Sgt. Ma'am nearly fell from her chair. "Stay out of my life! Do you hear me!" she shouted. "Always meddling. Damn you! You thought what? That I'd be as mean and hateful as you? Owen was a cheating piece of trash the entire time we were married!"

Alice turned to Gemma. "Did he promise to marry you?"

Gemma nodded.

"You weren't the first or the last, honey, believe me. Did you have the baby?"

"Yes."

"Boy or girl."

"Girl."

"Where's she now?"

"Buried in Arlington National Cemetery."

She stopped. "Oh, my word," she whispered, scanning Gemma's tight face. "I'm so sorry."

"Thank you."

Lisa asked Alma, "Did you know this?"

"No."

"Of course not! Why would you care about anyone else's pain? How'd you find out about her? You weren't even living in Franklin back then."

"Astrid Wiggins told me a few months ago."

"Seabiscuit? Another piece of trash." The disgust on her face mirrored Gemma's and she made a mental note to have Astrid's name added to the sheriff's list of possible tire slashers.

Lisa said to Gemma, "I heard you'd left Franklin during your pregnancy, but had no idea where you went. No offense, but at the time, I didn't care."

"None taken. My parents sent me to an aunt in Chicago."

"Owen was a bastard. We both deserved better. Just like we both deserved better than to be ambushed by this person who calls herself my sister," she snapped, glaring at the stunned Alma. "She told me you were an old friend from my high school days who wanted to reconnect, so I drove up from Plainville."

Gemma asked, "Where's Owen now?"

"The last time we spoke, he was selling cars in California, but that was twenty years ago right after the divorce. Haven't heard from him since."

Gemma wondered if the colonel was watching this on his monitors. Alma's left cheek still bore the bright red splash of her sister's fury.

"My apologies to you, Gemma," Lisa said sincerely.

"Thank you."

Lisa picked up her purse and without a word or a glance back at her sister strode from the office.

In the silence that followed, Gemma asked, "Anything else?"

"Get out!"

Keeping her satisfaction hidden, Gemma complied.

For the rest of her shift, she didn't see hide nor hair of Alma. At lunch, she heard that Sgt. Ma'am hadn't been feeling well and had gone home. That she'd set a trap for Gemma only to have it blow up in her face. Priceless. Gemma hoped she'd be unwell until the cows came home.

Driving to the rec after work, Gemma thought her interview with Gary went well. In spite of the crazy day, she felt as though she'd answered all the questions to the best of her ability. He'd been impressed by the letters of recommendation she'd given him from some of her co-workers. Although they didn't count as references, she thought the letters would show how the employees felt about the possibility of working under her in the position. He advised her that he had a few more applicants to interview but promised to let everyone know who'd be getting the job by the middle of the next week. She was still worried about the incident with her tires, though, and hoped the sheriff found the person soon.

Gemma picked up the kids from the rec, made them a quick dinner of hamburgers and fries, then hurried off to her class.

Taking her seat, she felt herself relax for the first time that day. In class, there'd be no slashed tires or ambushes from Sgt. Ma'am. The meeting with her team last Saturday went well, so there were no worries concerning their ongoing build-a-business-assignment. Seeing Professor LeForge enter, and fielding the smile he shot her way, buoyed her also.

Once class began, LeForge said, "Okay everyone, I want you to get with your groups and continue working on your businesses."

Earbud Brad Young hadn't shown up, so Gemma, Josh, and Carrie pulled their desks close and began working. They were discussing how many employees their tat shop would need, and how much they could afford to pay, when a woman entered the room. She was a young redhead. Even though Gemma had never seen her before, she thought the woman might be a class member until she said, "Honey, I locked my keys in my car. I need your extra set."

Gemma froze. LeForge sent Gemma a quick glance before opening his bag and began searching inside.

He handed her a key. The woman asked the

class, "Isn't my hubby an amazing instructor?"

If Gemma had any doubts about who the woman was before, there were none now. She turned to Josh. He met her eyes, and sadly shook his head. Pushing her disappointed feelings aside, she returned to the discussion.

When class was over, a melancholy Gemma gathered up her possessions and headed to the door.

"Ms. Dahl."

She stopped, but didn't turn.

"Um. Can I walk with you to the parking lot?"

She shook her head and left.

Driving home, she supposed she owed the fates a thanks for revealing LeForge's true status. All they'd shared were a few smiles, nothing more, but the potential for more had been simmering like a pot on the back burner of a stove. Finding someone to spend time with might have been nice, but the last thing she needed was to hook up with another married man. She had enough on her plate with a job, raising three kids, and school; she didn't need drama.

CHAPTER
16

Bernadine nodded approvingly as she, Lily, and Luis Acosta were walked through a presentation put together by Trent and Barrett Payne in response to Gemma's tire slashing incident yesterday. Their subdivision was going to be outfitted with security cameras and Bernadine couldn't be more pleased with the decision. No one thought such precautions would be necessary when the homes were initially built. Sadly, they were wrong. Once the new system was up and running, all future perpetrators would be caught on film.

"How long will this take?" Lily asked.

"No more than a couple of days," Trent replied. "We're going with the same company that wired Gary's store. We have a good relation-ship with them and they have some new outdoor prototypes they've been wanting to test. They're coming out tomorrow to lay the groundwork for the installation."

Bernadine liked the time frame.

Luis asked, "Who's handling mainte-nance?"

"They are. They'll also store copies of the digital records on their site in case we lose our backups for whatever reasons, weather, fire, hackers, et cetera."

Barrett asked, "Any other questions?"

Bernadine turned to Luis and Lily but both appeared satisfied by what they'd heard.

Trent said, "We'll let you know when they arrive."

The men filed out, leaving Bernadine and Lily alone. "I never thought we'd have to do this."

"True, but there are crazies everywhere. Even in small towns like ours."

"I hope Will finds out who did this to her. I don't want us constantly looking over our shoulders wondering who might be next."

"Trent's going to take the cost of her new tires out of his budget. He says she shouldn't have to foot the bill."

"She's not going to be happy about that. Gemma is serious about paying her way."

"I know but she's got three kids to feed now, and she's in school. Even with the stipend from the Herman kids, she's not rolling in dough."

"No, and that reminds me. I need to hook her up with a financial adviser so she'll have help managing their funds."

"Good idea. Do you need me for anything else here? I promised Tamar and Gen that I'd help them move some of the food out to her place for the August First get-together."

"No, you go ahead. I think I can turn the world without you for the rest of the day."

Lily searched her face. "You look tired, girl."

"Worried about Mal."

"Are you getting any sleep?"

"Sleep is overrated," she replied with a bittersweet smile. She hadn't had a full night's rest since this all began. Crystal being gone seemed to make sleeping even more of a challenge. "I'll be fine. You go help Tamar."

Lily didn't look convinced, but she made her exit, leaving Bernadine alone. What Bernadine hadn't told anyone was that PI Sandy Langster hadn't found anything related to Mal's whereabouts. When they spoke on the phone last night, Sandy said either he'd registered at one of the hotels under an assumed name or he wasn't in Vegas at all. She had a few ties to some of the police and private investigators there and planned to call in some favors to track him down, but Bernadine found it all very discouraging. *Where are you Mal? What made you take off? Why are you breaking my heart?* Bernadine was still waiting on word from the computer people in LA. She was at the point of almost hoping they wouldn't be able to crack the password either for fear of what the data might reveal.

Hearing what sounded like the chop of helicopter blades, Bernadine went to her window.

The sight of the all-gold chopper hovering over Main Street put a smile on her face. Tina Craig had come to town.

"So, you really want to build and open a bed and breakfast?" Bernadine asked her as they sat having lunch at the Dog.

"I do. I like entertaining people, at least for short stays, so a B&B would be perfect." She glanced around. Gina the Jukebox was playing Chaka Khan's "Stop on By," which could barely be heard above the noise of the lunch rush.

"Is it always this crowded in here?"

"Lately, yes." Bernadine then told her about the new restaurant she wanted to open.

"If you need another investor, count me in."

Bernadine saw people staring curiously at Tina. "Everyone in here wants to know who you are. When you're done eating, would you mind meeting a few people?"

"I'd love to."

"Most of the ladies are out at Tamar July's place getting ready for our annual August First gathering, so for now, I'll introduce you to some of the men."

"Lucky me."

After their meal, she took Tina over to meet Trent and Barrett, who was on his lunch hour from the store. Both were gracious.

Bernadine explained to Trent, "Tina may be moving here to open a bed and breakfast. Can you stop by my office later so we can fill you in?"

He eyed Tina for a second as if he weren't sure what to make of her, but agreed. "Sure. Text me when you're ready to meet up."

"Will do."

Then she steered Tina over to Bing and Clay. Bing gave her a big smile of welcome. Clay just nodded.

"What's up with the Clay guy?" Tina asked as they moved on.

"Still pouting because his lady friend found someone else."

"He's kind of cute."

"Neanderthal brain where women are concerned, though."

"Oh. I don't do Neanderthals. Not even cute ones."

"Exactly."

In the kitchen, she met Rocky and Siz, and received a big hug from Crystal. "Aunt Tina! What are you doing here?"

"Just dropped by to check on your mom. Are you staying out of trouble?"

Crystal grinned. "Pretty much."

"That's no fun."

"Tell me about it, but I have my own place now. You'll have to come see it."

"Will do."

They left the kitchen and stepped back out into the sunshine. "Now where?" Tina asked.

"Now. The grand tour."

While Bernadine drove her around the countryside, she told Tina about the history of Henry Adams, the Exodus and the founding Dusters. She and Tina had discussed the subject before but this was the first time she'd seen the town with her own eyes.

Tina said, "I'm from Minnesota originally, and I look at all this flat land and think about the snow, and the wind that had to be blowing here during the Dusters' first winter. It must have been awful, especially for those from the south. They were remarkable people to have survived."

Bernadine agreed. "And to live in dugouts underground?"

"Unbelievably remarkable."

"Are you sure you want to live here?"

"Positive. We need to build an airstrip long enough for our jets, though."

Bernadine laughed. "Check!"

They went back to her office. She sent Trent a text and a short time later he joined them to talk about potential building sites.

Tina studied the large map he'd rolled out. "How about here, near your rehabbed hotel?"

"There's probably enough space. Any idea how big you want the place to be?"

"Five, maybe six bedrooms. Bernadine said you have out-of-town contractors and such going in and out of here a lot." She glanced at Bernadine. "What do you think?"

"I think you could fill that easily. There're also people coming into Franklin for funerals and weddings all the time. This might give them more options when deciding where to stay."

"How long do you think it'll take you to get it built?" Tina asked him.

"We could maybe get it up by the first of December, depending on the weather and how long it takes your architect to finish the design. We'll need to get the site cleared, pull permits, and all that."

"That would be great. I'll pay for extra crews if that will help?"

"It will."

She looked pleased. "Then make it so, Captain."

"You got it."

Trent left to get started.

"So," Bernadine asked, "Are you spending the night? I have plenty of room."

"No. I'm going to head home and get started on hiring an architect. So, what's happened with Mal? Anything new?"

She told her about the discouraging call from the PI.

"That's not very good news, is it?"

"No."

"Do you really believe he's been embezzling?"

Bernadine let out a loud sigh. "My heart says no way, but my brain doesn't know what to believe at this point."

"I'll keep a good thought for you, honey."

"Thanks." Tina called her chopper pilot, who'd been chilling at the airport in Hays.

When he arrived, the two friends shared a parting hug.

Bernadine said, "I can't wait for you to move here."

"Me, too. Tell Crys I'll see her place next time. I'm so excited to get this off the ground. I'll be in touch."

A few minutes later, Tina was gone and winging her way home.

Bernadine was pleased that her good friend would be moving to town but still saddened by the drama surrounding Mal.

The August First celebration began with the parade of the family flags. As the kids marched onto the field, the large crowd stood silent, pride shining in their eyes. The flags debuted Father's Day as a tribute to the men of Dads Inc. Back then, the fatherless Wyatt led the procession with the big blue and gold Henry

Adams flag, but this time he held high one Bernadine and the adults had never seen. It was pale yellow and had the crest of the United States Army prominently displayed in the center. Gemma's hand flew to her mouth and tears filled her eyes. Flanking the army crest were two others: the black and gold shield of Alpha Phi Alpha, founded in 1908 as the first African American fraternity, and the blue and gold shield of Sigma Gamma Rho, the African American sorority founded in 1922. The Herman kids walked proudly behind Wyatt.

Bernadine turned to Crystal, standing with her. "Did you make their flag?"

"Yes. We worked on it the nights Ms. G had class. The Army crest is for Wyatt's mom, of course. The Alpha crest is for the Hermans' dad, and the Sigma is for their mom. Did you know Martin Luther King was a member of Alpha Phi Alpha?"

"No."

"Neither did I, but Lucas knew."

"That's outstanding."

Behind Lucas marched the other kids bearing the flags with their family crests: July, Acosta, Garland, Payne, and Clark. Eli was in California so there was no one to carry the James's standard. Bernadine saw Rocky gently rub Jack's back as if acknowledging his son's absence.

One by one the flags were set in stands on the far end of the field and fluttered in the wind like a display of nations. The attendees cheered loudly.

When the applause ended, Tamar walked out to the center of the field. "Welcome to our August First celebration. We gather on this day as our Ancestors did to commemorate Emancipation. To honor that fight, the children of Henry Adams will recite Francis Ellen Watkins Harper's iconic poem 'Bury Me in a Free Land.' As many of you know it's the most famous poem of its time—recited at abolitionist meetings, in churches of all faiths, and memorized by schoolchildren." She paused a moment before adding, "This was not an assignment they were given. They came to me and asked if they could make this part of the program. I'm proud to have them represent us." She gave Amari a short nod and he stepped up and recited the poem's opening verse.

"Make me a grave where'er you will,
In a lowly plain or a lofty hill;
Make it among earth's humblest graves,
But not in a land where men are slaves."

Devon took up the second verse:

356

"I could not rest if around my grave
I heard the steps of a trembling slave;
His shadow above my silent tomb
Would make it a place of fearful gloom."

Jasmine had the third verse:

"I could not rest if I heard the tread
Of a coffle gang to the shambles led,
And the mother's shriek of wild despair
Rise like a curse on the trembling air."

Alfonso Acosta spoke the fourth:

"I could not sleep if I saw the lash
Drinking her blood at each fearful gash,
And I saw her babes torn from her breast
Like trembling doves from their parent nest."

Tiff Clark continued:

"I'd shudder and start if I heard the bay
Of bloodhounds seizing their human prey,
And I heard the captive plead in vain
As they bound afresh his galling chain."

Leah Clark stepped up, her voice clear and pure:

"If I saw young girls from their mother's arms
Bartered and sold for their youthful charms,

357

My eyes would flash with a mournful flame
My death-paled cheek grow red with shame."

Then it was Lucas's turn:

"I would sleep, dear friends, where bloated might
Can rob no man of his dearest right;
My rest shall be calm in any grave
Where none can call his brother a slave."

They all lined up to recite the last verse as one.

"I ask no monument, proud and high,
To arrest the gaze of the passers-by;
All that my yearning spirit craves,
Is bury me not in a land of slaves."

In the silence that followed, Bernadine and many of the adults wiped their damp eyes. The performance had been so moving it took people a moment to recover. Once they did, the applause echoed to the heavens, and the kids executed a solemn bow.

After that it was time for fun. There was music, sack races, egg tosses, push-up contests—led by the colonel—checkers, and chess. Jasmine had yet to beat Leah, Brain, or Amari in chess, but she was determined to do so and challenged them to matches every chance she got.

The weather was unseasonably cool, but perfect for the outdoors gathering, so rather than wait for the sun to drop to play the highly anticipated Little Brother of War, they decided to start right after lunch.

As the teams gathered and prepared, the honoree, Eula July, was given a prominent seat at midfield. Accompanied by Thad in his motorized chair, she appeared frail as she made her way slowly on her cane, but her smile beamed like a young girl's.

Bernadine carried her lawn chair over to a spot on the sidelines and saw Crystal a few feet away talking to Diego July. She didn't know if her daughter still carried a torch for the motorcycle-riding bad boy or not. He'd already broken her heart once; admittedly through no fault of his own, but she prayed his visit didn't lead to Crystal's Heartbreak: The Sequel.

Lily set her chair down next to Bernadine. "Lord, is Crystal going back for more heartache."

"I hope not."

They watched as the girl who'd ridden into town with Diego, a beauty named Marissa, walked over to join them. She was no longer wearing the revealing halter top and booty shorts she'd arrived in, and was instead conservatively dressed in a black tee and jeans.

Lily said, "The wardrobe change was Tamar's suggestion."

Bernadine chuckled. "I figured that." Bernadine was taken aback seeing how easy the conversation appeared to be going with the three. In fact, at one point, Crystal laughed and Marissa laughed, too.

Lily said, "I'd love to be close enough to hear what they're talking about."

"Me, too. I'm pleased nobody's taking off earrings or searching for Vaseline."

They shared smiles and directed their attention to the field.

Even though the Henry Adams team out-numbered the Julys two to one, it didn't help. Griffin, Trent, and the three Julys on the Henry Adams team did their best to score and defend, but the opposing team was too fast and too skilled. Leah caught a pass on her stick from Griffin and went streaking to the goal only to be blindsided by a body check from one of the younger Julys that hit her so hard, she was knocked to the ground. He laughed, she got up, gave him a smile, and viciously kneecapped him with her stick. He dropped like a stone and was rolling on the ground in pain when she turned on her heel and walked to the penalty box. The Henry Adams supporters roared approvingly.

The home team did score one goal, however. Lucas. He caught the pass on his stick and somehow managed to elude Team July. He would tell Gemma later he thought about the flying squirrel in the myth, and, using the moves he'd learned in soccer, threaded his way to the goal. When he threw the ball past the July goalie, he was so ecstatic, you'd've thought he'd scored for the win in the World Cup finals. But, it was the only point his team would make. Final score: Henry Adams 1, Team July 12.

After more music, food, and dessert, everyone lined up for Marie Jefferson's iconic game of Simon Says. It was a tradition they all enjoyed. There were about fifty people at the gathering; forty were eliminated in the first ten minutes. One of whom was Zoey, who when eliminated, angrily took the Lord's name in vain in a voice loud enough to be heard in Chicago. "Goddamn it!"

Time stopped.

Everyone froze.

Tamar eyed her.

Zoey shrank.

Mama Roni called out, "Marie. Ms. Miami will be at your house in the morning to do some painting."

"No problem," Marie called back.

Zoey's eyes went wide as saucers. "Mom!"

Roni wasn't having it. "How many times have I told you about keeping that mouth and temper of yours in check?"

With everyone staring, Zoey looked down at her green tennis shoes.

Reg, also frustrated by her behavior, said in a calm voice, "Your mom and I have talked to you. Reverend Paula and Tamar have talked to you. Everybody in town has, too. Maybe a little paint will make it stick."

Bernadine almost felt sorry for Zoey. Almost. But the Garlands were right. Their daughter was headstrong and fearless in a way that would serve her well in the future, but a game of Simon Says didn't warrant that kind of language from an adult, let alone an eleven-year-old child. Particularly in Henry Adams.

The now sobbing Zoey sat down next to her parents. Roni draped an arm across her daughter's shoulders, placed a kiss on her forehead, and settled in to watch the rest of Simon Says.

As the game progressed, Trent and Gary were the last two players still standing. They'd both been Marie's students back in the day, and she had a tough time eliminating them. She used every trick in her book but neither would bite. In the end, she gave up and declared them co-winners.

Fireworks would close out the August First fun once darkness fell, but in the meantime, the big cleanup got underway. When Bernadine and Lily cleared tables, it made her think back to her first year in town. There'd been a celebration for Marie's birthday and during the cleanup, Mal quietly confessed his battle with alcoholism. She'd been so moved by the admission, that he ceased being the caricature of an old player, and instead became a man of flesh and blood. Lord, she missed him.

"Mom. Do you think you can talk to Zoey's mom for me?"

It was Devon. Bernadine and Lily looked up from their trash bags.

"About what, Dev?" Lily asked.

"Letting me help Zoey paint Ms. Marie's fence in the morning."

Lily scanned his earnest face. "Did you ask her?"

"Yes. She said, no."

"Then, that's your answer, baby. This is between Zoey and Ms. Roni. It's not my place to try and change her mind."

"But she helped me when I had to paint it."

"I know she did." All the kids had painted the fence at some point but Zoey had managed to avoid the novel punishment until now.

"But it's not fair," he argued, looking miserable. "That fence is like a thousand miles long."

"I can't help, Devon. Maybe ask Ms. Roni again in a few days. Okay?"

He sighed. "Okay."

Bernadine and Lily watched him walk back across the field to where the rest of the kids were gathering up the folding chairs. They all stopped to listen as Devon apparently relayed his conversation with his mom. Amari gave him a consoling pat on the back and they returned to their task.

"Poor Dev," Lily said. "Last year he'd wanted Zoey boiled in oil and she felt the same way about him."

"Maybe Roni will change her mind at some point." But Bernadine had no plans to intervene either because this was the wake-up call their beloved Ms. Miami needed.

Under the supervision of fire chief Luis Acosta, the fireworks filled the night sky. There were reds, blues, streaks of white, and lots of oohs and ahhs from the crowd. Tamar watched the show from her back porch along with Eula and Thad. Although she didn't want to admit it aloud, she was exhausted.

Eula said, "This is wonderful. You've quite the town here, Tam. Wish I could stay and visit until the cows come home."

"Did you have a good time?" Tamar asked, pleased by Eula's words.

"I did, indeed. How about you Thad?" Eula asked him.

"Ditto."

"Thanks again for the ball game," she said as a golden palm tree flared to life above the field.

In rapt silence, they watched the show for a few more minutes until Eula struggled to her feet. "Tammy, I think it's time for this old lady to get to bed. I had more fun today than I've had in years. Decades maybe. And your children are simply outstanding."

"Do you need help?"

"No, I'll be fine. See you both in the morning."

As the door closed behind her, Griffin stepped out of the darkness and onto the porch. He'd taken his cousin Harper to the ER to have his Leah-bashed knee looked at.

"How'd it go?" Thad asked.

"Fracture of the tibia just below the knee. They put him in a cast."

"He should be glad she didn't break that stick over his head," Tamar said. "He had no business hitting her that way."

"I agree. He wants to know if she'll date him."

Tamar rolled her eyes. "First he'll have to go through Preston and then write her an essay on string theory."

Griff chuckled. "I told him probably not. Although he may be able to write the essay. Kid's pretty smart when he's not being an idiot." He then asked his grandfather, "Are we heading home tomorrow?"

"Yes."

"Okay. Good. I'll see you in the morning. Good night."

"Thanks, Griffin," Thad said.

Once they were alone again, Tamar said, "Your grandson is a blessing. Where would you be without him to handle things?"

"Dead already. For sure."

The fireworks ended a short while later, and as her neighbors and family members left to seek their beds, a weary Tamar closed up the house, looked in on the sleeping Eula, and climbed the stairs to seek her own. "I'm getting too old for this," she groused to the night. "Way too old."

As soon as her head hit the pillow she slid into sleep.

She was walking through a large cave. Was she inside the mountain, she wondered. She sensed that she was. Off in the distance drums called softly. The air was filled with the faint, sweet scent of wood smoke flavored with the smells of sofkee, the traditional Seminole corn soup, and tetta poon, a sweet spicy pie made from yams. The now familiar caw of the harpy eagle drew her eyes up to see it perched on a rocky niche high above. No longer wearing a woman's features, it unfurled its massive wings and took flight deeper into the interior. Tamar followed and noted raptors of all types watching her from the cracks and crevices of the cave's surrounding walls. Snowy owls, falcons, red-tailed hawks, golden eagles. As she passed them, they each sounded a cry before flying off in the direction the harpy eagle had taken.

The passage progressively narrowed until she was standing in a room carved out of the rock. In the center, a large cooking pot sat atop a small fire. Stirring the contents was a tall thin woman dressed in calico. Her hair was hidden beneath a red headwrap accented with cowrie shells. The woman turned, and a shocked Tamar stared into a face that was her own. The woman smiled. "Yes, it is you, but also me. I am the First. You are the Second, the me that walks the earth."

As Tamar tried to make sense of that, a young girl stepped out of the shadows. She appeared to be in her teens. Unlike First Tamar she wore a snow-white modern blouse and pleated skirt and on her feet were beautiful shoes made of feathers and jewels. She looked familiar but Tamar couldn't put a name to her face.

"Thank you for easing my passage,"

the girl said. "Let Julia know we will talk when her time comes."

Tamar's eyes widened and she scanned the young girl's features again. Eula!

First Tamar said, "You've been doubting your purpose, but you've done well by our clan. Go home now. We will meet again."

Tamar awakened the next morning to rain. Thunder rumbled in the distance. She had a vague sense of last night's dream. As she sat up in bed, the cobwebs of sleep finally parted, and she remembered. Eula! Grabbing her robe and pushing her feet into her slippers, she hurried down the stairs. The door to the bedroom was closed. She hesitated. She didn't want to go inside even though she knew she must. Turning the knob, she entered. Eula was lying in bed. "Eula?" she called softly.

Hoping the dream had been wrong, Tamar crossed to the bedside. Eula wore a peaceful smile, which Tamar met with a bittersweet one of her own. Bending over, she placed her ear against Eula's chest and heard only silence. She straightened and gently stroked a finger down her cheek. "I wish we'd found each other before you got sick. We would've had such a good time. Rest in peace, cousin."

Leaving the room, Tamar walked across the hall to tell Thad that Eula was gone.

Eula had asked for cremation so Tamar and Thad honored her wish. And because Eula specifically asked that there not be a lot of fuss, as she termed it, Tamar chose not to wait for the widespread clan to arrive. Instead, she, Thad and his cubs held a simple ceremony for her in Henry Adams. Seated in the church and listening to the singers raise their voices in the traditional songs meant to ease a soul's journey into the next world, Tamar thought about her dreams. She hadn't told Thad or anyone else about them. First Tamar had visited Amari a few years ago, so maybe she'd talk with him about them when he got older, but for the moment, she kept the memory in her heart and wondered how long it might be before she once again looked into the face that was her own.

CHAPTER
17

L ucas!"
  Lying in bed, Lucas opened his eyes and stared sleepily up at Wyatt. "What?" he asked groggily.

"Zoey's mom said we can help her paint today. Do you want to come?"

"Not really," he replied without thinking, but Wyatt looked so disappointed, Lucas pushed the covers aside and sat up. "What time is it?"

"Six forty-five. Gram said she'd drop us off on her way to work, but we have to be ready so she won't be late."

Lucas groaned inwardly. "Zoey was the one cussing, Wyatt. Not us."

"I know but she's my girl. I have to help. Wait until you see the fence. It's a mile long."

Lucas had planned on going to the pool, hanging out at the rec, and diving into Harry Potter number five. Painting a fence had not been on the agenda. "Is Gram already up?"

"Yes. She's cooking breakfast."

Lucas could smell bacon frying now that it was pointed out. "Okay. Let me brush my teeth and get dressed. I'll be downstairs in a minute. Is Jaz going, too?"

"I don't know. I came to you first. I'll ask her. Hurry up so we don't miss our ride."

"Okay. Okay," Lucas said.

"Thanks, man."

Guessing this is how brothers were supposed to support each other, he smiled. "You're welcome."

Downstairs, Gram and Wyatt were already at the table when Lucas entered the kitchen.

"Morning, Lucas," she said.

"Good morning."

"You're going to help Zoey?"

"I guess. Yeah." He got a plate and added scrambled eggs, bacon, and two pieces of toast. He sat and poured himself some juice. "Is Jaz going?"

Wyatt shook his head.

Jaz came in on the heels of that. "I told Ms. Gen I'd help her and Tamar get ready for the movies tomorrow."

Lucas wished he had a legitimate excuse to blow off paint duty but again reminded himself that he was doing this for Wyatt.

They finished breakfast and piled into the car. Nothing in Henry Adams was very far away so the ride was a short one, but Lucas was still getting used to the wide tracts of open land and how quiet it was.

Gram dropped them off at Ms. Marie's, then she and Jaz went on their way. Zoey and Devon were already working on the fence, but paused when Lucas and Wyatt walked up. To Lucas it did look a mile long.

"Thanks for coming," Zoey said, looking miserable. She had specks of the white paint on her face, in her hair, and on her tee and shorts.

Wyatt asked, "How long have you been out here?"

"Not long," Devon answered. "Zoey was already here when my dad brought me."

She added, "I'm glad my mom said you guys could start helping today. This is hard, and there's still a bunch to do. I will never do this again."

"Me neither," Devon said. "I hated it when I did it."

"Where do we get brushes and stuff?" Lucas asked.

"Ms. Marie. She's sitting on the porch with my mom and Tamar."

Lucas saw them.

Wyatt said, "Okay. Be right back."

As they set out, Lucas asked, "You sure it's okay for us to help her?"

Wyatt nodded.

"How about the other kids? Amari and Brain? Are they coming to help, too?"

He shrugged. "They've had to paint this fence twice since they came to live here, so I'm not sure if they want to do it again."

"What did they do?"

"They got busted being on some adult websites.

Not sure what they did the other time, but this is how Henry Adams punishes kids. Amari said, when his dad was growing up back in the day he had to paint the fence, too."

Lucas had never heard of kids being punished this way. "Have you ever had to do it?"

"No. Not planning on it, either."

When they reached the porch, Ms. Marie said, "Morning, boys. Are you here to help?"

They nodded. Lucas gave Tamar a quick glance. He still worried that helping Zoey wouldn't be okay with the adults and expected her to say something to that effect. Instead, Ms. Marie handed them brushes, plastic paint trays, and some rags. "There's plenty of water down there. Make sure you drink it so you don't fall out in the sun."

Lucas wondered how long Wyatt planned to stay. They were supposed to be chilling at the pool, not risking heatstroke because some dumb girl couldn't control her mouth.

Zoey's mom said, "Thanks for being Zoey's friends."

Lucas didn't want to be a friend, he wanted to be elsewhere, but he walked with Wyatt back out to the mile-long fence and kept his grumbling to himself.

Having dropped Jaz off at the rec, Gemma turned in to the parking lot of the store and smiled upon remembering the annoyance on Lucas's face when he got out of the car at Marie's. He was obviously not down with helping Zoey handle her punishment, and Gemma understood. Back in the day Ms. Miami would've gotten the belt for pulling a stunt like that, but Gemma applauded him for agreeing because Wyatt asked him to.

The store hadn't opened the doors to the public yet, so once inside, she went through the regular check-in routine and made her way to her assigned checkout lane. So far, there'd been no news on the assistant manager job. She was doing her best to be patient and hoped Gary would make the announcement soon. The rumors were that three people had applied, including Wilson "Elvis" Hughes, but she didn't know how true they were.

She was signing in to her register when Gary Clark's voice came over the speaker system. "Good morning, everyone. Doors are about to open. Have a great shift."

And Gemma's day began.

It was a slow morning, but what it lacked in traffic it made up for in small-town drama. Mrs. Beadle was escorted from the store again for yet another incident of drinking while shopping. A pair of college boys were caught with packages of steaks stuffed down their jeans. Their wide-legged walks caught the attention of Colonel Payne's security crew, and the kids were collared before they made it to the exit. Pictures of someone's bare behind began appearing on the shelves a few days ago, and so far, the high-tech cameras had been unable to identity the culprit, who, from the pictures, looked to be a hairy white male. A few more were found that morning nestled in the freezer amongst the bags of frozen corn and beneath bottles of fabric softener. The amused staff had taken to calling the derriere selfies *butties* and couldn't wait for the person responsible to be exposed.

On Gemma's way to lunch, she was stopped by head cashier Sybil Martin. "Mr. Clark wants to see you in his office," she said, and without further explanation, rushed off. Sybil seemed to be in a constant rush lately, probably because Alma still hadn't returned and Sybil was being forced to do her job. Alone.

Gemma smiled at Gary's secretary, Myra, and knocked lightly on his closed door. When he called her in, she stepped inside. "Thanks for coming. Have a seat please."

With butterflies in her stomach, she complied and wondered if this was about the job opening or if she was going to be blindsided by something terrible.

"First, congratulations. You're my choice for assistant manager."

Her jaw dropped. She wanted to jump with

joy but forced herself to stay seated. "Thank you."

"You're an outstanding candidate and I'm looking forward to working with you."

Gemma didn't know what else to say other than thank you, seven hundred more times, so she sat and listened.

"And, so you'll know, I'm going to be letting Sybil go."

Gemma stilled.

He continued. "With Alma gone, it's clear just how unqualified she is to be head cashier."

Gemma agreed. With her in charge, the cashier schedule was in chaos. A few days ago, they'd been short three people and yesterday, too many people had shown up for the morning shift. She asked hesitantly, "Is Alma coming back?"

"No. She's resigned. Apparently, there are family issues needing her attention."

His tone made Gemma wonder if he'd seen the playback of the visit by Alma's sister but she didn't ask.

"In reality though, I fired her. For harassment. I saw the tape of the two of you in the break room and the one of you and her sister. It wasn't the first time she's tried to bulldoze her way over an employee, and she'd been warned."

Gemma hated being petty but she was pleased she'd gotten the axe. Sybil's fate gave her pause though, mostly because of her status as a single mom. "Everyone knows Sybil isn't qualified to be head cashier and truthfully, she and I don't get along, but how about she be moved back to a cashier position? She has a son. She needs her job."

Gary studied her silently for what seemed like such a long time, she thought maybe he hadn't wanted her opinion, but finally he nodded. "And that's one of the reasons I chose you, Gemma."

She was confused.

"You're qualified on paper, but your empathy put you above the other candidates. The assistant manager deals directly with the staff. You hire. You fire. And even though Alma's mini me has been treating you badly, you're able to separate yourself from that and do what's best for her as an employee."

"I'm a single mom, too. I know how hard it can be trying to make ends meet."

"Your first duty will be to give me some recommendations on who should replace her."

Gemma paused. "Do I have to tell her?"

He smiled. "No. I will."

She blew out a breath of relief. "Okay."

"Myra has some paperwork pertaining to your new position for you to look over and sign. Your first full day on the job starts tomorrow at eight a.m., which will also be your report time from now on. Will that be a problem with the kids?"

She did some hasty thinking. "No. We'll work it out."

"What about your classes?"

"The term ends in about two weeks, and we only meet two evenings a week. Tuesdays and Thursdays."

"Then we'll work your training around that. There will be some night shift involvement too, so you can learn what goes on around here when we're closed. Stocking, maintenance, that sort of thing."

Her head was spinning. Amari, Preston, and Leah were part of the night stocking crew and she knew they'd help her get acclimated.

They spent a few more minutes discussing the ins and outs, and then Gary walked her into what would be her office. She looked around the space and fought back her tears. It was small with a window that overlooked the open field behind the parking lot, but she didn't care about the size or that it once belonged to Alma. It was hers now. A year ago, when she first moved back to Kansas without a job or a place to live, she never imagined ending up here. And as if having read her mind, Gary said, "You've earned it, Gemma. You've worked hard."

Emotion clogging her throat, she whispered, "Thanks for your faith in me."

"You made it easy. Now, go home, tell the kids. Have a celebratory burger at the Dog then be back here in the morning. Eight o'clock sharp."

Determined not to let the tears escape in front of him, she nodded. After he exited, she looked around the space again and a few tears did escape. Dashing them away, she took in the desk with its computer on top and the chair pushed in close. She eyed the coat rack and the small bare bookcase against the wall. *This is mine! Mine!* Walking to the window, she looked out and there below in the parking lot was her old gray Taurus. She still hadn't heard anything from the sheriff, but presently didn't care. The car now belonged to the new assistant manager, which meant she'd have a dedicated parking spot, and she laughed at the crazy change in her status. Gemma Dahl, former pregnant teenager and town pariah was now *somebody,* and it felt amazing.

She didn't know if Gary had made the announcement over the speaker system or what, but by the time she finished up the paperwork with Myra and went back downstairs to grab her purse from her locker, seemingly everyone knew about her promotion. Her co-workers applauded and shouted congrats as she made her way through the store, causing the customers to stare on curiously. She got a thumbs-up from Otto Newsome in the meat department, and a series of exaggerated bows from smiling butcher Candy Stevens, whose purple hair was now highlighted with strands of emerald green. She ran into Edith in the locker room and Edith hugged her tight. "Congratulations, Gem."

"Thanks, and thanks for being such a good friend. We're going to need a new head cashier. Do you want the job?"

The older woman shot her a look. "Like I told you before, I'm smarter than that."

Gemma laughed. "If you think of someone less smart, let me know and I'll add them to my list." She already had one candidate in mind.

"Will do."

Feeling like a million bucks, Gemma left the store and was on her way to her car when she heard someone call her name. Turning back, she saw Sybil approaching. Bracing herself because who knew what the woman had to say, Gemma waited for her to close the distance.

"What can I do for you, Sybil?"

"Mr. Clark told me how you went to bat for me so I wouldn't get fired."

Gemma thought he hadn't wasted time.

"Well, I don't need your help!" she snapped. "I just quit and so did Wilson. He's been offered a full-time Elvis job and we're getting married and moving to Vegas." That said, she turned and stalked back to the store.

Gemma sighed, chuckled, and drove away to pick up her kids.

They were ecstatic at her news.

Jaz asked, "Does that mean you get to boss people around?"

"No." Gemma laughed as they ate their carryout order of burgers and fries from the Dog in her kitchen. It was Thursday, so she had class in a few hours. A real celebratory dinner would have to wait until the weekend.

Professor LeForge had announced at their last class meeting that there'd be a test tonight, so although Gemma had studied, her promotion had her mind elsewhere. Forcing herself to focus, she answered the questions on accounting practices to the best of her ability and when she was done handed him her test paper. He smiled. She didn't. Some of the students were still working so she quietly gathered up her things and tiptoed out to head home. The other classes in the building were still in session, so as she made her way down the quiet hallway, she was stopped by someone calling her name for the second time that day. She turned to Professor LeForge.

"I was wondering if we could get together?" he asked.

"For?" she asked coolly and waited for his response.

He appeared uncomfortable. "Maybe have a coffee or something?"

She kept her voice bland. "Is your wife coming with you?"

He chuckled softly and looked away for a moment. "You're a very impressive woman, Ms. Dahl."

"And you're a very married man, Professor. I'll assume my choosing not to have coffee won't impact my grade."

"It won't."

"Have a good evening." She resumed her walk to the door.

Outside, she sat behind the wheel of her car for a moment, and wondered how many women would've agreed to his offer knowing he was married. Probably many considering how gorgeous he was, but she'd turned him down and had no regrets. She had to admit he had balls, though.

In the days that followed, Zoey and company finished painting Marie's fence, much to Lucas's relief, and she swore never to put herself in that position again. Devon and Wyatt planned to hold her to that by letting her know she'd be on her own the next time. Rocky and Jack skipped the rec's Friday night movie to have their own movie night at his place. They watched a remastered version of Akira Kurosawa's award-winning 1954 Japanese film, *Seven Samurai,* upon which the modern-day film

The Magnificent Seven was based. They ate popcorn, drank wine and had a great time. Once the movie ended, they stepped out onto the deck to view the heavens through Henry, the name Jack had given his powerful new telescope. Because the happy couple was counting down the days to their nuptials, they spent time with Sheila finalizing things like guest lists and details, and a lot more time on the phone with Jack's mom, Stella, who was determined to make changes in the plans wherever she could. After Eula's memorial, Thad and the cubs returned to Oklahoma. Out of respect for the pact he'd made with his sister, he didn't lay a hand on Olivia. However, Deputy Davida Ransom laid two speeding tickets on Tamar two days in a row, which sent the officer's stock plummeting further in the eyes of the furious town matriarch, but Ransom didn't appear to care. Will Dalton and his children held the area's second memorial, this one for his wife, Vicky, and seemingly everyone in the county came to her memorial to pay their respects.

Bernadine spent the morning looking over the town's map for the perfect location for her new restaurant. She thought the best place might be on the end of the town where the Power Plant was so as to put as much distance between it and the Dog as possible.

She was about to hit up Lily on the intercom to get her opinion when Lily walked into her office.

"Just got an e-mail from the computer place out in LA. They were able to break the password and get into the files."

"Hallelujah!"

"They want to know what you want done with the data?"

"Can they send it here, so we can review it?"

"I asked the young man on the phone and he said that wouldn't be a problem. None of the files are damaged as far as they can tell."

"Good, have them e-mail it to us or send a thumb drive or whatever works best."

"Will do."

They sent the files as an attachment and Lily downloaded it to her computer. Two hours later, after going over the numbers, twice, she came into Bernadine's office. Bernadine took one look at her face and said, "Should I pour myself a drink first?"

"Maybe."

Bernadine drew in a calming breath.

"There's roughly one hundred and twenty thousand missing. And it was withdrawn in big chunks. The first was for seventy-five grand and another for forty-five."

She thought she might be sick, but said, "Maybe he was helping somebody in need, maybe—I don't know, Lil." Without him to personally explain there was no way to know the truth.

"This doesn't look good, Bernadine," Lily said softly.

"I know, but as dumb as it may make me sound, I can't believe he'd do something so underhanded. He said he'd be back to give Rocky away at her wedding."

"And if he doesn't show?"

"Then I'll have to overlook the fact that he's the man I love and turn this over to law enforcement."

"Lord," Lily whispered.

"I know, but I don't have much choice."

"I know. Okay, let me go and tell Trent."

"I'll call Rocky and then Tamar."

After Lily departed, Bernadine did her best to set aside the mountain of unanswered questions and picked up the phone.

After getting Bernadine's call, Tamar decided it was time to stop pussyfooting around and get some answers. Like Bernadine, she didn't want to believe her son was a coldhearted thief, so she drove out to Clay and Bing's farm. Rocky had already questioned Clay and gotten nothing, but he and Mal had been friends since they were little. If anyone knew where he was, Clayton Dobbs was that person.

When she walked up, shotgun in hand, he was

out in the pens filling the feed troughs for his hogs.

"Where's my son?"

Clay froze.

"If you lie to me, so help me Clayton, I will take this shotgun and put it right between your eyes. Where's Mal?"

"Oklahoma. Oil fields."

"Why?"

"He—he's trying to make back the money he borrowed."

"Borrowed?" she shouted.

Clay wouldn't meet her eyes.

"Why'd he *borrow* it in the first place?"

"It's hard to explain, but a man has his pride, Tamar. When he and Bernadine got back from Key West last Christmas, he told me, having to stand aside while she paid for everything hurt—you know—made him feel less than himself."

"So, he stole one hundred and twenty thousand dollars!"

"He wanted to invest it, and make enough money to pay back the cash he borrowed—"

"It wasn't borrowed, Clayton! Borrowed implies he had consent."

When his jaw tightened and he glared, she wanted to shoot him just for having the nerve to be mad that she kept correcting him. "What did he invest in?"

"I'm not sure."

She blasted the ground less than six inches from his feet, and he jumped, cried out, then yelled, "I'm not some little child! I'm over sixty years old! Don't you—"

She fired at his feet again. "And I'm over ninety and I have a shotgun. Don't you dare lie to me! Where'd the money go?"

Bing came hobbling out of the house on his cane. "What the hell is going on out here!" Seeing Tamar, he stopped. "Oh. Hey, Tamar."

"Hey, Bing. Just trying to get Clay to tell me the truth about Mal's thievery."

Bing glared at his seething, tight-lipped housemate. "I told those two from jump it was a dumb idea, but nobody wanted to listen to the old man with the cane. All I ask is that you leave enough of this one for me to bury. I owe him that much." He turned to make his return to the house and called back, "They invested in a condo complex in Kansas City. Builder disappeared. Left them both holding an empty bag."

Muttering, Tamar returned to her truck. After locking the shotgun inside the gun case in Olivia's bed, she got in the cab and drove away

"A condo complex?" Bernadine yelled, jumping up from her desk's chair.

Tamar, who'd just shared Bing's revelation,

looked fit to be tied. Rocky shook her head and Trent ran his hands down his face in disbelief.

Lily asked, "Did he know which oil field he's working in?"

"I was so angry I didn't even think to ask," Tamar admitted. "Had I stayed one minute longer I was going to need bail money."

"But why did he invest the money in the first place?" Trent asked her. "Does he have gambling debts he needed to cover? What?"

"No. Pride."

Trent's confusion was mirrored on the face of the others in the room.

She explained, "Clay said when Mal and Bernadine went to Key West last Christmas, Mal's pride was hurt by her paying for everything."

Bernadine dropped back down into her chair. "Good lord."

"I suppose that makes sense," Trent said, then had to come to his own defense in response to Tamar's heat-filled glare. "I'm not saying it's a valid excuse, but it's how society has men wired. We're the protectors and providers. We pay. I'm kind of surprised, though. He always claimed to have no problems with your money, Bernadine, and he was the one who raked Reg over the coals something fierce when he was acting out over the money Roni makes."

Lily asked him in a cool voice, "So if I made more money than you, you'd lose your mind, too?"

He shrugged. "I say no, but in reality, maybe at some point I would. But, as I said, before I get tarred and feathered, it's how men, especially OGs like Mal, are wired."

"In a way, I understand," Rocky tossed out. "But it's still stupid."

Trent didn't argue. "I'm not saying it isn't, but it is what it is."

Bernadine had a question. "Can he make over a hundred grand in a less than a month working the oil fields?"

"Maybe, if he was younger. No way he can put in enough hours in such a short time at his age."

Bernadine understood Trent's explanation of why Mal had taken the money, but he'd never expressed any problem with her wealth. She supposed his pride played a part in that, too. So where did this mess leave her and their relationship? And was she supposed to be the villain for wanting to take a nice vacation so they could spend some time together? She didn't think so.

Rocky asked, "What do you want to do, Bernadine? The wedding is ten days away. Do we call Will's office and have Mal picked up? Do we ride to Oklahoma and drag him back?"

"A part of me wants to find him and strangle him, while the part that loves him wants to wait and see if he shows for your wedding so he and I can talk. Maybe he can pay it back. Maybe—I don't know. I'm just so blown away by this, I'm having trouble telling up from down." She looked to Tamar for advice.

"It's your money and your relationship. You get to decide."

Bernadine's eyes met Trent's. "Up to you. I can probably find him now that we know where he is. Might take a few days of calling sites to figure out which field he's working though, but it's doable."

Bernadine turned her attention to Lily. "Your call, Bernadine."

Although Bernadine knew her response might come back and bite her in her butt, she made the decision with her heart. "I'll wait for the wedding. And afterwards, if I must tie him to a chair to make him talk to me, that's what I'll do."

CHAPTER
18

Gemma drove home from work and thought about the surprise and joy on Edward Plainwell's face when she offered him the job of head cashier. She'd recommended him to Gary because he was a hard worker, took his job seriously, and the other cashiers liked him very much. Everyone agreed he should've been given the position during Alma's tenure but she'd given it to Sybil and to this day no one knew why. A new dairy manager had been hired to replace Mr. Elvis. Her name was Celeste Koppelman. She'd held a similar position at a store down in Hays and it was working out well. Now that Gemma had finished night shift training she was back on days. Although unloading the trucks and shelving the stock had been grueling work, she'd enjoyed learning the ropes from the night supervisor Melvin Green. A former high school phys ed teacher and football coach, he was gruff on the outside and an old softie in the middle. He'd been up front about his dislike for Alma. He said she always thought she knew more about the operation than he, and he was retired Navy, which Gemma took to mean the two branches of the military didn't get along. She'd also been correct about how helpful Amari and his crew would be.

As she pulled into her driveway and got out, she looked up at the security cameras on the utility pole in front of the house. They'd been mounted on all the poles in the neighborhood but were small enough to be unnoticeable unless you knew they were there. Will Dalton's office still had no leads in her tire slashing incident and although she really wanted to know the person's identity it didn't look as if she ever would.

Inside, she found the kids playing Scrabble with Genevieve. If she didn't love Henry Adams enough already, her feeling for the town soared when Tamar's crew offered to keep an eye on them not only at the rec but at home too until school started. Wednesdays were Gen's day. She was a literary tutor and loved word games as much as the kids.

"Who's winning?" Gemma asked as she put her purse on the couch and walked over to where they were gathered around the kitchen table.

"Ms. Gen, of course," Jaz groused. "She never lets us win."

Gen said, "If I just let you win, you won't have a sense of accomplishment. In life, you have to work to get what you want." And she set down the word *conundrum*.

The kids groaned and Lucas asked, "Is that even a real word?"

Wyatt already had the dictionary open and read aloud. "Conundrum. A challenging riddle or a situation where there is no clear answer or right solution."

Gen smiled. "And on that note, I'm going home."

Lucas said, "Geez. She got like a thousand points on that word."

She replied, "And you now know the definition which'll give you big points on your SATs."

Gemma chuckled softly. Everyone in town adored Genevieve.

With a wink to the kids, and a quick hug for Gemma, she made her exit.

The Scrabble board was put away and they made dinner together—pork chops, mashed potatoes, and broccoli.

As they ate, they talked about their day. Gemma said, "We finally found out who's been leaving the butt pictures around the store."

The kids laughed. They'd enjoyed hearing about the ongoing search for the person behind the mysterious *butties*.

Wyatt asked, "Who was it?"

"One of the knuckleheads in the dairy department."

"How'd he get caught?" Lucas asked.

"He made the dumb mistake of leaving one

on the chair of his new supervisor. She rounded up her whole department and threatened to fire everybody if she didn't get answers." Elvis had run the department like a clown car. The work got done but they liked playing pranks on each other. Celeste Koppelman was the taskmaster dairy needed, and when she threatened firing they believed her.

"Was he fired?"

"No, but he's on probation. He said he thought it was funny."

"Ew," Jaz said. "Pictures of his butt? Not funny. Ew."

"I agree," Gemma said. Gemma didn't tell them about the teenagers caught doing some heavy necking in the bean-bag chairs in the store's small Home section. They were escorted out and warned that if they ever entered the store as a couple again, their parents would be called and shown the security footage. Being the assistant manager meant she got to know more about what was going on in the building than she cared to.

Lucas asked, "Is tonight the night you Skype with the financial planner Ms. Brown got for me and Jaz?"

Work had been so crazy she'd all but forgotten about it and was grateful for the reminder. "Yes, and I want you and Jaz to sit in on the conversation."

Wyatt said, "Mr. James said he got in some new maps of the moon. Can I go over while you guys are talking?" Wyatt had dreams of being a cartographer.

"Were you invited?"

He nodded. "He sent me a text earlier."

"Okay. You can go over after your dinner chores. I'll text you when we're done with the financial person."

He did a fist pump. "Thanks, Gram."

After the meal, they cleaned up. Wyatt left to visit with Jack and Gemma booted up her laptop for the Skype conference set for 7:00 p.m.

Lucas asked, "Do Jaz and I really need to listen in? It's not like we can do anything with the money until we turn eighteen. I wanted to see the moon maps, too."

"Yes, you do. It's your money and you need to hear what's going on and learn about it, just like I do. Mr. James can show you his maps another time."

He didn't look happy but didn't argue further.

At seven the laptop beeped, signaling the start of the session. A middle-aged brown-skinned woman with natural hair and perfectly applied makeup came on screen. She introduced herself as Nadine Iler.

Gemma introduced herself and kids, and the meeting got under way.

"I've looked over the portfolio," Ms. Iler said.

"Mr. and Mrs. Herman made some very smart moves financially, so we'll just leave everything the way it is for now. I'll send you copies of everything I have for your files."

"They have college funds?"

"Yes. One for each, and both are growing at a good rate. With the way college costs are skyrocketing, this will help them immensely when the time comes."

Lucas had a question for Gemma. "Does Wyatt have a college fund?"

"Yes. I put his mom's life insurance into a savings account." She explained to Ms. Iler who Wyatt was.

Lucas asked Ms. Iler, "Will it grow as big as the ones Jaz and I have?"

She showed a kind smile. "I don't know, Lucas. I'd have to have Ms. Dahl's permission to check that out."

"Will you let her, Gram? I want Wyatt to have enough money, too. And if it's not enough, Jaz and I can give him some of ours. Can we do that, Ms. Iler?"

"When you get eighteen you can use your money however you want."

Jaz said, "I think we should give some money to Wyatt, now."

Lucas agreed. "I think we should, too."

Gemma said, "Thanks for your generosity, you two, but I think Wyatt will be fine. I'll have

Ms. Iler check his account though, just to be sure."

They spent a few more minutes talking about life insurance, stocks and the rest, and Jaz, who'd began looking bored with the dull conversation, asked, "Can we go back to Hawaii for Christmas?"

Gemma was confused. "Hawaii?"

Ms. Iler rifled through her papers. "Ms. Dahl, the Herman family owns a condo on Maui and one at Disney in Orlando. Both are paid for and mortgage free. Have you ever been to Maui?"

"No."

"Then you might consider taking them. I'm sure Ms. Brown knows a quality travel agent and she can speak to any concerns the court may have about taking them out of state."

"But I don't want to be accused of frittering away their money."

"My office has charge over their estate until they're eighteen, and believe me, we'll be keeping an eagle eye on every penny. A trip to Hawaii is not a misuse under the circumstances. They've been in foster care for some time and since there are more than enough discretionary funds available to pay for the time there, you might want to go. It makes no sense to let the condos sit vacant unless the kids want to put the places up for sale and it doesn't sound as if they do."

Gemma glanced Lucas's way and he smiled. She now better understood the earlier conversation they'd had about his wanting to take Wyatt to Disney.

"Please," Jaz pleaded. "Maui is so awesome! We can go surfing."

Gemma laughed. "You two surf?"

"Yep," she boasted proudly. "Lucas and I have our own boards, too. They're at the condo. Or at least they were."

Lucas added, "And we can go snorkeling and kayaking, and do a bunch of other stuff."

Amazed by them and their former lifestyle, she replied, "Okay, let me think about it and we'll talk."

Ms. Iler asked, "Do you have any other questions for me?"

No one did.

"Then I'll sign off. After you get the financial statements and paperwork, if you need any-thing, or have any questions at all, send me an e-mail or give me a call. Great meeting you."

Once she was gone, Gemma again wondered what their parents would think of her being the person raising them. She hoped they'd be pleased. She encouraged the kids to read, made them do chores, and keep their rooms clean, like a good parent should. They all watched family-friendly television and DVDs together, played board games, had spelling bees, and she did her best to make them feel safe again. She also tried to be an easy person for them to talk to and not be scary like their aunt Wanda had apparently been. Truthfully, Gemma wanted to adopt them so their home would always be with her and Wyatt, but knew it was too soon in the process to petition the courts. Her foster parent certification was still making its way through the bureaucratic maze. In the meantime, she just wanted them to enjoy being in this place called Henry Adams, make friends with the other kids, and be as content as they could be.

Jaz asked, "Are you thinking about Maui?"

Gemma grinned. "Yes. Do you think I'm too old to learn to surf?"

Jaz laughed but Gemma read something weightier in Lucas's eyes. It was almost as if he knew what she'd been thinking.

And as if to prove her point, he said quietly, "I think our parents are glad we're with you."

That night while Gemma slept, she was awakened by sirens and blue lights flashing over her bedroom walls. *Police?* Throwing back her bedding, she went to her window and looked down at the street below. There was a strange van parked in the driveway behind her Taurus, and two county sheriff cars parked in front of her house. Numerous deputies, Trent, Barrett, Reg, and Jack were there as well. She pushed her feet into her flip-flops, quickly threw her robe on over her pajamas, and left her bedroom to investigate. The kids were in the darkened hallway.

"What's going on?" Wyatt asked, sounding anxious.

"No idea, but you three stay up here."

"But—"

"Don't argue with me, Wyatt. I'll be back."

Through the screen door, she watched a deputy lead someone wearing dark sweats and a hoodie over to one of the cruisers. Leaving the porch, she smelled gasoline as she walked up to Barrett and Trent. "What happened?"

Barrett said grimly, "We think we caught your perp."

Over by the cruiser, the person was being cuffed. Before she could ask questions, Will Dalton appeared. "Evening, Ms. Dahl. Can you come with me, please? I want you to tell me if you know her. She refuses to identify her-self."

Her? A woman?

He added, "Barrett saw her on the camera feed on his laptop. She was splashing gas around the base of your place."

Her mouth dropped.

At the cruiser, Will used the beam of his powerful flashlight to illuminate the suspect's furious face and Gemma was so stunned, it took her a few seconds to speak. "Krebs," she said in a wondrous voice. "Aretha Krebs. She works for the Kansas Department of Children and Families."

"I used to!" she snarled. "Until you got me fired!"

"You got yourself fired!" Gemma shot back. "You didn't do your job! You sent my kids to a monster, and now you want to burn down my damn house? Go to jail, witch!" She was livid.

Krebs's curse-filled response lasted only seconds before Will snarled, "Read Krebs her rights and get her out of here."

After the deputy drove away, Will had a few remaining questions, then informed her that a tow truck was en route to haul away Krebs's van. "My office will be in touch."

"Thank you, Sheriff."

"You're welcome. I'm just glad Barrett caught her before she did any real damage."

She was, too. Thinking about what might've happened infuriated her all over again.

He departed and Gemma was left standing with Trent, Barrett, and the other men while their wives and children looked on from their porches.

Trent said, "I'll take care of the gasoline in the morning. Are you okay?"

"No, I want to snatch her ignorant behind into next week. She'd better ask somebody."

Barrett chuckled. "Whoa."

WITHDRAWN

She glared.

He went still.

Holding his gaze by the light of the street-lamps, she told him, "You can take the girl out of the South Side, but you can't take the South Side out of the girl. Thanks a million times for your help. You saved our lives. I'll be better tomorrow." Seething, she went back inside.

The day of the wedding dawned sunny and bright. Tamar was dressed in a sweeping indigo-colored caftan shot through with gold. On her wrists were her signature silver bangles but she was having trouble finding the earrings she wanted to wear. After searching the numerous jewelry boxes she'd accumulated over her long life, she finally located them. Putting them in, she grabbed her fancy black pocketbook and her keys and hurried out to Olivia. She didn't want to be late.

She headed out at full speed. As far as she knew no one had heard anything from Mal. She hoped he'd keep his promise to Rocky and not make Bernadine have him hauled off to jail. *What a mess.*

She was rolling along at eighty when she saw Davida Ransom swing in behind her. Sighing angrily, she pulled over and waited for the day's citation. Tamar now had a glove box full. She did plan to pay them, but it wouldn't be today. She had more important matters to attend to.

"Morning, Ms. July."

"Deputy Ransom."

"Are you on your way to the wedding?"

"Yes, so can you just give me my ticket? I don't want to be late."

"Yes, ma'am."

Ransom wrote it out and handed it over. "You think I'm targeting you, don't you?"

"As a matter of fact, I do."

"You're right, and do you know why?"

Tamar pinned her with her hawklike eyes. "No. Why?"

"Because you're the county's matriarch. You're loved, respected, and there may not be enough of you left for your family to bury if we have to extract you from a flipped over, burning truck. Don't put your people through that."

Tamar flinched.

"Slow down," Deputy Ransom said softly. Touching her hat respectfully, she walked back to her vehicle and drove off in the opposite direction.

A pensive Tamar sat there for a moment and thought about the young deputy's words. She was right, and no, she didn't want her family and friends to have to deal with such a horrific outcome. Starting Olivia up again, she continued the drive to town. She stayed well within the posted speed limit and vowed to do so for the rest of her days.

Rocky looked at herself in the mirror in the school's art room and almost didn't recognize herself. Being beautiful had been her cross to bear her entire life, but today, decked out in her white wedding leather, she didn't mind. Kelly had spent hours braiding her hair into a gleaming work of art, and Crystal's makeup application was flawless. She was getting married. The idea that the day had finally arrived made her want to weep with joy.

Sheila, standing beside her said, "Don't you dare cry and ruin that gorgeous face."

"Rocks don't cry," she whispered emotionally.

Sheila looked confused.

"It's what my daddy used to tell me whenever I fell off my bike or fell out of a tree and hurt myself. He wanted me to grow up tough."

Sheila hugged her gently. "Today, once you start down that aisle, Rocks can bawl if she wants."

Rocky met Sheila's eyes in the mirror. "Thank you for all you've done. No way would this have happened had it not been for you."

"It was a labor of love. I'll never have a daughter of my own to help on her wedding| day, so you've been sort of a substitute. Hope you don't mind me saying that."

"Not at all. My mom's not here anymore, so having you with me has sort of made up for that. Thank you." Rocky thought about her mother and pushed the painful memories aside.

A knock sounded on the door. Sheila went over and peeked out. When she stepped aside, Stella James walked in. She eyed Rock's attire critically. "You're getting married in leather?"

"Go away, Stella."

She had the nerve to look offended.

"Now!"

"Fine," she huffed out and left.

"You're gaining an interesting mother-in-law," Sheila said.

"Only if I let her live."

There was another knock and Rocky growled, "If that's her again."

But it was Mal. In his tuxedo, he was tall, dark, and handsome. Rocky was torn between hugging him and treating him to a right cross. She took the high road and went for the hug. "Glad you made it."

"Told you I would. You look way too good to be marrying a professor."

She grinned. He did too, but his eyes said he was uncomfortable and she thought that only right, considering.

"How mad is everybody at me?"

She waved a hand dismissively. "Not doing that now. I'm getting married."

He nodded. "Okay."

The strains of the "Wedding March" drifted into the space.

He extended his arm. "You ready?"

"I am."

Sheila held the door wide. Rocky gave Sheila a kiss on the cheek as Mal escorted her by, and then they were on their way to the kiva.

Bernadine stood with the rest of the guests as the "Wedding March" played, and thought Rocky was probably the only woman on the planet who could rock a white leather bustier, duster, and pants as wedding attire. She looked fabulous, but the man escorting her drew most of Bernadine's attention. Mal. In his black tuxedo, he was as fine as ever. As they moved up the aisle and passed her row, his eyes brushed hers but didn't linger. She still had no idea how she was supposed to feel in response to what he'd done. Rather than tie herself up with angst and worry, she let go of her warring emotions and opted to enjoy the ceremony instead.

And it was lovely. Roni sang beautifully. Jack choked up reciting his vows and had to start again. The usually unflappable Rocky dropped his ring while sliding it on his finger, and Eli, the best man, had to chase it down, much to the crowd's delight. In the end, Reverend Paula pronounced them Mr. and Mrs. Jack James. The kiss they shared made the kiva erupt with applause and cheering loud enough to be heard around the world.

Mal approached Bernadine as everyone was leaving the school to head to the Dog for the reception.

"Can we talk?"

"Sure."

They moved out of the fray and found a quiet place in one of the empty classrooms.

"So," he said. "I guess you know about the money."

"I do and Clay told Tamar the reason why. You never seemed to have a problem with my money, Mal. Why now?" She really wanted to understand this.

"I don't know. I was good until we went to Key West. Watching you flash that black card and me getting side-eyes from the hotel people when we checked in, and then at the restaurants. It made me feel small."

"That was never my intent. I just wanted us to have some time together—some fun."

"It wasn't much fun, believe me."

"So, I'm the villain in this?"

His lips tightened.

Trying not to get upset, she waited.

A well-dressed and pretty middle-aged woman stuck her head in the room. "Oh, here you are,

Mal. Honey, I need the keys to your truck so I can get my phone."

Bernadine's heart stopped.

"Hi. I'm Ruth," the woman said to Bernadine. "And you are?" she asked with mild suspicion.

Bernadine's eyes flared like a forest fire at Mal. "Bernadine Brown."

Mal cleared his throat. "Ruthie, let me finish talking to Bernadine. Be there in half a sec."

Ruth eyed them both and said, "Sure. Make it quick though, baby."

"I will."

When they were alone again, Bernadine said, "Really?"

He didn't respond at first, then replied, "I figured you'd be so mad about the money, you wouldn't want to be with me anymore."

"She's your date for the wedding?"

He nodded.

She wanted to rage, scream, flip over tables. Her heart was shattered into a thousand pieces. She wanted to ask him why he hadn't picked up the phone so they could've tried to work through this. Instead he'd taken what seemed the coward's way out and just simply replaced her as if she were a pair of socks he no longer liked. Now it was her turn to feel small.

"Look. I have almost half of the money and you'll have the rest before Christmas."

She viewed him icily. "Good."

He met her eyes. "Bernadine—"

But she was already on her way out of the room.

"Bernadine!"

She went to the reception because she knew it was expected and forced herself to have a good time. Mal didn't show.

She left early and walked into her empty home and felt just as empty inside.

She took a shower, put on her pajamas and allowed herself an hour-long pity party. When the hour ended, she walked to her vanity table and viewed herself in the mirror. Red, tear-swollen eyes stared back out of her makeup-free face. Life offered two choices. She could either wallow or lick her wounds and go on. It was a given that she'd be dealing with hurt and heartache for some time to come, but she chose the latter. Hers was the hand that turned the world. Henry Adams needed her.

She crawled into bed and turned out the lamp on her nightstand. Lying in the dark while the pain leaked through, she reminded herself that she'd lived through Leo's betrayal. She'd live through Mal's, too.

Across the street, Lucas Herman sat out on the deck watching the stars. He'd never seen so many. Wyatt told him that sometimes Mr. James had sky-watching nights and everyone brought

411

their telescopes. Lucas thought he might like to be a part of that so he could learn all about the planets and be able to name the stars. It looked like he and his sister were going to be in Henry Adams permanently, and he was okay with that, even while he wished they were still with their mom and dad. He wondered where people went when they died. Did they really go to heaven to be with God and if so what did they do while they were there? He liked to think that his parents were in heaven together and were smiling down at him right now. "I miss you guys," he said quietly to the night. "But Jaz and I are good. We like it here. Can you send me some kind of sign to let me know you're up there? It doesn't have to be right now, but just sometime?"

As soon as the words left his lips a shooting star went streaking across the horizon and his mouth dropped. "Wow!" he whispered. He watched it disappear and grinned. "That was awesome!"

Feeling content, safe, and loved, he sat and watched the sky for a few minutes longer before rising and going inside.

Ms. Gemma was seated in the living room with the TV on. She was watching the show about the teeny tiny houses, and she had her laptop on the coffee table. Wyatt and Jaz were upstairs. "I got my grade from my class."

"What did you get?"

"An A!" She jumped and did some old people dances like the Running Man and the Robot and a few other moves with names he didn't know. "I'm so happy!"

He laughed. Hard.

She stopped. "I enjoy hearing you laugh."

"Why?"

"Because it makes me think you're going to be okay."

He looked at her and thought about that for a moment. "I think I will be."

"Good. And that makes me want to dance some more!"

She started up again and he laughed. He was going to be okay.

Author's Note

I hope you enjoyed this latest visit to our favorite small town. Many of you have asked for new children and a story arc for Tamar, so we welcome Lucas and Jasmine Herman to the Henry Adams family. Putting them through so much turmoil was heartbreaking for me as writer, but over the years I've learned to follow where the words lead. I was so happy to see Bernadine's jet waiting for them at the airport—a bit teary too. After all they'd endured, they were finally heading home. Previously Gemma Dahl had been a marginal side character, but this book put her front and center. Her dream to carve out a better life showed her strength, tenacity, and huge heart. It was great learning more about her. She's inspiring.

Tamar July has been a force of nature since *Bring on the Blessings,* the first book in the series. *Chasing Down a Dream* added layers to her personality, past, and dealings with her family. I was pleased that she and Eula came to closure before it was too late, and that she's finally made peace with her brother, Thad. Seeing the legendary First Tamar was a treat, too.

Another new character, Deputy Davida Ransom, played a small but important role in

Tamar's story. We'll see what the future has in store for her, and if Tamar will really stop driving like she's qualifying for the pole at Indy.

Rocky and Jack are finally married. Her dream to find love is now fulfilled and she couldn't be with a better guy than her professor, Jack.

Dreams and family were our theme this time, but Mal's dream warped into a nightmare. Will he and Bernadine be able to repair their relationship? Are the new coffee shop owners really as nice as they seem? Will Tina Craig open her B&B? Stay tuned.

Until next time,

B

Books are produced in the United States using U.S.-based materials

Books are printed using a revolutionary new process called THINKtech™ that lowers energy usage by 70% and increases overall quality

Books are durable and flexible because of smythe-sewing

Paper is sourced using environmentally responsible foresting methods and the paper is acid-free

Center Point Large Print

600 Brooks Road / PO Box 1
Thorndike, ME 04986-0001 USA

(207) 568-3717

US & Canada:
1 800 929-9108
www.centerpointlargeprint.com